"A well-developed, long-lived series that remains as welcoming and entertaining as it was in the beginning, this story will keep readers returning to Hemlock Falls time after time." —*The Mystery Reader*

"Always a great reading experience . . . Claudia Bishop writes an enthralling amateur-sleuth mystery."
—*The Best Reviews*

"A great cozy series." —*Books 'n' Bytes*

"An entertaining, quirky, and offbeat mystery . . . A special treat for amateur-sleuth lovers." —*Midwest Book Reviews*

"The reader can settle in Hemlock Falls comfortably."
—*The Armchair Detective*

"Fine local color and interesting characters."
—*Murder Ad Lib*

continued . . .

"Chock full of quirky characters and offbeat situations."
— *MyShelf.com*

"Delightful, unique characters." — *TwoLips Reviews*

"Engaging . . . Keep[s] the reader enthralled."
— *Fresh Fiction*

Praise for the Beaufort & Company Mysteries by Claudia Bishop writing as Mary Stanton

"I was hooked from page one . . . This book should give Mary Stanton the same kind of cult following usually reserved for Charlaine Harris."
— Rhys Bowen, author of *The Twelve Clues of Christmas*

"Engaging and charismatic . . . Will be a breath of fresh air for fans of paranormal cozy mysteries."
— *Publishers Weekly* (starred review)

"Spooky Southern charm and a wonderfully inventive approach to the afterlife."
— Madelyn Alt, national bestselling author of *In Charm's Way*

"An elegant enchantment with a delightful heroine and a historic setting."
— Carolyn Hart, author of *Death Comes Silently*

Berkley Prime Crime titles by Mary Stanton

DEFENDING ANGELS
ANGEL'S ADVOCATE
AVENGING ANGELS
ANGEL'S VERDICT
ANGEL CONDEMNED

Titles by Mary Stanton writing as Claudia Bishop

Hemlock Falls Mysteries

A TASTE FOR MURDER
A DASH OF DEATH
A PINCH OF POISON
MURDER WELL-DONE
DEATH DINES OUT
A TOUCH OF THE GRAPE
A STEAK IN MURDER
MARINADE FOR MURDER
JUST DESSERTS
FRIED BY JURY
A PUREE OF POISON
BURIED BY BREAKFAST
A DINNER TO DIE FOR
GROUND TO A HALT
A CAROL FOR A CORPSE
TOAST MORTEM
DREAD ON ARRIVAL
A FETE WORSE THAN DEATH

Casebooks of Dr. McKenzie Mysteries

THE CASE OF THE ROASTED ONION
THE CASE OF THE TOUGH-TALKING TURKEY
THE CASE OF THE ILL-GOTTEN GOAT

Anthologies

A PLATEFUL OF MURDER
DEATH IN TWO COURSES

A Fete Worse
Than Death

Claudia Bishop

BERKLEY PRIME CRIME, NEW YORK

THE BERKLEY PUBLISHING GROUP
Published by the Penguin Group
Penguin Group (USA) Inc.
375 Hudson Street, New York, New York 10014, USA

USA / Canada / UK / Ireland / Australia / New Zealand / India / South Africa / China

Penguin Books Ltd., Registered Offices: 80 Strand, London WC2R 0RL, England
For more information about the Penguin Group, visit penguin.com.

A FETE WORSE THAN DEATH

A Berkley Prime Crime Book / published by arrangement with the author

Berkley Prime Crime Books are published by The Berkley Publishing Group,
BERKLEY® PRIME CRIME and the PRIME CRIME logo are trademarks of
Penguin Group (USA) Inc.

For information, address: The Berkley Publishing Group,
a division of Penguin Group (USA) Inc.,
375 Hudson Street, New York, New York 10014.

ISBN: 978-0-425-26279-5

PUBLISHING HISTORY
Berkley Prime Crime mass-market edition / March 2013

PRINTED IN THE UNITED STATES OF AMERICA

10 9 8 7 6 5 4 3 2 1

Cover illustration by Karen Strelecki.
Cover design by Diana Kolsky.
Interior text design by Laura K. Corless.

ALWAYS LEARNING   PEARSON

Once again, for Whit and Cee

Acknowledgments

Most country fairs feature competitions for the best in local food preparation. When I put out the call for prizewinning recipes for the (fictional) Finger Lakes Autumn Fete, my friends and family responded with wonderful things. My special thanks to Rebecca Monroe, Julie Schwartz, and Whit Hairston.

I'd also like to thank the skilled professionals at the New York State Wine and Culinary Institute in Canandaigua, New York, for inspiring the creation of La Bonne Goute Academy of the Culinary Arts.

Cast of Characters

The Inn at Hemlock Falls

Sarah "Quill" Quilliam-McHale . . . . *innkeeper*

Margaret "Meg" Quilliam . . . . *the Inn's master chef*

Jackson "Jack" Quilliam-McHale . . . .
. . . . *Quill's five-year-old son*

Myles McHale . . . . . *Quill's husband, a government agent*

Doreen Muxworthy-Stoker . . . .
. . . . . . *Jack's nanny, formerly the Inn's head housekeeper*

Dina Muir . . . . . *the Inn's receptionist, a graduate student*

Kathleen Kiddermeister . . . . *head waitress*

Bjarne Bjarneson . . . . *head chef*

Elizabeth Chou . . . . *under chef*

Mike Santini . . . . *the groundskeeper*

Nate . . . . *the bartender*

Cast of Characters

Linda Connelly . . . .
. . . . *a guest and an event planner who owns Presentations*

George McIntyre. . .*a guest, and Linda's general factotum*

Mickey Greer . . . .
. . . *a guest, Linda's assistant, and a former football player*

Nolan and Althea Quince . . . .
guests, retired from a food brokerage business in nearby Rochester

Jeeter Swenson . . . . *a guest*

Porter Swenson . . . . *an attorney, and Jeeter's son*

Melbourne Swenson . . . .*Porter's wife*

Max . . . . *a dog*

And others

Citizens of Hemlock Falls

Elmer Henry . . . .*mayor*

Adela Henry . . . .*Elmer's wife*

Davy Kiddermeister . . . . *the sheriff*

Howie Murchison. . .*town attorney and justice of the peace*

Justin Alvarez . . . *an attorney, and Howie's junior partner*

Miriam Doncaster . . . .*the librarian*

Marge Schmidt-Peterson. . . . .

a businesswoman, and the wealthiest person in Tompkins County

Harland Peterson... *a dairy farmer, and Marge's husband*

Betty Hall .... *Marge's partner in the restaurant business*

Harvey Bozzel. . . . . *Hemlock Falls premier (and only) advertising executive*

Dolly Jean Attenborough ....*president, the Crafty Ladies*

Nadine Peterson ...... *owner of Hemlock Hall of Beauty*

Esther West . . . . *president, the Craft Guild*

"Shady" Brady Beale . . . . *owner, operator, Peterson Automotive*

The Rev. Dookie Shuttleworth . . . . *pastor, the Hemlock Falls Church of the Word of God*

Andy Bishop, MD. . . . .*physician-in-chief, Hemlock Falls Clinic*

Lt. Anson Harker. . . . .*New York state trooper*

Austin McKenzie, DVM. . . . . *a veterinarian*

And others

Employees of La Bonne Goute Culinary Academy

Clarissa "Clare" Sparrow ....*a chef, pastry, and Director*

Sophie Kilcannon . . . . *a chef, fruits and vegetables*

Cast of Characters

Pietro Giancava. . . . .*sommelier and chef, sauces*

Raleigh Brewster. . . . . *chef, meats and stews*

Jim Chen. . . . . *chef, fish and seafood*

Madame LeVasque . . . .*owner*

Bismarck. . . . .*a Maine coon cat*

And others

Prologue

Jeeter Swenson sat in a rocker between his son and his daughter-in-law on the porch of his cottage overlooking Cayuga Lake. He was ninety-eight years old today, and there was a lot to like about that. For one thing, he was looking at the prettiest view in upstate New York. It was an afternoon in late August and the sun was that rich antique yellow that meant autumn was closing in. The placid surface of the lake shrugged a little under a mild breeze. The shoreline was thick with trees. A little sailboat—Jeeter pushed his spectacles up his nose and squinted—looked like a Hobie Cat, or maybe a Sunfish—tacked merrily back and forth on the aluminum-colored water. She tacked leeward and Jeeter squinted once more. A Hobie Cat. He knew it. Nothing wrong with his eyesight that a good pair of glasses couldn't fix.

Nothing wrong with the rest of him, either. He'd outlived his enemies, buried a nagging wife, and his digestion worked just fine. The little aide that came to see him three days a week was a pip. His relatives didn't bother him much, except to plague him on his birthday. And that was more about wondering if he was ready to give up the lake house than a bid for his attention.

Which was why they'd showed up today, wasn't it?

He turned his head and glared at his son, Porter. The kid was what—sixty-three now? Maybe even sixty-five? He'd never been good with crap like birthdays. And look at the flab on him. They should have named him Portly.

Jeeter giggled, smacked his own flat belly, then thumped his cane on the porch floor, narrowly missing Porter's tasseled loafers. "Buzzards," he said with sudden ferocity.

Porter's wife Melbourne leaned forward in her chair and peered up at the sky. "Buzzards, Dad? Where?"

Truth to tell, Melbourne scared Jeeter a little. She was more bullheaded than a decent woman ought to be, and although he knew for a fact she was drawing her Social Security check, she didn't look much more than forty-five. Unnatural. Unnatural and bullheaded. Porter sure'd gotten himself a prize.

"You see any buzzards up there?" Jeeter demanded. "Me, neither. But there's a couple of them buzzarding around me, you bet your life."

Porter Swenson rolled his eyes at his wife. Melbourne acknowledged the look with a slight nod, then leaned forward and placed a solicitous hand on Jeeter's knee. "You okay, there, Dad?"

Jeeter looked at his watch. It was a thirty-one-year-old Rolex and it ran like he did; a little hitch in its git-along now and then, but mostly worked just fine. "They gave me this watch the day I retired."

Melbourne Swenson added an extra layer of warm sincerity to her voice. "So they did, Dad."

" 'To Alfred Swenson: In recognition of forty years dedicated service.' Says so right on the back."

Melbourne couldn't resist an overly patient sigh. She'd heard it all before. Over and over again. She adjusted the tasteful little sapphire stud in her right ear. "Yes, indeedy."

"Forty years chasing buzzards in the fraud unit of the New York state controller. Which means I know a buzzard when I see one." He hefted the cane and narrowed his eyes at his son. "And that's what I'm looking at now. Buzzards."

Porter moved his feet out of the way. "We're just very concerned for your welfare, Dad. The lake house is too isolated. It's miles from anywhere . . ."

"Red Tail Winery's just down the road. Got busloads of tourists running up and down Route 14 all hours of the day and night. Seneca's a popular spot. And that Red Tail wine's damn delicious."

". . . That offers any kind of emergency services. And there's no denying the fact that you're getting on a bit . . ."

". . . Which makes this place worth roughly twenty-two times what your mother and I paid for it in 1986 . . ."

". . . And we want you to make that century mark!"

"A hundred, hell." Jeeter grinned at Melbourne. "Article in the *Wall Street Journal* this morning said the oldest living American's a hundred and seventeen. Figure I can break that record if I put my mind to it."

Melbourne's answering smile was stiff. She removed her hand from his knee. "We're just very, very worried that something will happen in the middle of the night . . ."

"Now I'll tell you something about the middle of the night. Best part of being old is getting up at two in the morning." Jeeter waved at the lake. "Seneca Lake by moonlight is something to see."

". . . A fall, for example." Melbourne blinked her heavily mascara'd eyelashes in an effort to summon a few tears. "And there you'd be . . . all alone. In pain. Perhaps dying. I just can't stand to think of it, Dad. I lie awake nights worrying about it."

"If you're up at night, you ought to get up and do something useful," Jeeter said. "Surveillance, that'd be useful. Hike on out to that big backyard of yours in Rochester. You'd be pretty amazed at what you can see along of two o'clock in the morning."

"Surveillance," Melbourne repeated. "Right."

For a long moment, all three of them were silent. The lake sparkled in the mellow August sunshine. The remains of Jeeter's ninety-eighth birthday cake sat on the teak picnic table. Melbourne was dressed for the country in white linen trousers and a blue linen camp shirt that hid that frustrating roll of flesh at her waist. Porter had on worn chinos (Melbourne forbade shorts) and an Izod golf shirt. Jeeter himself wore shorts, a Cornell University sweatshirt so old it was transparent in places, and a John Deere tractor billed hat.

Anyone boating by would figure them for a nice happy family celebrating the summer afternoon at their lake stone estate.

Estate.

Jeeter huffed to himself. Well, maybe estate was too pretentious a word for the comfortable old house. But the price that pushy little Realtor had given him just last week would have bought an estate in his day. And that's what the greedy buzzards sitting on *his* porch, in *his* rocking chairs, after stuffing themselves with *his* cake, were after. His estate. His retirement fund. His *savings*. Dammit.

Porter broke the silence. "Surveillance? What do you mean exactly?" He and his wife exchanged more meaningful looks. Jeeter was getting pretty sick of the conversation they weren't having, as opposed to the one they were. "If Melly did venture out into the backyard on a summer's night, what do you think she'd see, Dad?"

Jeeter shrugged. He never should have sent the kid to law school. Once Porter had graduated, he'd starting talking like he was running for office and he hadn't shut up since. "You never know," he said mysteriously. "You just never know. You know Seneca's the deepest lake in the state. Close to nine hundred feet. That'd bury a sixty-story skyscraper so you'd never know it's there. Fact is, along of a summer's night, you just might run across something like the Loch Ness Monster."

Melbourne and Porter digested this for a moment. "Is that so," Porter said.

"Damn straight." Jeeter clamped his lips shut tight. They weren't getting another word out of him, not if they fell flat on the porch deck and begged like a dog.

~

It took another twenty minutes to get the story out of him. And after they did, the younger Swensons couldn't suppress the faintest glow of satisfaction as they made their farewells.

~

"Oh dear Lord." Melbourne sank into the Lexus's passenger seat with a sigh and tossed her straw tote in the back. "I knew it. I just knew it. He's losing it, Porter. We've just got to get him out of there and into somewhere safe." The look of concern on her face wouldn't have fooled Jeeter for a minute.

" 'Not so much like a reptile as a seal,' " Porter quoted his father. "Swimming along the shoreline, crawling up the rocks. The Seneca Lake Monster. And he's thinking about calling the papers." He put the Lexus into gear and drove slowly down the cobbled drive. The lake house was a good half mile off Route 14, a road that ran for eighteen miles up Seneca Lake's west side. Porter signaled to pull onto 14. They drove without speaking until they passed the Seneca Shores winery.

Porter cleared his throat. "We've been fortunate so far. Very, very fortunate. Dad's physical health is splendid. Splendid. But that can't last forever. And as you know, a decent nursing home's going to run six thousand, seven thousand dollars a month. His estate's not going to handle that kind of expense, not without us kicking in. He's got Medicare, which doesn't cover long-term care, and so he's going to have to pay for it himself."

Melbourne smoothed her hair over her ears with nervous jerks of her fingertips. "Do you suppose he was right? About that guy who's lived to be a hundred and seventeen?"

"He's usually right where numbers are involved. Life's a giant general ledger to him. Always has been." Porter wasn't particularly perturbed by this. Life was a general ledger to him, too.

Route 14 had taken them into the heart of Geneva. Porter would have bet there were more nineteenth-century brick buildings in the village than in the whole of Tompkins, Ontario, and Wayne Counties. He stopped at the intersection of 41 and 5 and 20, and signaled a left turn. "Town's looking a little seedy. Seems like there's another dozen FOR SALE signs every time we come through here."

"Oh, I don't know," Melbourne said. "There's some marvelous Greek Revival buildings here, and a couple of stunning examples of Carpenter Gothic. The Finger Lakes wine industry's made a huge difference in the econ—"

"What I'm getting at, Melbourne, is that Dad's lakefront property might not be worth what he thinks it is."

"He won't sell it to us, Porter, and he's not about to get his scrawny butt out of there unless we make him, and you've been harping on the fact that the state is going to take all his assets if he ends up in a nursing home until he finally kicks off at a hundred and seventeen, and then go after our assets, maybe, and we've got to do something." She stopped for breath. "This business about the lake monster, for instance. It's ridiculous. Isn't there something we can do? The old geez . . . I mean poor old guy is losing it. Can't we hold a competency hearing or something?"

Porter winced.

"Sorry," Melbourne said. "That'd make it pretty public, I guess. But what else are we going to do? We're concerned for him, that's all. Both of us. Honestly, how are we going to feel if that little aide calls us up one morning and tells us she's found him dead as a doornail in the lake? Or," Melbourne continued, since Porter's face had a "might be the best thing" sort of look on it, "with a broken hip or some other totally disabling problem. Honestly, the best thing for him is a nice little nursing home somewhere. But he needs to sell the lake house to us first for a rational price so the nursing home can't get its paws on it. That will let him live out the rest of his life on his savings in a protected environment. Honestly . . ."

Porter held his hand up. "I hear you. I'll think about it. These things aren't as easy as you might think."

"What things?"

"Competency hearings. The state's not all that anxious to lock people up, believe it or not."

"I'm not talking about locking him up. I'm talking about seeing that he's safe and . . ."

"Be *quiet*, Melbourne. I know what I'm doing."

The red light clicked to green, and Porter pulled onto 5 and 20 with a squeal of the Lexus's tires. "We don't want to try something like this in Rochester or Syracuse. We need a small town, where these kinds of cases aren't as usual and maybe some personal influence will help."

Melbourne smiled a little.

"There's an old classmate of mine from Cornell. Howie Murchison. He's got a small-town practice. I think it's over near Ithaca. Place is called Hemlock Falls." He reached over and squeezed Melbourne's knee. "Howie will sympathize. The Loch Ness Monster in Seneca Lake. Right."

1

Sarah Quilliam-McHale sat in the tasting room of La Bonne Goute Culinary Academy and wondered if she could find a doctor who'd excuse her from committees, based on the very sound medical reason that she was going to go stark staring crazy if she had to volunteer for another one.

She had a charcoal stick and a sketch pad in her lap. She sketched a tiny Quill swollen up with hives. Then she sketched a tiny Quill in a straitjacket. Then she sketched a tiny Quill sprawled in hopeless resignation with a stake through its heart that read: KILLED BY COMMITTEE.

She'd promised to sit on three Finger Lakes Autumn Fete committees this year. She couldn't back out. She wasn't that kind of person (although she sure wanted to be).

She was doomed.

"These guys on the advisory committee remind me of the second act of *Oklahoma!*" Miriam Doncaster said to her. "You know, that song that goes 'Oh, the farmer and the cowman can be friends.' But the cowboys and the farmers hate each other, right? Let's say the cowmen in this case are from Hemlock Falls and the farmers are from Summersville. They're pretending to agree but they want to shoot each other dead." She rolled her eyes. She was an attractive divorcée in her fifties and ran the town library with brisk efficiency. Quill had always admired her air of cozy sensuality. She had large blue eyes and curly, gray blond hair. She raised her eyebrows suggestively. "You know that song ends in a shoot-out. The cowboys shoot at the farmers. Blam! Blam! Blam!"

Quill made a face. "Yikes. Keep it down. We don't want to give these guys any ideas."

The Finger Lakes Autumn Fete had been held in the village of Hemlock Falls for thirty years. The fete was hugely popular with thousands of tourists. Every year, one or more of the local villages from the surrounding lakes made a bid to host it. Hemlock Falls always prevailed.

But this year, Brady Beale, whose car dealership lay between Hemlock Falls and Summersville, New York, had done a lot of behind-the-scenes politicking. The move-the-fete minority was larger than usual. The routine bickering at this particular meeting of the fete's advisory committee had escalated into quarrels.

Quill sighed and looked at her watch; evening meetings in this rural part of upstate New York almost never ran past ten o'clock. It was close on eleven, now.

Clare Sparrow, who sat on the other side of Quill, leaned forward and whispered, "Madame is going to have my guts for garters. She's never going to let me offer our tasting room for meetings again. Or if she does, she's going to want a humongous security deposit. The cleanup is going to take hours and half the staff's in bed."

Madame LeVasque, Clare's boss, was a notorious penny-pincher. Clare was the recently appointed director of La Bonne Goute Culinary Academy. The academy sat directly across Hemlock Gorge from Quill's own small hotel, the Inn at Hemlock Falls.

Clare was right about the cleanup, Quill thought. Committee members had thrown stuff in exasperation. They'd pounded the table in dudgeon. Disposable coffee cups and balled-up paper napkins lay all over the polished oak floor. Smears of raspberry jelly and brioche crumbs littered the long refectory tabletop that was (usually) such an attractive feature of Bonne Goute's vast and impressive tasting room. There were fifteen people in the room, and twelve of them were really mad at each other.

The annual Finger Lakes Autumn Fete, hosted by the Hemlock Falls Chamber of Commerce for thirty years, was a huge tourism draw in the increasingly popular Finger Lakes region of upstate New York. The planning for the fete was a big pain in the neck. Until this year, Quill had managed to keep her own participation in the fete at a merciful minimum. She didn't mind the work involved in volunteering, but the spats, the feuds, and temper tantrums drove her crazy.

Brady Beale sat coiled in his chair, his eyes narrowed in an unfriendly glare at the fete chair, Adela Henry. Brady owned the local car dealership, Peterson Automotive, which he'd bought from his uncle's estate after a hitch in Iraq. Peterson Automotive lay between Hemlock Falls, which was close to Cayuga Lake, and Summersville, which was right on the shores of Seneca Lake.

Adela was the mayor's wife. Quill (who had painted

oils and acrylics for a living before buying the Inn with her sister Meg) often visualized Adela as a three-masted schooner, the kind with cannons on the foredeck. Adela stood at the head of the table, her considerable bosom huffed out like a topsail.

"The committee," Adela said with ominous calm, "is not going to consider your suggestion, Brady Beale, and that's that."

"You aren't the committee," John Swinford heatedly pointed out. He and his wife Penelope owned the Swinford Winery, which overlooked Seneca Lake. "A committee's more than one bossy bi—" His wife Penelope poked him hard. John swallowed the word, shut his eyes for a moment, and then said, mildly, "Brady's suggestion has merit. As I say, Adela, you aren't the committee, not the whole committee, anyway."

"And you, sir," Adela said majestically, "are not from Hemlock Falls."

"Well, no, I'm not. But Summersville isn't at the other end of the Earth. We're only ten miles from you."

"Eight-point-six miles, in fact," said the elderly gentleman next to him. "I would like to add my voice in support of Brady's suggestion to move the fete to Summersville."

Adela's lower lip jutted forward in a dangerous way. "You aren't a Hemlockian, either, Dr. McKenzie."

Dr. McKenzie, who was small, fit, and sported an admirable salt-and-pepper mustache, said tartly, "My veterinarian practice extends to your village, madam. I've always considered myself an honorary Hemlockian. The fete brings a great deal of money to village businesses. It is time to spread the wealth."

"Dr. McKenzie's judged the Furry Friends competition for *years*," Dolly Jean Attenborough piped up. She was shorter, rounder, and older than Adela by some ten years, but she generated the same forceful personality. "Brilliantly, I might add."

Adela smiled coldly. "I'm sure anyone with a pet entered into the Furry Friends pet show would feel that way, Dolly Jean. Before the judging results are in, at least."

Brady Beale waved his hand in the air. "Hey! Look, people. Can we get back to the point here? This is the fete steering committee, right? I mean, all of us here have got a stake in the ground with this fete. I'm going to make a motion, okay? To move the fete to Summersville instead of Hemlock Falls. And then we can vote."

Quill didn't know Brady Beale very well, except that he was a distant relative of her friend Marge Schmidt (the richest person in Tompkins County), who was married to Harland Peterson, the biggest (and most good-natured) dairy farmer in the five-county area. She had the impression that the dealership did pretty well, despite the inevitable nickname bestowed on him—"Shady Brady Beale." He'd recently added a line of high-end imported cars after a trip to an international car show in Miami. "The thing is," he'd confided to Quill when she'd brought her Honda in for a tune-up, "we've got all these rich guys moving in from Toronto and New York to spend the summers here. And rich people like luxury vehicles, if you get my drift."

Quill got his drift. Her own Inn was thriving, mostly due to an affinity the wealthy had for her sister Meg's gourmet cooking.

"The group assembled here is not the official steering committee," Adela said. "This is the advisory committee." Her gaze swept the room, like a foretopman searching the sea for enemy vessels. "Fortunately, all the members of the steering committee are here. If you wish, Mr. Beale, to put this absurd suggestion to a vote, we will do so. Do I hear a motion?"

"I just *made* a motion," Brady shouted. "Dammit!"

Everybody glanced sideways at the Reverend Dookie Shuttleworth. Dookie raised one hand in gentle absolution.

"The motion has to come from a member of the steering committee," Adela said stubbornly.

"That is godda . . . I mean absolutely unfair," Brady snapped. "The steering committee is stacked with your toadies."

Quill straightened up in indignation. She was on the steering committee.

"They vote the way you tell them to vote."

"They will vote their conscience, Mr. Beale. Elmer! You were about to make a motion to move the Finger Lakes Autumn Fete to Summersville."

Elmer Henry, mayor (in name at least) of Hemlock Falls, and Adela's devoted, if somewhat oppressed, husband, jumped to attention and said, "I so move."

"Mrs. Quince, you were going to second?"

Althea Quince, a large, colorful lady of a certain age, nodded amiably. "I second the motion."

"Any discussion?" Adela asked with a dangerous look in her eye.

"We about discussed this to death," somebody muttered.

Adela drew herself up. She was fond of pantsuits in

noticeable colors. She had matched today's purple with a bright yellow silk blouse. She looked like an infuriated pansy. "Members of the steering committee? How say you?"

"Nay," Elmer said.

Althea Quince nodded decisively. "Nay."

"Quill?!" Adela demanded.

"Nay."

"Reverend Shuttleworth?"

"Abstain."

"I myself . . ." Adela paused dramatically. "Vote nay. Your motion is defeated, Mr. Beale."

~

"So everybody went home mad," Quill said cheerfully to Marge Schmidt. The meeting had finally wound down close to midnight. Quill invited Miriam for a glass of wine at the Croh Bar before going home, in the hope of finding Marge there, too. If she plied her friends with wine, maybe she could convince one or both of them to take her place on at least one of her other committees.

She was in luck. Although it was late, Miriam thought that a cool glass of her favorite Chardonnay would erase some of the tensions of the evening, and the Croh Bar was on the way home for both women.

Nothing was very far from anything else in Hemlock Falls; Quill's Inn was less than a mile away from the village, and Miriam lived in a pleasant old Federal brick home just off Main. Marge Schmidt, along with her partner Betty Hall, owned the Croh Bar and was there to gather up the night's receipts and drop them off at the bank.

"Ha! Everybody went home mad?" Marge slapped the bank bag onto the bar top. "Big surprise, that. The whole town spends the month of August being mad every year, and I'm getting sick of it. I'd be home watching *American Idol* with Harland tonight instead of closing this place if Betty wasn't on that committee."

"Since the alternative was being on the advisory committee yourself, you tell me which you'd rather be doing," Miriam said cynically. ·

Marge's lips twitched in a smile. She was short, with ginger-colored hair, and beady gray eyes that put most people in mind of a Marine sniper on the not infrequent occasions when she was in a temper. "Good point. So Shady Brady led the charge to move the fete this year?"

"I buy my cars from him," Quill protested, "he's never seemed shady to me."

Marge snorted. "You know that old oak tree sits in front of the dealership? He used to do deals for George under it in the summertime. Oak? Shade tree? Get it?"

Quill raised her hand in protest. "I get it. I get it."

"Brady worked for old George when he was in high school, went off to the navy and when he came back, George was dead. You wouldn't remember about the 'shady' part because you've only been here fifteen years. You're still a flat land foreigner." Marge took a swallow of wine and expanded. "Now, I've never thought much of Brady in the business way of things, that's true. Doesn't have a lot of what I'd call common sense." (For Marge, this translated into the successful conversion of opportunity into cash.) "What the heck did he expect, trying to change the location of the fete at this late date? It's only two weeks away and the advertising's been out for months."

"He offered to cover the costs of letting everyone know the location was changed."

Marge rolled her eyes. "Like I said. Not a lot of common sense. Thing about Shady Brady is, he gets an idea stuck in that noggin of his, he won't let it go."

"Adela squashed him good and proper," Miriam murmured. "He didn't so much let it go as have it wrenched away."

"That Adela," Marge said with reluctant admiration. "Now, there's another one without a lot of common sense, but when she wants something, she gets results."

Like a steamroller flattening a house, Quill thought. She decided to change the subject and edge into the actual reason she'd stopped at the Croh Bar. It was late. She was tired. Her husband Myles had left for a monthlong assignment overseas that afternoon, and she'd moved back into the Inn for the duration. So in addition to being tired, if she thought too much about him being gone, she'd get depressed. Her four-and-a-half-year-old son Jack got her up early, and she had a full day tomorrow, committee after committee after committee. "Since you skipped out on the advisory committee this year, Marge, how's about giving me a hand with the booth assignments?"

Marge looked startled. "How's about I sign up for a peacekeeping mission in Beirut? It'd be a lot safer."

Miriam snorted into her wineglass.

"You could help out, too, Miriam. We're almost finished with the site map. Just a few more booth assignments to make."

Marge and Miriam looked at each other, grinned, and shook their heads simultaneously.

"Let me guess," Miriam said sweetly. "Dolly Jean Attenborough wants to put the Crafty Ladies booth right at the main entrance."

"Well, of course . . ."

"And the Crafty Ladies' most bitter rivals, the Craft Guild, want the very same space . . ."

"In a manner of speaking," Quill admitted.

Marge slapped the bar top and slung the bank bag into her purse. "I'd rather eat a rat than be on any of those committees. Forget it. I'm off to the bank."

"Me, too," Miriam said decisively. "Not to the bank, but home to bed. And if that's why you offered to buy us a glass of wine, forget it."

"There's a couple of openings on the Furry Friends committee," Quill said desperately. "You guys like pets, don't you?"

"That's the pet show stuff?" Miriam said. "My dog's better than your dog? I don't think so."

"Fine," Quill said crossly. "Just fine."

"You've got only yourself to blame," Marge pointed out. "Thing is, Quill, you're a pushover. Always have been. Always will be." She swung her arm around Quill's shoulder in a companionable way, and led the way out of the bar and into the parking lot. "Go home. Let Doreen off her babysitting duties, take a hot shower, and go to bed. Things will look better in the morning."

Actually, Quill thought as she got into her car, except for the fact that she couldn't con anybody else onto her committees, things looked pretty good right now. The full moon floated overhead, seeming to bob gently in the soft dark sky. The air was filled with the scent of late roses. Myles was off on another assignment, but they'd both known when they'd married that his job took him away from her and Jack. She accepted that because she loved him. Not only that, but their son was a joy, a miracle in a world too often short of miracles.

She drove up the long circular driveway to the Inn.

The gracious old building sat on five acres on the lip of Hemlock Gorge. Carriage lamps gleamed at the corners of each of the three stories, washing the mellow stone walls with yellow light. Beyond the circle of the main driveway, the rush of the falls was familiar and unutterably soothing. Her collection of Oriental lilies was just starting to add their perfume to the air, mingling with the smell of freshly cut grass.

On impulse, she parked in front, rather than going around to her usual spot in the back, and used her key card to go in through the big oak door at the entrance.

The night-lights were on in the foyer. The mahogany reception desk sat at the right. The PLEASE RING FOR ASSISTANCE sign stood on the polished desktop. The two hip-high Oriental vases that flanked it were empty; Mike the groundskeeper would fill them with late-blooming dahlias in the morning. To the left, the beige leather couch faced the cobblestone fireplace. She paused on her way upstairs and ran her hands over the back. It was looking worn, and they had the money to replace it, but there was a comfort in old things, and she'd resisted that small change in her life.

When she and Myles had married, she'd moved into

Myles's house, which sat on a tributary of the Hemlock River, some three miles away and out of the small suite she'd lived in on the third floor. After Jack was born, they had all decided—Myles, Quill, her sister Meg, and their much-loved housekeeper Doreen Muxworthy-Stoker— that when Myles was away, Quill and Jack would come back to the Inn and stay.

Quill barely admitted to herself, much less to her family, how important her rooms upstairs were to her. She had to make some adjustments—her large walk-in closet, which had a window, was converted to a bedroom for Jack. Doreen moved into the connecting room next door to care for him. And, of course, her sister Meg had the suite opposite her own.

She decided against using the elevator and walked upstairs.

Quill had just re-carpeted the third floor in a navy-and-celery-green patterned plush that shouldn't have worked but did. The new-carpet smell was faint but persistent as she walked down the hallway. Her sister's door opened just as she put the key card into her lock.

"Hey," Meg said.

"Hey, yourself."

Meg was small, a whole head shorter than Quill, and dark-haired where her own was perilously close to carrot-colored. Myles, in his tender moments, assured her it was red-gold. Meg was also the best gourmet chef in the northeastern United States, and the Inn had the satisfied diners to prove it.

"How was the committee meeting?"

Quill rolled her eyes. "Dire. Contentious. Awful. How was your date with Justin?"

"Fine."

"Just fine?"

"Nice. But then Justin's nice."

"Yes, he is," Quill said readily. Some part of her hoped her gypsy sister would decide to settle down with Justin; the more rational part of her brain knew this was unlikely to happen. Justin Alvarez was the junior partner in Howie Murchison's law firm and a little too steady for her volatile sister. On the other hand, he was a younger, cuter version of the actor Benjamin Bratt, and for Meg, who was always attracted to lawlessness, his gorgeousness went a long way toward mitigating his excellent character.

Quill glanced at her watch. It was well after one o'clock. "Shouldn't you be asleep?"

"Bjarne's got the breakfast shift tomorrow. I've got a light day in the kitchen. Clare Sparrow's coming over in the morning to finish up some work for the fete."

"The fete! Aha!" Quill clapped her hand over her mouth. If she woke Jack up, she'd never get to bed herself. She dropped her voice to a whisper. "How's about if you give me a hand with the Furry Friends committee?"

"How's about if I smack myself silly with a sauté pan?" Meg said amiably.

"Then maybe you wouldn't mind helping out with the booth assignments."

Meg patted her sister on the back in a kindly way. "Everybody in town knows that Dolly Jean Attenborough is gunning for Esther West and the ladies at the Craft

Guild. I'd just as soon *not* be witness to the start of a land war."

"I'll make you a deal . . ."

"Forget it. I've already exposed myself to unfriendly fire by agreeing to select the judges for the food competition. This is me saying good night, Quill." She slipped back inside her room before Quill could think of a bribe big enough to get her sister to change her mind. She made a face at the closed door and let herself in to her suite.

~

Moonlight flooded in from the French doors to the balcony, bathing her small living room in silvery light. She put her tote on the kitchen counter. The door to Jack's bedroom was ajar. She edged it open and looked in on her sleeping son. Here, the moonlight touched his face and hair. He slept hard, the way that little boys do, his mouth slightly open. Max the dog stirred a bit at the foot of the bed. Quill rumpled his ears and hushed him.

In the living room, the connecting door to Doreen's room was also ajar, and the sounds of Doreen's snores were a soft purr. She closed the door, drew the drapes in the living room, and prepared herself for bed.

Fine, she thought as she drifted off to sleep. If she couldn't get anyone to take over a couple of her committees, she could at least take a solemn oath not to get on any more. Marge thought she was a pushover, did she? Ha.

2

Esther West was sitting on the worn leather couch in front of the cobblestone fireplace in the foyer when Quill came downstairs at nine-thirty the next morning.

It had been a wonderful day so far. The weather was warm and sunny. She'd eaten a leisurely breakfast with Jack. She'd checked in with the head of the housekeeping staff and Mike the groundskeeper. The only thing left to do as far as Inn management was concerned was to return yesterday's phone calls left for her by the Inn's excellent receptionist, Dina Muir. She now had an hour and a half to do that, before her first committee meeting. The Chamber of Commerce meeting was at eleven and the Furry Friends committee meeting was in the afternoon. Then the day would be hers and Jack's. He would be starting pre-school in a couple of weeks. Each day she could spend with him was a gift.

Esther was an old acquaintance, and she greeted her happily.

Esther ran the local crafts store, which she called, in her direct and unambiguous way, Esther West's Kountry

Krafts! For many years, it had been West's Best Dress Shoppe! but the rise of the nearby Pyramid Mall in Syracuse and the new Walmart out on Route 15 near Ithaca had driven even her most loyal customers away. With practical good sense, she'd taken advantage of her former customers' love of knitting, quilting, beading, and sketching and opened a craft store.

Esther was a great believer in advertising her own wares. This morning she wore a patchwork quilt skirt, handmade beaded earrings, and a quantity of beaded bracelets. She clutched a large, thin package wrapped in brown paper.

She got up as soon as she saw Quill coming downstairs. "I'm so glad I caught you. I just happened to be passing by and I thought I'd drop off those sketch pads you ordered. I brought a nice new package of charcoal pencils, too. Don't worry about paying me for them, dear. I consider them a contribution to the arts." She dropped the package onto the couch and clutched Quill's arm companionably. "I know how busy you are with your dear little boy and your many, many duties at the Inn, but I was hoping you had a few minutes to spare to consid—"

"Ha!" Dolly Jean Attenborough rolled through the big front door with the determination of Sherman advancing on Atlanta. "I thought I'd find you here, Esther West. It's just like you to go sneaking around behind my back." She put her hands on her hips. "Sarah Quilliam, if you've gone over to the Craft Guild, all I have to say to you is shame, shame, shame!"

Esther retained her grip on Quill's arm and wagged her finger in Dolly Jean's face. "I cannot believe that you are

addressing one of the finest artists of our generation in
that rude way, Dolly Jean!"

The two women glared at each other. Esther, president
of the Craft Guild, was tall and thin and reminded Quill of
a great blue heron. Dolly Jean, chairwoman of the Association of Crafty Ladies, was short and round. With her
fluffy white hair and hand-crocheted skirts, she looked a
bit like a doily.

Quill had been an innkeeper for more than fifteen
years, and she had a highly developed sense of survival.
She looked at her watch and exclaimed in dismay, "My
goodness, is that the time?! How nice to see you, Dolly
Jean. And, Esther, thank you so much for bringing the art
supplies by. I'll drop by the store later to pick up the in-
voice, shall I? Now, if you ladies will excuse me, I have a
ton of . . ."

Dolly Jean grabbed her other arm. "Just one minute. I
have been sent here by the Crafty Ladies to offer you an
honorary membership on our board of directors." She shot
Esther a triumphant glance. "The membership comes with
a modest stipend, naturally."

"Quill was just about to agree to become the honorary
chair of the Ladies Craft Guild Auxiliary," Esther snapped.
"Which also carries a stipend." She thought a moment. "A
stipend much less modest than yours."

Quill gently disengaged herself from both women.
"Now, look," she said kindly. "You both realize that as a
judge on the arts committee, I'm forbidden to associate
with any artists who've entered their work in the fete. As
much as I would love to be on the boards, I just can't. The
rules simply won't allow it."

"Damn," Esther said.

Dolly Jean bit her lower lip and said crossly, "That's not it. It's because you're one of those big-city artists who sneers at the crafts of the common people."

"I am not!" Quill said, astonished.

"Huh!" Esther said. "For once in your life, you're making sense, Dolly Jean."

Quill clutched at her wildly springy hair. "That is absolutely not true!"

~

Twenty minutes later, Quill stamped into the kitchen and sat down in the rocker by the fireplace in a huff.

Nobody paid any attention to her.

Meg's two sous chefs, Bjarne Bjarnsen and Elizabeth Chou, were finishing up the breakfast service. Meg and Clare Sparrow were hunched over the birch-topped prep table in a sea of pens and yellow pads. Dina Muir, the Inn's receptionist, perched on a stool in front of the twelve-burner stove. Mellow sunshine flooded the large, comfortable room. Bunches of fresh herbs hung from the wooden beams that crossed the high ceiling and the air was filled with the scent of drying lavender, basil, oregano, and thyme.

Quill addressed the indifferent air. "I cannot believe I did this. I just joined another committee."

"This is good," Bjarne said. "As long as I, myself, do not have to join any committees, I approve of others joining committees."

"I hate committees," Quill said. "But it was the only way out. I am now director of the Associated Crafts Association of Hemlock Falls. I did not," she continued darkly, "choose the title. But at least the Crafty Ladies and Craft Guild are in temporary alliance . . . nobody cares about this, do they?"

"You're a pushover, Sis. Always have been. Always will be." Meg's small, slender body was hunched over her notebook with the ferocity of a mamma bear defending her young. Clare, who was equally slender but much taller, leaned back against the counter, her arms folded defiantly. The tension between the two would make a marvelous line drawing. Quill decided to stop beating herself up for getting onto yet another committee and get the shapes onto paper before the two either subsided into amicable squabbling or erupted into open warfare.

Dina Muir was at Clare and Meg's meeting mostly because she didn't have anything better to do before graduate school resumed in three weeks. She was texting somebody with indignant jabs of her forefinger, ignoring all three of them. Quill had allowed her to forward phone calls to reception to her cell phone, and it'd given her the freedom of the Inn.

"I give!" Meg said. "I'll judge the flipping Jell-O architecture contest. But I am not, not judging pies. No way, no how. No, ma'am."

"Why not?" Clare asked suspiciously.

"For one thing," Meg said, "you are a far, far better pastry chef than I will ever be."

Although this was true, everyone in the kitchen knew that Meg would rather dye her hair blue than admit it.

Clare looked at her best friend and chief competitor with a skeptical eye. "There's something going on here I don't understand," she said. "This is a simple job, assigning judges to the food competition. We've been at it an hour or more. And it's turning out to be not so simple. What kind of baloney are you trying to pull on me now?"

"You are the empress of pastry, Clare," Meg added. "I've always said so, haven't I, Quill?"

Quill didn't bother to answer. If nobody cared that she was hostage to yet another committee, she wasn't going to jump into this. Clare and Meg could work it out themselves.

Clare made a sound like "phooey."

Meg flung her hands apart. "I concede your preeminence in pastry. You should be flattered! *You* should judge the Homemade Pies division at the fete. Besides, there's nothing sneaky or underhanded about my preference for judging the Jell-O architecture contest. Let's face it. Buildings made out of food are cool."

Clare squeezed her arms closer to her chest. "First of all, neither one of us thinks Jell-O is food. Food is a perfectly balanced bouillabaisse. Or individually crafted *tartes au chocolat*. Jell-O's processed by machines that kick out tons and tons and tons of the stuff every minute. Second, food is something you eat, not something you make bricks with. We're both master chefs and the food part of this fete is an opportunity to get a little PR for the both of us. You're telling me you're happy to get publicity for judging the quality of a town hall made out of horse's hooves flavored with lime?"

Dina looked up uneasily. "You're kidding me, right? Not horse's hooves." She flipped her phone shut and shoved it into her skirt pocket. "Ick."

"Cow hooves, anyway," Meg said carelessly. "Whatever. Don't be such a wimp, Dina."

Dina resettled her red-rimmed spectacles farther up her nose. "I'm not a wimp, Meg, thank you very much. I find it perfectly disgusting that people eat the boiled hooves of animals. Anyone would. And to answer your question, Clare, Meg doesn't want to judge the fete pie contest because it's a suicide mission. Think about it. Every home cook in Tompkins County—and we're still very much a rural economy here no matter what the Chamber of Commerce thinks, so there's a *ton* of farmwives—takes pride in her piecrust. You really want to be the one who picks Mrs. Kiddermeister's pie over Marge Schmidt-Peterson's? Or even worse, Carol Ann Spinoza over Adela Henry, the mayor's wife?"

Clare paled. "Carol Ann Spinoza enters the Homemade Pies competition?"

"Every year," Dina said.

There was a moment of respectful silence. Carol Ann Spinoza was a persistent, annoying dermatitis on the village skin. When she'd been tax collector, she'd risen to the status of a lethal disease. As animal control officer, she'd posted a wanted poster in the Hemlock Falls post office that featured Quill's dog Max as Public Enemy Number One. For a brief, horrible couple of weeks, she'd been a food inspector for the State of New York. There was a lot more that was horrible about Carol Ann, including her deceptively cheerful blond good looks, but Quill didn't want to think about it.

"She's unemployed at the moment," Dina said darkly. "And you know Carol Ann. She's power mad and competitive. She's probably Googled prizewinning pie recipes from the entire planet and is going to enter every single one of them. It's going to be one heck of a contest this year."

Clare tossed her pencil onto the prep table, folded her hands over her middle, and looked at the floor.

A minute passed, then two.

Meg couldn't stand the silence. She leaped to her feet and yelled, "Gaah! What the heck are you doing?"

Clare smiled serenely at her. "You just can't stand a peaceful meditative silence, can you, Meg? I'll tell you what I'm doing. I'm centering."

"Centering," Meg said flatly.

"Some sort of yoga thing, I expect. Or maybe Zen." Dina swung her forefinger into the air for emphasis. "You're going to need more than yoga to get you through the homemade pies. Vodka, maybe. Lots of it. That'll help."

Clare settled back onto the stool. "How did you guys talk me into this, anyway? I get that the fete is an annual event . . ."

"A tradition, really," Quill said.

"Right. So for the past umpty-ump years . . ."

"Fifteen for the Inn," Quill said. "Ever since Meg and I bought it. The fete itself—gosh, probably since the War of 1812. Adela Henry's been running it for years. She's been so successful that the last five years or so we've had thirty thousand people show up for fete week. It's pretty amazing, when you think about it."

"Whatever. I'm from New York, remember? Crowds don't bother me." Clare, that rarest of birds, an unflappable chef, was showing signs of agitation. "I'm new here, right? I've only been director at the culinary academy for a year. So of course I want to do my bit. You're Food Booth Liaison, Quill, right?"

"Yes. I'm judging the art show, too. And I'm in charge of the Furry Friends booths." Quill sighed and clutched her hair. "Which is another huge mistake. You think people get passionate about their homemade pies? You should see how they feel about their pets."

"What's that? What? Oh. Right. The pet thing. Kittens, puppies. Whatever. So are you guys still with me here? Okay, fine. Meg is doing her bit as chair of the selection committee for the food judges and asks me to be on it, too. Easy peasy, right?" She slapped her yellow pad with a little more emphasis than was necessary. "We have fifteen food contests. We have twelve candidates for judges of those self-same food contests including you and me, Meg. This should be a no-brainer."

"It is a no-brainer, really," Meg said in a kindly way. "You just have to remember that Dolly Jean Attenborough can't judge cakes because she's president of the Crafty Ladies and every single one of the Crafty Ladies puts a cake into competition. And that Nadine Peterson has to judge Pickles and Preserves because she won twelve years running and the other picklers and preservers want a chance to win, too, and if she's judging she can't enter anything into competition. Stuff like that. And you are the best possible person to judge Homemade Pies because you haven't been in town long enough for anyone to hold anything against you."

"Don't do it," Dina muttered. "The losers will ride you out of town on a rail."

"Wait, wait, wait." Clare wasn't a pretty woman, but she had distinctive features, and when she chose, a true air of command—a necessity in her job as director of La Bonne Goute Culinary Academy. "Carol Ann Spinoza? Marge Schmidt? Adela Henry? They all enter the Homemade Pies competition?"

"Berry and fruit division," Quill said. Using her thumb, she smudged the shadow under the Meg-figure's chin, then closed her sketch pad and slipped it under her rocking chair. "In the years before you came to take over the academy, we always got a chef from Syracuse to judge the pies. We always recommended that they beat feet out of town before the results were announced."

Meg waved her pencil in the air. "Clare'll be fine."

"I'm not doing it," Clare said firmly. "Sophie will judge it. Not me. Put that down in the notes, Dina, judge for the Homemade Pies, berry and fruit division, is Sophie Kilcannon. She's the new fruits and vegetables," she said in response to Meg's questioning look, "I recruited her out of Miami and she's starting this week. Nice kid. Eager to learn, which is good, since she's not quite up to snuff in a couple of areas."

"I hope she's good at self-defense," Dina muttered under her breath. "Okay, Sophie it is. Pie judge."

Quill got to her feet. "Is that it? You guys settle all the food judging items? The Chamber meeting started ten minutes ago, and I promised to hand the assignments over to Adela today. The fete's two weeks away, and she's already antsy. If I don't give her a list, she'll have my head on a plate."

Meg ran her hands through her short dark hair, which made it stand up in spikes. "I think so. Good enough for a first cut, anyway."

"What do you mean, a first cut?" Clare demanded. "We've spent more than an hour picking just the right judge for the preserves, and the quick breads, and the pickles and everything else. We're the best experts in a five-county area, if I do say so myself. Who's going to second-guess us?"

"Adela," Quill said. "The whole fete is Adela's baby from start to finish. She's organized it for thirty years— maybe more than that. She's terrific at it, too." She glanced at her watch. "I'm late for the chamber meeting. Does somebody have the list written up so that I can take it with me? You do, Dina? Thanks. I'll see you all later."

Dina followed her out the swinging doors to the dining room. "Do you want your messages before you go into the meeting?"

Quill paused to rearrange the small bouquet of Pink Lady roses at table twenty-six, partly because one of the roses drooped unattractively, but mostly so she could stand and appreciate the room. She'd given up on the wall-to-wall carpeting (something she should have done long before) and restored the narrow-plank pine flooring. Then she'd replaced the tabletops, which had required tablecloths, with natural stone instead of wood. The project cost as much as the annual budget of a small African country, but the Inn had done well over the past three years, and she was glad they'd spent the money. The dining room featured floor-to-ceiling windows that faced the falls outside. The wood floors, the shale tabletops, and the cut-stone walls made it seem as if the falls and the Inn were a warm and natural part of each other.

Dina waved a fistful of pink While You Were Out messages in the air. "Hey, Boss? You want to take a look at these?"

Quill dabbed impatiently at the curl over her left ear. She didn't want to take a look at a thing. She wanted to finish the sketch she'd started of her sister and Clare. She wanted to go up and take Jack down to the Hemlock River so they could play in the summer sunshine. Anything but attend to the myriad, pesky details of running her Inn.

Instead, she held her hand out for the messages. "Anything that won't keep?"

"You might want to call the Golden Pillar travel people. They're bummed about the Inn being booked until after Thanksgiving and they're threatening to take us off their website as a desired destination, or whatever they call it."

"We're booked until after Thanksgiving?" This was good news.

"Yep. This Long-Term Let idea is turning out to be a bummer."

Quill grimaced. "Maybe."

Their financial guy, John Raintree, had suggested the Long-Term Let as a hedge against the ups and downs of their vacancy rate. Quill and Dina had posted reasonable monthly rates for the high-priced suites, which were usually the last to be booked by guests. It had seemed like a great idea at the time—but the suites were snapped up almost immediately, leaving no vacancies for at least six months. There were only three: the Provencal, the Federal, and the Colonial. A couple named Quince had promptly booked both the Federal and the Colonial. A very, very old fellow named Jeeter Swenson had the Provencal. Mr. Swenson made Quill a little nervous. The Provencal Suite was on the third floor with a balcony one guest had already fallen off of. Since the apparent accident had turned out to be a murder, Quill supposed that didn't really count.

"Maybe we should tell the Golden Pillar people that we've given up the Long-Term Let idea."

"Okay," Dina said.

"But maybe the Long-Term Let idea is a good one. This travel boom can't last forever."

"Okay," Dina said.

"Maybe I should discuss it with Melody Brodie at Golden Pillar and see what she thinks."

"Sounds like a Scarlett O'Hara moment to me."

Quill stuck the message in her skirt pocket. "Right. I'll think about it tomorrow—or maybe after the Chamber meeting." She looked at her watch. The morning had started so well—and now look. She'd volunteered for another committee. The Golden Pillar people were threatening a boycott. And like the White Rabbit, she was late, late, late for the Chamber of Commerce meeting, which meant somebody had probably volunteered her for another committee.

"Grrr," she said, to Dina's confusion. "We'll just see about that!" She straightened her shoulders, stiffened her spine, and prepared to go to the meeting.

3

The Hemlock Falls Chamber of Commerce meetings had been held at the Inn's conference room since Meg and Quill had opened for business. At the time, the Inn was the only business in the village with room enough for all twenty-four members to sit down together. This wasn't true anymore. Tourists had discovered that upstate New York—with its vineyards, boutique distilleries, local food and craft stores, and amazing natural gorges—was one of the most beautiful places on earth. And as the tourists came, so came the construction crews.

The first building of note was the Resort, a lavish hotel complex about a quarter mile downriver from the Inn. La Bonne Goute Culinary Academy followed some years later—and although its internationally acclaimed master chef had been murdered not long after its ornately carved doors opened to the public—the academy's cooking classes attracted even greater numbers of out-of-towners under Clare Sparrow's stewardship. So there was plenty of room to hold the Chamber meeting elsewhere. But tradition was a matter of principle in the village, and not even Carol Ann Spinoza had the nerve to suggest a change in venue.

Quill walked through the dining room to the reception foyer and turned left down the short hall to the conference room. The space had been a keeping room in the inn's distant past, but instead of barrels of flour, sacks of apples, and huge hams, the room now held a long refectory table with seating for twenty-four. Whiteboards were fastened to the stone walls and a long credenza held the coffee and tea services. It wasn't Quill's favorite space at the Inn, but it served a very useful purpose.

Quill tapped at the door as she opened it.

As she'd thought, nobody noticed the tap, much less her belated entrance. The room was overcrowded and at first glance, it seemed as if everyone was yelling at everybody else. Quill propped the door open with the kick plate, and took a moment to sort things out.

Mayor Henry, his round face bright red either with heat or temper, sat at the head of the table, whacking the gavel for order.

Adela, his wife, stood nose to nose with Carol Ann Spinoza.

Carol Ann's outward appearance belied her inner Idi Amin. She was small and curvy with big blue eyes, naturally curly blond hair, and pink-cheeked cheerleader good looks. She smelled like shampoo and soap. She believed that clothes made the woman. During her tenure as animal control officer, she wore a unique uniform of black pants, black T-shirt, and black billed cap. She'd sent her original design for the animal control officers' weapons belt to

Albany, with a suggestion that it be adopted statewide. The only organization to express interest had been the NRA. She'd had a brief, terrifying term as a New York state food inspector. Quill wasn't sure what career Carol Ann was pursuing at the moment. She was very sure she didn't want to know.

Whatever it was, it had gotten up Adela's nose.

Adela hollered. Carol Ann hollered back. Her blond ponytail bobbed loosely up and down as she danced with rage.

Adela jabbed her fist in alarming proximity to Carol Ann's pert, freckled nose. Her cheeks matched the violent purple of her blouse. If Adela had a heart condition, it was going to manifest itself speedy quick.

Farther on down the table, Marge Schmidt roared vehemently into her husband Harland's ear. The Reverend Dookie Shuttleworth, pastor of the Hemlock Falls Church of the Word of God, appeared to be praying aloud. Nadine Peterson, owner of the Hemlock Hall of Beauty, sat with crossed arms and a glowering expression while she harangued Esther West. Harvey Bozzel, Hemlock Falls' best (and only) advertising executive chewed on his tie and looked desperate.

Quill scanned the ranks of members—it appeared as if most of the twenty-four had turned out in force—and settled on Miriam. The town librarian leaned back in her chair, watching the fracas in mild bemusement. Her large Sierra Club tote occupied the chair next to her. She caught sight of Quill and lifted the tote off the chair. Quill sidled around the end of the table and sat down. "Hey, Miriam."

"Hey, Quill."

"So, anything special going on?"

Miriam had a sort of knowing centeredness about her character that Quill greatly admired. "Adela quit."

"Adela quit what?"

"Adela resigned her chairmanship of the Finger Lakes Autumn Fete."

"No!" Quill turned and stared at the mayor's wife. Adela's large bosom heaved in indignation. "She's run the fete for thirty years. We can't do it without her. She doesn't mean it."

"Order! Order! Order!" Elmer hollered. He whacked the gavel on the table several times for emphasis. Adela ignored him. Carol Ann ignored him. Both women were shouting, and Quill was hard put to make out what the argument was about. The exchange seemed to consist of the "you will not," "I will so," "can't make me," "old bat," "little witch" variety.

"This meeting will come to order!" Elmer roared. "Adela, you're making a fool of yourself. Sit down, dammit." He made a grab for his wife's arm.

Adela, who was, Quill judged, quite senseless with fury, swung around, leaned down, and punched Elmer in the shoulder. Elmer, startled, swung the gavel and connected smartly with Adela's backside.

Miriam, Nadine Peterson, and Esther West gasped.

Quill jumped halfway out of her chair and sat down again.

A shocked—and covertly delighted—silence descended on the room like a wet blanket falling off a clothesline.

Harland Peterson rose to his feet and extended one

meaty hand. "Give me that damn thing, Elmer. You don't want to be a-hitting on your wife with it."

Elmer was perfectly white. He gazed at the gavel in his hand in horror.

Adela took three deep breaths. "Well," she said in a trembling voice. "Well! The next communication you have with me, Elmer Burton Henry, will be through my lawyer."

She burst into tears and ran out of the room.

The gavel dropped from Elmer's nerveless fingers onto the table. Nobody said anything. After a long moment, the slam of the Inn's heavy front door rolled down the hallway.

Marge Schmidt stood up and leaned across the table. "Gimme that thing, Elmer."

Elmer blinked at her.

"The gavel, Elmer. Give it here."

He shoved it across the table with the palm of his hand. Marge picked it up and whacked it on the table, once, twice, three times. "Meeting adjourned."

For a long moment, nobody moved.

"Come on," Marge ordered. "Meeting's over. Get on back to whatever you need to, folks. Except you, Quill. You and Miriam come with me. We got to find Adela and pound some sense into her."

Minutes later, Quill stood in the parking lot at the front of the Inn with Dina, Miriam, and Marge, looking for Adela's red Camry. The dining room opened for lunch at eleven and the lot was already full. The lot was directly across from the massive pine door of the Inn's entrance and was a small paved area that held a total of eight cars.

The Henrys' Toyota wasn't there. The larger lot was behind the building and it was where Quill, Meg, and the staff parked, in addition to most of the guests.

"My guess is she took off for home," Miriam said. "We can check around back, if you like."

"No, she was parked here in front," Dina said. "She slammed out the front door and in about two seconds I heard a car peel out of here." She slipped the rubber band off her ponytail, rewound her hair, and put the rubber band back in. "Should I call Davy, or something?"

"Don't be an idiot," Marge said. "There's no call to get the sheriff involved."

Dina made a sound like "huh!" Miriam nudged Marge reprovingly. Marge swung her turret-like gaze onto Dina. Marge had the steady calm of a seasoned tank gunner and she was the richest woman in Tompkins County, and for all Quill knew, the rest of upstate New York. "Sorry, I guess, Dina," Marge said. "But this just goes to show you."

"Just goes to show you what?" Miriam said tartly.

Marge shrugged. "I don't know."

"I *meant*," Dina said, "that Adela might try to do something to herself, you know? I mean, she was pretty upset. Here she was assaulted by her own husband in front of practically the whole town, and like, what could be more humiliating?"

"Now you *are* being an idiot," Miriam said, even more tartly.

Quill sighed. "I think we could all do with a glass of wine. And maybe a little lunch. Marge, do you think Harland would take Elmer home? The Henrys' car is gone, and it's likely that Adela went home and I'm sure they can work this out. It isn't as if Elmer's a batterer or anything. The gavel just sort of . . . slipped."

"Huh!" Dina said, with a good deal of spirit. "That's what they all say."

"What d'ya mean, 'they'?" Marge demanded.

"Abusers. For all we know, Elmer could have been beating up on Adela for years and years."

Quill thought of Elmer, who was five foot six in his elevator shoes and Adela, who topped Quill's own five foot seven by a good two inches.

"Adela outweighs him by sixty pounds and always has," Miriam said. "I'd hate to have their little fracas end up as wild gossip, Dina. You know what small towns are like. And you weren't even there! As a matter of fact, I don't know why you're here now!"

"You guys all pounded past me like you were headed for a fire," Dina said. "My goodness. I couldn't just sit there."

"Stop," Quill said. "Let's go into the Tavern Lounge. It'll be quieter there. Then maybe you guys can tell me how this all started."

Quill led the way across the lawn to the other side of the cobblestone building. The Inn was set so that the entrance looked out over the village; the east side, which faced the falls, had sixteen of the twenty-seven rooms. The Tavern Lounge was on the south end. The flagstone patio was almost filled with diners; Quill knew that on a pleasant day like this, very few guests would opt to eat inside. When they walked in, the only guest was a small old gentleman sipping a cup of coffee at the bar; Jeeter

42

Swenson, the elderly man who had taken the Provencal Suite on a Long-Term Let. He turned and waved spiritedly at Quill, who waved spiritedly back.

A table for six was set up apart from the others, to the right of the large hearth. Quill led her party there and signaled Nate the bartender for menus.

Marge took the corner chair, so that she faced the rest of the room. Dina settled next to her. Marge narrowed her eyes. "Aren't you supposed to be at the reception desk?"

Dina held up her cell phone. "I route the calls through here."

"I'm sure Quill knows how to run her own business, and if she wants Dina to go back to work, she'll say so," Miriam said pleasantly. "Lay off, why don't you?"

Nate laid menus in front of them. Marge picked hers up with a grunt, and then set it down again. "Now what the hell are we going to do? Adela's quit. The fete's in two weeks. There's no director. You know how many folks in town have money invested in this thing?"

"I was a little late to the meeting," Quill began. "Could you tell me how all this happened?"

"You're always late," Marge snapped. She glared up at Nate. "I'll have a hamburger with fries. Can't screw up a hamburger. You got Stroh's on draft? Then I'll have one of them."

Nate nodded. He was tall and bearlike and fiercely protective of Meg's reputation as the best gourmet chef in the northeastern United States. His teeth glinted in his dark beard. "Meg made chicken salad today. With avocado, grapes, and pecans. She didn't screw that up, either."

"I'll have the chicken," Miriam said hastily. "And a glass of white wine, Nate. Whatever you have that isn't too sweet."

Quill and Dina both ordered the chicken salad, and as soon as Nate ambled away, Miriam blinked at them all. "What *is* it with you, Marge? You're rude, but not usually this rude. You want to tell us about it?"

Marge's irritation left her like air leaving a balloon.

Quill was lost in admiration of Miriam's technique. Whether it was the tone of her voice or her body language, Miriam somehow managed to pull the thorn from Marge's paw. Marge even had the grace to look abashed. "Sorry," she grunted. "Got a funny feeling about this, is all. None of it makes sense. Makes me jumpy."

Quill raised her hand, partly as a calming gesture and partly to get their attention. "Why don't we start with why Adela resigned in the first place?"

"Carol Ann," Miriam and Marge said in unison.

Miriam got in first. "It was outrageous, Quill, it really was. We'd barely gotten through the Pledge of Allegiance when Carol Ann jumped to her feet and demanded that Adela make a . . ." She turned to Marge. "What did she say, exactly?"

"Complete and full disclosure of how she was handling the funds for the fete."

"The funds?" Quill repeated. "You mean the money?"

Marge snorted. "Of course she means the money. She practically came right out and accused . . ."

Miriam pounded the table. "She *did* come right out and accuse Adela of appropriating moneys for her own use."

Nate put a draft beer in front of Marge. Marge took a

long swallow and banged the mug down. "Thief. She accused Adela of being a thief. Although it's not theft. It's embezzlement. Maybe."

"Holy crow." Dina looked longingly at Marge's beer, then at Quill, and then took a sip of her water. "Holy *crow*."

Quill shook her head. "That's absurd. Adela as an embezzler? I don't believe it for a minute."

"Maybe," Marge said, "and maybe not. And maybe that's the burr under my saddle. You three don't realize how much money flows through the fete."

"I do, actually," Quill said. "I mean, I didn't before I agreed to be on the steering committee, but we're talking several hundred thousand dollars here."

Miriam's mouth dropped open. "You're kidding me."

Marge looked grim. "I don't kid about money. Think about it. The booth fee is two hundred a day, for three days. There are a hundred and twenty booths. That's . . ."

"Seventy-two thousand dollars," Dina said.

"Right." Marge's grim expression relaxed a little. She had a soft spot for quick minds. "Then there are advance ticket sales. Three-day pass is ninety bucks, the fete's sold more than two thousand of those already and that's . . ."

"Nineteen thousand dollars. Holy *crow*." Dina looked at Quill. "I think I need a beer."

Quill smiled. "I think not. Not until your shift's over."

"Listen up, here." Marge rapped her knuckles on the table. "What with this and that, Adela's got a hundred k in that fete account, easy. A hundred grand is a powerful temptation."

Quill looked at the plate of chicken salad in front of her

that Nate just served, picked up her fork, and set it down again. "I don't believe it."

Marge took a large bite of hamburger and said, rather thickly, "I don't believe it, either." Her face reddened a little. "On the other hand, there are those that find a hundred k kind of pocket money, so to say, and then there are those that see it as a substantial pile. I'd put the Henrys in the second category."

"That's outrageous, Marge," Miriam said furiously.

"Hang on to your pigtails, Miriam. I'm not accusing Adela of a thing. All's I'm saying is that there are some folks who'd be more tempted than others."

"I see Marge's point, Miriam," Quill said in as even-handed a way as she could manage. "The mayor's salary is what, forty thousand a year? And Adela doesn't have an outside job. It's not all that much to live on these days." Quill leaned forward, controlling her voice with an effort. "What you're overlooking, Marge, is the kind of dedication the Henrys have to the village. They're the most . . . the best . . ." Quill floundered. "They'd never do a thing to harm us. What kind of proof did Carol Ann offer, anyway?"

"Not a shred," Miriam said promptly. "What she did is call for an investigation."

"Just like the Republicans plugging up the senate. That's Carol Ann all over," Dina said, with a surprisingly objective tone. "Mean as a snake." She caught, too late, the scent of Prell shampoo, and clapped her hand over her mouth.

"Thank you so much, Miss Dina Muir."

Carol Ann's poisonously sweet voice came from somewhere behind Quill's left shoulder. She turned around. "Hello, Carol Ann."

Carol Ann ignored her. "I see you ended that Chamber meeting pretty darn quick, Marge Schmidt. Is it maybe because you know something about Adela Henry? You want to let the rest of us in on your sneaky little secrets?"

Quill discovered she was furious. "Sit down, please. There are a couple of things we'd like to discuss with you."

Carol Ann's perfectly arched eyebrows rose. "Like what?"

"Like what kind of proof you have Adela's involved in anything at all."

"Love to, Quill. But I haven't a minute. I came to fetch Marge and you, too, since you're on the committee."

Quill took a moment to sort this through. She was on too many committees. Booth committee. The Furry Friends committee. The arts committee. And now this committee to keep the Craft Guild ladies from whacking each other to pieces. "Which committee?"

"The steering committee, of course." Carol Ann sat down next to Marge, picked up a fork, and poked at Marge's hamburger. She pursed her mouth disapprovingly. "That's a lot of animal fat you're gorging yourself on, Marge Schmidt. You need to sign up for my nutrition classes. I'll give you the friend's rate, since I know you. Best thing you'll ever do for your high cholesterol. But first, you have to come with me." She clapped her hands, like a particularly officious gym teacher. "Chop-chop! Right now."

"I don't *have* high choles—" Marge smacked herself on the forehead. "What the heck am I doing, talking to you about anything? And I don't have to go anywhere with you."

"You do, too, unless you want to be in big trouble with the sheriff. It's the sheriff that wants you. Both you and her." She jerked her thumb at Quill.

"For what?!"

"We're going over the fete accounts at the bank, and Mark Anthony Jefferson wouldn't do it without a legal presence so he called the sheriff, and the sheriff can't make head nor tails of the accounts and wants you to interpret for him. I don't know what he wants *her* for." This time she actually looked at Quill, as if diagnosing an insect problem.

"This is all most irregular," Miriam said in her bossiest librarian tone. "Did anyone call the judge? And Davy's not a legal presence, he's a police presence. Big difference, Carol Ann."

Carol Ann's eyes narrowed to icy blue slits. "If by judge you mean your boyfriend, Mr. Howard Murchison, Esquire, he's not a judge, he's a town justice. Big difference, Miriam Doncaster."

Quill had a pretty good idea why Davy Kiddermeister wanted her at the bank, but she didn't enlighten Carol Ann. She squashed a cowardly desire to run upstairs to her room and hide under her queen-sized bed with Jackson and a box of chocolate-covered cherries. She folded her napkin and got to her feet. "I think we'd all better go to the bank, don't you? Except you, Dina. I'll need you here at the front desk."

"That," Dina said, with a sideways glance at Carol Ann, "is way okay by me."

4

The Hemlock Falls Savings and Loan stood at the corner of Main and Maple. Like many of the buildings on Main Street, it'd been built in the boom years after the Civil War. It was a solid cobblestone building, three stories high, designed in an architectural style somewhere between Greek Revival and Georgian. There were a few modern touches; the big doors opening into the main lobby were glass and an ATM kiosk sat under the portico. The parking lot was at the rear of the building, sharing space with a 7-Eleven that had been tucked well out of the view of tourists.

At Quill's suggestion, the three other women drove to the bank separately, and by the time she had talked to Meg and checked with Doreen to make sure Jack's activities were covered for the afternoon, everyone Mark Anthony Jefferson had called to the meeting was there. She walked into the small conference room—which smelled like fresh paint for some reason, and had for years—and sat down in the corner.

Mark Anthony sat at the head of the table, his laptop opened in front of him. Davy Kiddermeister stood behind him. Davy had been promoted to sheriff after Quill's husband Myles decided to work for the government. He was well past thirty, but his fair hair, red cheeks, and mild blue eyes made him look years younger. Davy Kiddermeister didn't look anything like a sheriff, in Quill's opinion. He looked like he'd just graduated from high school. He blushed easily and often.

Howie Murchison sat at the opposite end of the conference table, Miriam at his side. In his late fifties, with a comfortable paunch and a fringe of gray hair, Howie looked exactly like what he was, a village lawyer who took on town justice duties once a month.

Marge stood by the room's only window, looking out at the parking lot. Carol Ann, her ponytail restored to glossy perfection, sat upright in the chair across from Miriam. She watched Mark Anthony with the intensity of a cobra after a mouse.

"Hello, Quill," Mark Anthony said. "Glad you could make it."

"I'm not glad to be here, under the circumstances," she said honestly. "I'm sure we can get this all cleared up quickly." She looked at Howie. "And should we be doing this without Adela? I think she would want to be here, too."

"She took off in that underpowered little Toyota and no one's seen her since," Carol Ann said. "She's on the lam."

Quill looked at her watch. "Marge adjourned the Chamber meeting at eleven thirty. It's twelve thirty now. I doubt that she's on the lam. She's probably at home."

"Crying her eyes out," Miriam agreed. "This whole thing is shameful."

Quill nodded. "I think so, too. Adela should be here to

answer these ridiculous charges. Besides, don't you need her permission to access the fete account?"

"Well, no, we don't," Mark Anthony said. "We just need the written permission of someone on the fete committee. Everyone on the committee is signatory to the account."

"Oh," Quill said. She'd been afraid of that.

Mark Anthony passed his hand over his skull. He'd recently taken to shaving his head and his skull shone like polished ebony under the fluorescent lights. "You're on the committee," he added.

"True." She bit her lower lip.

"So if you could just sign this?" He picked up a legal-sized piece of paper. "We can proceed. Perhaps you'd like to join us at the table?"

Reluctantly, Quill abandoned the safety of her corner and sat down at the table. She cast a quick glance over the permission affidavit, and then scrawled her name at the bottom.

Mark Anthony nodded gravely, filed the affidavit in a manila folder, and then tapped at the computer. He waited a moment, his eyes on the screen. "Any idea how much should be in this account?"

Quill patted at her skirt pockets and withdrew the sketch pad she used for Chamber meeting notes. The fete committee notes were on it, too. "I don't know why everyone insists on making me secretary. I'm not a very good one."

"No kidding," Carol Ann said.

"It's because you never say no," Marge said. "And you shut up, Carol Ann."

"I don't recall making any notes about the budget." She flipped through the pages and paused. "Okay. This is it. At the last meeting Adela reported that all of the booths had been sold and that eighty percent of the fees had been collected. So at a hundred dollars a day . . ." She trailed off.

"Sixty thousand dollars, give or take," Marge said.

Quill flipped the page. "There's ticket money, advertising revenues for the program . . . Aha! Here it is. I have a subtotal here of one hundred thousand seven hundred and twenty dollars and sixty-five cents."

Mark Anthony frowned. Davy leaned over his shoulder and frowned, too.

"What's the balance in the account?" Quill asked.

"Twenty sixty-five," Davy said.

"Twenty thousand and change?" Marge snorted. "She could have paid the tent bill and the landscapers already. I wouldn't call that definitive."

"No," Davy said. "Twenty dollars and sixty-five cents."

The room was filled with a shocked silence.

Carol Ann shot her fist into the air in victory. "I knew it!" She whirled, her eyes glittering in triumph, and faced Davy Kiddermeister. "Sheriff, I demand you arrest that woman."

"There could be a good explanation for this, Carol Ann," Howie Murchison said testily. "Mark, when was the money moved?"

The banker tapped at the computer. "Late last night. The transaction was recorded at 3:14 A.M."

"Where to?"

Mark shook his head and muttered to himself. He continued to tap at the keys.

"Right to that woman's bank account, that's where," Carol Ann said. "And then into her pockets. She's on her way out of town right now, with a suitcase full of cash in the trunk of her car. Sheriff, I demand you put out an APB."

Davy leaned against the wall, his face a careful blank. "Mr. Jefferson?"

"We don't have any proof that a crime's been committed yet," Mark Anthony said. He looked at Davy. "This is going to take a while. We're a local, privately owned bank, as you know, and we don't have a fraud unit as such."

"You don't have a fraud unit at all." Marge snorted. "I've got somebody you can hire as a consultant, Mark."

"We'll see." Mark moved his shoulders uncomfortably. "I've got to call a meeting of the board of directors. I think it would be a good idea to talk to Mrs. Henry. I've got some questions, certainly."

"Questions!" Carol Ann was almost bouncing with anger. "I've got a question for you. Why aren't you sending a squad car for her right this minute?!"

Mark sat back in his chair with a relaxed air that didn't fool Quill at all. "Ms. Spinoza, Mrs. Henry has sole discretion over this account. The money was moved to a bank in North Dakota. I've just sent an inquiry about the balance. They'll get back to me. Maybe it's an interest-bearing account, and Mrs. Henry decided that the fete funds would be better served with a bank that can afford to do that. I just don't know. To go any further than that, I'm going to need to talk to the other people signatory on the account. That's right, isn't it, counselor?"

Howie nodded.

Mark folded his arms across his chest. "As president of this bank, I will go so far as to say, I'm concerned enough to ask that the fete steering committee grants permission for an investigation."

Davy nodded. "Sounds good to me. Quill? Who all's on the steering committee?"

"Me, Reverend Shuttleworth, Elmer, and Althea Quince." Quill pulled her cell phone from her pocket. "I'll see if I can get them all here, shall I?"

"Cover-up!" Carol Ann shouted. "I am so sick of you people thinking that you run this town. You know what? I'll tell you what. It's time we fixed that." She narrowed her eyes to a threatening glare. "There's quite a few of us ready to change things around here. We've been, like, totally pissed off at the high-handed way you've been running things, and the theft of this money is just the tip of the corruption iceberg, the tip!"

"The what?" Miriam asked.

Carol Ann took a deep breath and smiled; the effect was a lot scarier than her threats. "You'll see. You all might want to make a point of watching the six o'clock news." She looked at her watch. "Pardon me. Better make that the eleven o'clock news. I've got a lot of phone calls to make."

Without another word, she walked out of the room and slammed the door behind her.

Miriam threw up her hands. "The woman's crazy." Mark Anthony Jefferson looked uneasy. Marge rubbed her chin thoughtfully. Davy muttered, "What the hell?" and punched a number into his cell phone. Howie put his pen into his sports coat pocket and his yellow pad into his briefcase.

Quill, who had been sending and receiving texts, slipped her own phone back into her pocket. "I reached Dookie. Althea Quince is off on a wine tour with her husband, and she's more than an hour and a half away, but they've turned around and headed back. Harland is bringing Elmer back here right now. That's three of us, Mark. Is that going to be enough to authorize whatever we need to authorize?"

"Sure. I'll just need you to agree to remove Mrs. Henry from the account and maybe file an official request to move the inquiry forward."

"We can do that," Quill said sadly. "Davy?"

"Yeah," Davy said. "I'll go out and talk to her."

~

"I don't think I've ever spent a more awful afternoon, Myles," Quill said into her computer screen. "The whole village is in an uproar."

It was late, well after midnight, but Myles had e-mailed her the only time he was available for his call, and they were both hostage to his schedule. "That's not the worst thing. I told you Carol Ann said she was going to make the eleven o'clock news? Well, she did. She and Brady Beale have started something called Citizens for Justice. They managed to organize some of the people who've been unhappy about having the fete here in Hemlock Falls all these years. The first meeting was out at the car dealership and Carol Ann talked the anchor from Channel 11 out of

Syracuse into covering it. They're claiming corruption, cronyism, and all kinds of inflammatory things. Oh! And conspiracy. That's what caught the attention of the TV people.

"Davy had to send the patrol cars out to Peterson Automotive—Carol Ann kept insisting that the Citizens for Justice needed police protection. Of course, the presence of the patrol cars made really great TV." Quill shook her head in disgust. "Some citizens' movement. There were twenty or so people there, at most, none of them with anything substantial to say. Brady kept shoving people in front of his store sign so the TV cameras would pick it up. If you ask me, he's in it for the free advertising. Too bad for us it was a slow news night. Oh! And Carol Ann's started a Twitter campaign. She's calling it fete-fraud. Very catchy, which is also too bad for us."

"What does Adela have to say?"

Quill rubbed her forehead. "Nobody can find her, poor thing. Dookie, Elmer, and I signed all the permissions to launch a bank inquiry. Elmer's a mess. Davy let all the deputies know we needed to talk to her . . . in an informal way, since there's no evidence a crime's been committed yet—but then they got diverted with this protest Carol Ann organized.

"Marge and I went over to Adela's three times today, but her car wasn't there. Then I had to go to Syracuse to see about renting those crates for the Furry Friends booths, and by the time I got back, Carol Ann was blatting away about the conspiracy. Don't ask me what kind of conspiracy. It doesn't make any sense. She's named herself president and the whole purpose seems to be to hang poor Adela out to dry. It's awful. I went down to the Croh Bar for a glass of wine after Doreen put Jack to bed, to kind of get a feel for things. Everybody shakes their head and says: "I always knew there was something funny about those Henrys" and "I didn't want to say anything before, but . . ." And then they go on to say the most dreadful stuff. She's got a few supporters, all of us at the Inn, and Marge, and Miriam, and Clare's people up at the academy, but everyone else is just nasty. I've been an innkeeper too long to be disillusioned, but still." She rubbed her hands over her face. "Ugh."

Her husband shook his head slightly in sympathy.

Myles was in an airport lounge, she could tell that much. But where the lounge was located and where he was going was a complete mystery. She never wanted to know, in case it was one of the hot spots featured so terrifyingly in the *New York Times* and the *Syracuse Herald*. He'd been traveling for at least twenty-four hours, so it had to be halfway around the world. Beyond that, she didn't want to speculate.

"This will blow over, dear heart." Myles's voice was deep and resonant, even through the distortion of the speakers. Quill's heart turned over. Somehow, phone calls had been easier than the video conferencing and she wished, briefly, that she'd never set up the video software. She missed him less when she couldn't hear him and see him at the same time.

"I suppose you're right. The big question is the fete. Elmer keeps saying the fete's the responsibility of the steering committee, which it is, of course, except that Adela took care of everything. I got a little ruffled when

Brady Beale accused us of being doormats and rubber-stamping everything, but he's right! And it's not that big a committee. Just me and Adela and Elmer, who's a mess, of course. Dookie Shuttleworth is so gentle he can never put his foot down about a thing. So guess who's been elected temporary chair?"

Myles bit his lip.

"It's not funny, Myles! I was perfectly happy being a doormat. I'm totally fine with rubber-stamping. I do not, not, *not* want to run another damn committee!"

"What about this Althea Quince?"

"What about her?" Quill said crossly. "She was just super sympathetic when she and her husband finally got here, but she's not a native, and she's clueless about what needs to be done next."

"Do I know her?"

"You met her. She's that woman who's renting the Federal Suite at the Inn for three months. That's *not the problem*!" Quill wanted to pound the desk, which would wake up Jack, or throw something against the wall, which would also wake up Jack. Instead, she dug her fingers into her temples and took a long breath. "Where's the money? If Adela moved it, where did she move it to? If she didn't move it, who did?

"None of us had access to the checkbook. Adela guarded it like a lioness. She's always been so proud of how much we've been able to donate to the literacy program. Handing over to the charity was one of the highlights of her year. No. Something else must have happened to the funds. A computing error, maybe, although Mark Anthony got really ruffled when I suggested that."

"I should think he would. If it is a bank error, it'll show up soon enough."

"Mark Anthony won't talk to me about it. I called him at home. All he said was: 'the bank end checks out,' whatever that may mean. And then 'we've hired a fraud consultant,' which says to me that the money's actually gone and somebody actually took it."

Myles maintained a diplomatic silence.

"Marge is going to put one of her tech guys on it, if she can get the bank to agree. Doesn't think much of the bank's consultant. Anyhow. All this will take enormous amounts of time, and since the money's gone, and we can't find Adela, it's pretty clear that the fete will be toast if we don't find the thief pretty soon."

"So you're pretty sure you're looking for an embezzler."

"But who?! Out of Adela, Elmer, Dookie Shuttleworth, and me, who would you pick? I didn't do it. And for God's sake, literally, we can't suspect Dookie of all people . . ." She stopped and said, with emphasis. "Althea Quince."

Myles smiled. "Tell me about Althea Quince."

"Sure. Well, you've met her. She and her husband were the first to sign up for the Long-Term Let. They moved into the Federal Suite and the Colonial Suite last month."

Myles looked a little startled. "Both suites?"

"Althea said she's been happily married for forty years and living in two suites would insure that she and Nolan would make it forty-one." Despite her agitation, Quill laughed. She'd liked the flamboyant Althea Quince. But not if she was a thief. "There's your suspect, Myles. The day after she and Nolan moved in, she asked if there were any openings in community service. They've taken the suites for three months, and she said she'd go stir-crazy if she didn't have something interesting to do. And you know how hard it always is to get local people to serve on the fete committee. It's strictly rubber-stamp. Adela's show. Only wimps allowed, which is why Dookie and I get drafted every year. But we did need another body, and Althea was more than happy to take on the more tedious tasks, like the ads and the mailings. I could just kick myself." She grabbed her hair with both hands and tugged at it. "Who likes to spend their time collating mailing lists? Nobody. I can't believe I was so mistaken about her."

"Quill . . ."

"I'll bet she's flown the coop—and she prepaid for the three months, too!"

"Quill!"

Quill released her hair and sat up. "I know. You're right. I'm jumping the gun. I'm theorizing ahead of the facts. You just wait. I'll get Marge to dig into her background and we'll get that money back."

The computer screen was high res, and it didn't obscure Myles's slight frown.

"Don't worry. I'm not getting involved with anything like murder. I promised, remember? But I've got to find out who took that money. If I don't—I'm chair of the fete steering committee."

"I've said it before so I don't need to say it again."

"Leave it to the professionals. Right. I will. Don't worry. I'll just make a few . . . inquiries. We have an emergency meeting of the committee tomorrow morning to decide what to do next." She sighed. "Let's leave it for the moment. How are you doing? Did you get the photos of Jack I sent in his bath tonight? I wish we didn't have to talk so late at night. You never get a chance to actually see him."

He held up his phone. "Received and stored. And the move back to the Inn went smoothly?"

"It did. We've got a lot of practice switching back and forth from the house to here. Mike brings the van and I've got it down to less than an hour." Suddenly, she felt tears at the back of her eyes. "I wish. Never mind. I love you, Myles. Stay safe."

5

The fete committee members had agreed that an early breakfast meeting was in order in view of the crisis.

Quill's office was small, but her Queen Anne conference table seated four and could accommodate coffee and small plates so at nine sharp, she sat down with Althea, Dookie, and a very haggard Elmer Henry.

"My dear, dear man." Althea Quince patted Elmer heartily on the back. "We will get to the bottom of this. Don't fear for a moment that we will fail."

Althea had a very loud voice. And it was hoarse. From years, she admitted, of smoking too many Gauloises in too many corners of Paris. She and her husband Nolan were retired from the food brokerage business, and it had taken them all around the world in pursuit of exotic and interesting foods.

Quill mentally categorized Althea's manner of dress as floaty. She swathed herself in long, gauzy, vividly colored scarves. She had a penchant for dangling earrings in various exotic designs. She reminded Quill of an African parrot, one of the brilliantly plumaged kinds.

She also wore a lot of Chanel No. 5, and the scent

wafted through the air every time she gestured. "Your dear wife is innocent of any malefaction. I'm as certain of this as I am of anything on this earth . . . or"—this with a gracious nod in Dookie's direction—"the next, if you forgive me, Reverend Shuttleworth."

Dookie blinked mildly at her. "None of us are certain of the next world, Mrs. Quince. We can only have faith. But I, too, believe in Adela's innocence. I'm sure that all will be explained in time."

"It doesn't make any sense," Elmer said in a very low voice. "None of this. It's like what they say about nightmares. I'm in one. I just can't b'live it. You heard about this Citizens for Justice gang?"

Althea clucked in sympathy.

"Bunch of yahoos," Elmer muttered. "Out to get my wife. It's a nightmare. A nightmare." He moved restlessly in his chair. Nobody ever called Elmer well dressed, but Adela always made sure that his button-down cotton shirts were neatly ironed, and he was never without a sports coat and tie. Today he was in a golf shirt, rumpled chinos, and his socks didn't match.

Quill sat up a little straighter in her chair. "I suppose we should call this meeting to order." Then with a hopeless optimism, "In Adela's absence, which I'm sure will be temporary, would anyone like to take the chair?"

Althea smiled, showing strong white teeth. "Wouldn't be appropriate for a flat land foreigner, my dear."

Dookie blushed and looked at his feet.

Elmer looked helpless.

"If no one minds, then I'll step in temporarily." Quill looked down at her sketch pad, where she'd made a short list of things to be done immediately. Actually, it was quite a long list. "Well. I'm not sure where to start, here. The fete's in two weeks and there's a ton of work to get through." She made one last stab at getting out from under. "I don't suppose Adela would consider stepping back in as an advisor, Elmer? We all know there's nothing to these nutty allegations."

To Quill's horror, Elmer started to cry. "She's talking to a lawyer. She texted me."

"That's a good thing," Quill said warmly. "That way she can refer any, um . . . inquiries from people to her counsel. All the best people do it, Elmer."

"A divorce lawyer," Elmer sobbed. "On account of that tap on her behind with the gavel."

"Oh." Quill sat back. "Yikes. I'm truly sorry."

Dina tapped at the office door and stuck her head inside. "Umm . . . Quill? Brady Beale is here to see you."

"Brady Beale the car dealer?" Quill said blankly.

Dina nodded, and glanced furtively over her shoulder and dropped her voice to a whisper. "Shall I let him come in? I can tell him you said no. He says now that there's a vacancy on the steering committee he wants to fill it."

"That son of a B!" Elmer said. "He's trying to hang my wife out to dry! You let him come in here, Dina, and I'll . . ." Elmer balled his fists. "I'll sock him, that's what I'll do."

Dookie cleared his throat. "Violence," he said gently, "is not the answer. I think, Dina, my dear, that we should invite Brady to the table."

Quill bit her lip uncertainly.

"Not a bad idea," Althea said briskly. "Best way to

know your enemy is close-up. I vote to let him in, too. As for you, old son"—she clapped Elmer briskly on the shoulder—"no socking, whacking, thumping, or hitting. Okay?"

Elmer's lower lip was stuck out so far, Quill thought he might trip if he got up too quickly. But he put his hands flat on the table and jerked his chin down in agreement.

Quill got up and sat behind her desk, leaving the fourth chair at the table free. "Okay, Dina. Let him in."

"I stuck him out in the foyer. Hang on."

Brady walked into the office with a broad smile that faltered under Elmer's glare. He was of medium height, thin, and his dark hair was thinning on top. Quill thought he was in his mid-thirties, perhaps older. He'd been married once or twice, although she was pretty sure he wasn't married at the moment.

He shook hands solemnly with Quill, and then Dookie. He nodded at Althea. "Brady Beale, of Peterson's Automotive."

"Althea Quince." She gave him a measuring glance. "I saw you on television last night."

His face lighted up. "Not bad, was it? I thought the coverage was a little light, myself, but Carol Ann thinks we can get the media down from Rochester at the next meeting. Too much to hope for national coverage, but there you are."

Elmer made a noise like a garbage disposal with a fork in it.

"Yes, well," Brady said hastily. "If you saw the news last night, Mayor, did you hear me say one word against your good wife? Or one word in support of those citizens who asked me to offer the space in my showroom for their meeting?"

"Are you telling us you didn't know the nature of the protest last night?" Dookie asked. His mild, inquiring gaze was steady.

Brady's eyes were flat brown. He widened them innocently. Then, since it was hard for anyone to lie to Dookie Shuttleworth, he said, "I had an inkling. No more. But as a neutral party, how could I say no to some concerned citizens who just asked for enough space to hold their meeting?"

You could say no to Hitler, Quill thought. Or Pol Pot. Not that Carol Ann's in the same category, but she's pretty darn close.

Dookie's gaze hadn't faltered, and Brady rubbed the back of his neck uneasily. "Besides, Carol Ann's been looking to buy an Escalade and when she called me up and said the TV people were headed this way . . . I guess maybe I made a mistake. I guess I'm sorry, Mayor, about the things they said about Mrs. Mayor."

Dookie nodded to himself, sat back, and folded his hands in his lap.

Brady edged around the table and sat down. "I know you folks aren't exactly glad to see me, but I was hoping you'd give me a chance to say my piece."

"If you think you got a place on this steering committee, you got another think coming," Elmer said.

"Now, Mayor, let's not be too hasty about this. I can bring a lot to this committee. You may be aware that there are several factions in town that haven't been happy with the way the fete has been run so far. I'm offering myself as a neutral party. We've all got a stake in the fete's success and I'm in a pretty good position to listen to both sides in a fair and honest way."

Elmer looked at Quill. "He's in, I'm out."

Althea and Dookie looked at her, too.

"You're chair," Althea finally said, with the air of urging a reluctant puppy outdoors. "We're leaving the decision up to you."

"Hm," Quill said, in a decisive way.

"It's not that I could even think of taking Adela's place. We all know how much she contributed to the success of this event. And I'll tell you right up front, I've given up this idea of moving the fete away from Hemlock Falls. It'd be like taking it away from Adela herself, and everyone in town knows how much we owe her. She is," Brady said, with passionate sincerity, "one of the best things that's ever happened to this town. You're a fortunate man in your marriage, Mayor."

Elmer's eyes filled. He sniffed.

"Now, no one can ever fill her shoes the way they should be filled, but I'd like to offer my services. In my own small way, I want to help. I'm willing to take on the hours and hours of responsibility until Adela is cleared and can join us once again."

Quill looked at Elmer's miserable face. She thought of the hours and hours (and hours) of responsibility involved in getting the fete up to speed. "I'm sorry, Brady"—and no one but Myles knew just how sorry she was—"but I think that any changes to the committee right now might be misunderstood."

Brady's smile vanished. For a moment, he looked mean.

"You're kidding me. How the hell are you going to manage it? No offense, Quill, but your administrative skills aren't exactly world-class. Everybody's got a lot of money tied up in this thing. You sure you're up to it?"

"I think so."

"Well, I don't, and neither do a lot of concerned citizens. We were pretty sure you guys were going to turn us down . . ."

"Who's we?" Quill asked.

"Concerned citizens," Brady repeated impatiently. "So I've been authorized to request that the committee hire a professional to take over."

Althea raised her eyebrows. "A professional?"

"An event organizer."

~

"Yep," Brady said briskly. "You need an event organizer. Best thing you could do. Bring a professional in."

Elmer mopped his eyes with a not-very-clean handkerchief, blew his nose and said, "What?"

"We even have a couple of suggestions." Brady dug into his sports coat pocket and produced a slip of paper. "Event organizers. Three of them. Take your pick."

Elmer looked around the office with a bewildered expression as if expecting to find an event organizer under Quill's chrysanthemum-patterned couch.

Althea reached over and took the paper. "One's in Buffalo, one's in Rochester, and one's in Syracuse. Which is closer, Quill?"

"Syracuse."

"You have a Syracuse phone book here? Or better yet, let's try your laptop."

Quill rose, went to her desk, and sat down. "I'll do an Internet search. If we can find somebody to step in, that'd be terrific."

Althea nudged Dookie. "A miracle, eh, Reverend?"

Elmer cleared his throat and smoothed the lapels of his seersucker jacket. "Those organizers cost a bundle, you know. We had one of them when the chicken people were here for the Fry Away Home contest. Took a percentage of the gate. Trouble is . . ." His nose reddened and a tear rolled down his cheek. "Paying for it might be a problem."

"There is no way Adela stole that money," Quill said. "Besides, a percentage of the gate means tickets, right? We always get a ton of walk-ins. If not, maybe we can pay this person from village funds, somehow." She tapped fruitlessly at her keyboard. "I'm not getting much action here."

Althea adjusted a pair of reading glasses onto her nose, then got up and made shooing motions. She had ornate rings on all ten fingers. "I'll handle it. I'm not bad at computers for a little old lady. You're talking to someone who shipped three hundred tons of yak's milk from Tibet through Marrakesh to Chicago all online. You all go see about breakfast. I'm starving, and the mayor here is going to be all the better for some calories. Right, Mayor? I'll work the computer and come up with a list of names, and then you can decide." She looked over her spectacles at Brady. "Not a bad suggestion, Mr. Beale."

"You're going to do it, then?" Brady said. "Spend all

that money for an out-of-towner to come in? I work for free, you know."

"I think it's probably best," Dookie said. "Perhaps next year, Brady, when we are creating the membership for the steering committee, you would consent to join us."

"Whatever." Brady got up. "I'll say good-bye then. Good to see you all," he added heartily. "If you're in the market for a car, you know where to find me."

Althea waited until the door closed behind him and winked at Quill. "I'll bet you're feeling a little better now, my dear."

"To be honest, I feel like a ten-ton weight's been lifted off my back." Quill smiled at them. "Althea's right about breakfast, Elmer. Let me go check on how it's coming along. I'll be right back."

Thankfully, Quill escaped to the kitchen, where she found her sister flattening veal with a large mallet.

"Hey, Quill."

"Hey, yourself." Quill resisted the temptation to sit in the rocker. If she sat down, she wouldn't want to get up for anyone except her son. "Guess what?"

"You decided to commit seppuku rather than chair the fete committee."

"They're hiring an event coordinator!"

Meg's face lighted up. "No! Hey!" She held her hand up and Quill slapped it gleefully. "You're saved, by God. I am like, totally psyched on your behalf."

"I don't know why we didn't think of it before. It'll be expensive."

"It'll be worth it. Besides, odds are good Adela will be back in harness soon, right?"

"As soon as I can find out who took the money."

Meg looked at her. "You're back in the detecting saddle again? How does Myles feel about that?"

Quill changed the subject. "I put an order in for four Eggs Quilliam in my office. I've come to see when it'll be ready."

"No, you didn't. You came to escape your fete. Get it? Fate. Fete."

"I got it."

"Of course your breakfast is on the way." Meg turned and shouted over her shoulder: "Elizabeth! How's Quill's order coming along?"

Elizabeth Chou didn't raise her head as she deftly sliced cantaloupe. "Another three minutes."

"Told ya." Meg whacked the veal even flatter. "Bet you wish it was thirty."

"I wish it was three years. Honestly, Meg, this is just a mess. What the heck could have happened to that money? And how did Carol Ann know anything about it?"

"Maybe she didn't. Maybe she was just being Carol Ann–ish, which is to say, she's a big-time troublemaker and lucked into the fact that the money's gone. Now she can dress up in jackboots and march around town calling for justice. It's a stunt, that's all it is."

"Maybe," Quill said dubiously. "And maybe she had something to do with it."

Meg shuddered. "If you're thinking about investigating Carol Ann, you can do it all by your lonesome. That woman's a walking *Titanic*."

"That makes no sense as a metaphor."

"Sure it does. She's a disaster waiting to happen to other people. Which doesn't include me."

Quill bent sideways and looked under the prep table. Meg wore clogs in the kitchen, and with the clogs, summer and winter, she wore socks. The color of the socks was a good indicator of her mood. Today's were a contentious green. "Actually, I wasn't thinking of Carol Ann so much as Althea Quince."

Meg put down the mallet, her attention finally caught. "Really?"

"The committee members are all signatory on the fete account. Surely you don't suspect Dookie. Or me. Or the mayor."

"And Althea's the only outsider? Very parochial. Not like you at all, Sis."

"Myles had that reaction, too. Honestly, though. I know I didn't do it, I can't believe our minister would do it, and Elmer wouldn't have the nerve."

"Yeah, but how would Althea access the funds? Adela holds on to that checkbook like it was her firstborn son. Speaking of which, how's my nephew this morning?"

Quill didn't answer that for a minute. There were shadows under Meg's eyes, and her little sister looked cross. It was clear that Meg didn't want to know much more about the problems with the fete. If there was something bugging her (and it was probably Justin, since the men in her sister's life didn't last long), Meg would tell her eventually. In the meantime, long years of experience with her sister told Quill it was time to back off. "Doreen's taking him to a playdate with Lily Peterson." Quill took a deep breath. "I should be on that playdate. I'm missing my son's childhood, Meg. Do you realize that?"

"You spend two hours every morning and three hours every night with him. Anyone who wants to spend more time than that with a five-year-old is insane."

Quill gritted her teeth. "Let's not get into it this morning, okay? I've got enough on my plate."

"You have Eggs Quilliam on your plate, or very nearly. Elizabeth!"

"Right here!" Elizabeth put two of the plates in Quill's hands and grabbed the other two. "C'mon, Quill. Eggs are lethal when they're cold."

~

Back in the office, Elmer was looking marginally better and Althea was beaming. Dookie sat comfortably on the couch, making notes in a journal in an abstracted way. Elizabeth cleared the conference table, whipped napkins and cutlery out of her apron pocket, and arranged the plates. After accepting Althea's generous praise for the presentation, she gave Quill an impish salute and left.

Elmer was the first to seat himself. He tucked his napkin into his collar, grabbed his fork, and said, "I do believe I found someone to take over the fete. She's coming in this morning for an interview."

"That's wonderful, Elmer." Quill touched Dookie gently on the shoulder to get his attention and shepherded him to the table. "Who is it?"

"Name's Linda Connelly. Runs an outfit called Presentations. I like the title, don't you? No fuss, no muss. Very professional. She'll be here at eleven. Said it wouldn't take more than an hour to get here from Syracuse."

"Her website was pretty impressive," Althea said. "She was laid off from Xerox about ten years ago and went into event planning."

"Done a lot of big dos," Elmer spoke between rapid and appreciative bites of egg and cheese. "Got a lot of references. Best of all, she's free."

"No charge?" Quill said.

"I mean that her schedule's free. She had some big wedding on for two weeks from now and the groom upped and went off with the best man."

"Oh, dear."

"So the folks had to cancel the wedding."

"I should think so."

"Lucky for us."

"Maybe not so lucky for the bride." Quill hesitated. "Do you want me to sit in on the interview?"

Elmer waved his fork. "No, no need. I can take care of it. I'll get Adela to sit . . ." He stopped. His face crumpled. He choked, and for an awful moment, Quill thought the eggs were going to come back up.

"Take a couple of deep breaths," Althea said kindly. She whacked him several times on the back.

Elmer took a couple of deep breaths. Then he folded his napkin and set it next to his plate with a decisive air. "There's one more thing I want to do this morning. I want to hire you."

"You want to hire me?" Quill had a number of immediate suspicions about what he wanted to hire her for, and she didn't like any of them. "For what?"

"You got to find out what's happened to this money.

You've been a pretty good detective over the years." He turned to Althea. "You wouldn't believe how many corpses this gal has under her belt."

Althea's eyebrows rose. "Is that so?"

"You betcha. Now, Kiddermeister hasn't done a half-bad job as sheriff, although he's not a patch on the Sheriff, of course, who never did take much to Quill's investigating so it's probably just as well he's in Kuwait or wherever he is. Otherwise Quill might have to stick to bein' a wife."

Althea rubbed her forehead. "What, what?" Then, rather pathetically, "This conversation makes no sense to me. None. I think my mind is going. My husband will be devastated."

Dookie looked up from his egg. "The mayor is referring to Sheriff McHale. Who is no longer sheriff but an antiterrorism agent. Memories are long in the country, Mrs. Quince, and many of us here view McHale as the sheriff qua sheriff, so to speak, even though he is serving his country in a much larger way at the moment. So he is, and always will be, the Sheriff. Sheriff McHale married Quill, after a long and affectionate courtship. He is a good man and naturally enough, he is concerned about Quill's unofficial forays into detection, both as an upholder of law and order and as a loving husband. That said, I must admit that as amateur sleuths go, the village has a healthy respect for Quill's abilities as a detective. She is quite gifted in that regard."

Quill opened her mouth, couldn't think of anything to say, and closed it again.

"I see. At least I sort of see." Althea hesitated. "I thought you were a famous artist."

"She is," Elmer said proudly.

"I thought you retired to the country to run this Inn."

"She did," Dookie said, just as proudly. "Partly, we surmise, to offer a diversion to her younger sister, who had been tragically widowed. But also because the burden of increasing fame in the arts was onerous for her."

Small towns! Quill thought furiously. I suppose everybody knows how much I weigh, too.

"And you're an investigator, too?" Althea fanned herself with her napkin. Her bracelets clanked. "Good heavens."

Elmer rapped the table impatiently. "Y'all need to get back to the point here. I want my wife back. I want my life back. So, Quill, can I hire you to get to the bottom of this fiasco?"

Quill glanced at Althea and away again. "Sure."

Elmer tucked his napkin back into his collar. "You wouldn't think of taking a fee, I'm sure of that."

"No, indeed," Quill said. "You can hire me for free."

"So when can you start?"

Quill blinked at him. "Right now, I guess. I'd like to talk to Adela first, if you don't mind. Do you know where I can find her?"

Elmer stared gloomily at his eggs. "At our house, I guess. If she's not at the lawyer's office. She won't answer her phone, and she's bolted all the doors from the inside, so I guess she's there."

Quill wanted to ask where Elmer had spent the night but didn't dare.

"I've been putting up at Harland Peterson's. They got that big old farmhouse and all his kids are grown so Marge said why not?"

Quill took his hand and gave it a gentle squeeze. "Then we'll wrap up here and I'll drop by and see her as soon as we're finished."

6

Elmer and Adela lived in a small, ferociously neat two-story house off Maple. Quill parked on the street and sat for a moment. The drapes were drawn. The morning paper sat on the porch. The house had an abandoned air. If the Hemlock Dairy still delivered milk, Quill was willing to bet the bottles would still be out and spoiling in the hot August sun. She had a sudden vision of a crowd of villagers picketing outside the waist-high wrought-iron fence yelling "Thief!" led by a gun-toting Carol Ann.

When Myles was away, at night she fell asleep to the television; as she walked up the trim brick pathway, horrific scenes from reruns of late-night crime shows kept nudging at her. Adela would be just fine. There wouldn't be a bloody corpse on the living room floor. Nobody would be hanging from the shower rod. This was Hemlock Falls. Stuff like that didn't happen here. At least not very often.

The front door was painted teal blue, to match the shutters. She pressed the doorbell, and didn't hear anything, but Adela opened the front door almost immediately.

"Quill."

"Adela."

Adela liked pantsuits, the more colorful the better. The one she wore this morning was a cheerful yellow. She'd matched it with a flowered blouse—the blossoms resembled poppies—and coral earrings.

"May I come in?"

Adela stood taller and peered over Quill's shoulder. "You're alone? That man has been setting siege to the place."

"Quite alone," Quill said gravely. "Elmer's back at the Inn. I've just come from a meeting of the fete committee."

Adela looked pleased. "I thought one of you might be along this morning. Come back through to the kitchen. I'll make a pot of tea. Oh! Good heavens. They finally delivered the paper." She bent down and picked it up.

Quill followed her through the foyer, past the living room, and into the Henrys' small eat-in kitchen. The round oak table showed the remains of a substantial breakfast. Adela gathered up her plate, rinsed it, put it in the dishwasher, and gestured. "Please sit down. Do you have a preference in teas? I have Earl Grey and a very nice herbal tea with hibiscus flowers."

"The Earl Grey will be fine. Thanks." Quill dropped her tote on the floor and sat down. Adela put the kettle on to boil and sat across from her. "I've been meaning to ask how the booths for our Furry Friends are coming along."

For a moment, Quill went completely blank. "The booths, yes. I went to Syracuse yesterday and checked out the crates. They'll be delivered two days before the fete opens so we'll have time to set up. As far as the entries go, we have . . ." Quill fumbled in her pocket for her sketch pad. "Let's see. Sixteen cats in the Purrfect Pet division. Twenty dogs in the Man's Best Friend division. Three chickens, four hamsters, one snake, and eight birds in the Exotic Expressions division. So I ordered the appropriate sizes for the crates. And a lot of wood shavings, too."

Adela coughed delicately. "And the manure disposal?"

"Up to the exhibitor," Quill said briskly, since she hadn't thought about manure disposal at all. "That's not why I'm here. Adela, we have to talk."

Adela nodded regally and steepled her hands. "Indeed we do. I take it you have come from the Chamber with an offer of a sincere apology. I have considered carefully what my response should be. First, I will accept it, as long as it is in writing. Second, I will resume my duties as chair of the fete committee if, and only if, that person is refused admittance to any Chamber of Commerce meetings now and in the future." She moved the sugar bowl, which was a small ceramic teddy bear, to one side of the table and back again.

"You mean Carol Ann."

"Who else?" Adela snorted. "She should be grateful I haven't demanded she be run out of town." She repositioned the creamer—a ceramic cow with a spout for a muzzle. "You don't think this sounds too much like blackmail?"

"Blackmail?"

"The fete is in two weeks. It means a great deal to this town. I would not like to force a cancellation."

Adela's calm was eerie. Quill's uneasiness grew. Carol Ann's demonstration had been all over the late-night news. Everyone in town was looking for Adela, including all six members of the sheriff's department. Maybe Adela had totally flipped out.

"Yesterday was stressful for all of us," Quill began.

"P'ah! After all these years, Sarah Quilliam, I know how to handle stress. After that insulting scene at the Chamber meeting, I went straight into Syracuse. I had a massage. I went to the Pyramid Mall." She smoothed the knees of her yellow pants. "Then I met my sister for dinner to counsel her about a problem she's having with her eldest grandson."

"You must have gotten home very late," Quill ventured. "Didn't you have a lot of messages waiting for you?"

"P'ah!" Adela repeated. "All of them from that man, I'm sure." She waved at the landline. The red message button blinked furiously. "He banged on the door repeatedly last night, too. I ignored him. I suppose many of the messages were from the Chamber members, offering apologies, but as you know, I prefer to deal with people face-to-face. I'll get around to listening to the phone messages later." She frowned. "I'm quite disappointed that you are the sole emissary. A delegation would have been appropriate, I think. As I say, under the right circumstances, I could be persuaded to return."

Quill decided that it was better to rip the bandage off fast. "The committee's talking about bringing in a professional organizer."

Adela's face fell. "I see." She cleared her throat. "I wish him luck. I doubt that he'll be up to the challenge. I doubt anyone else could do it. But I wish him luck."

The kettle began to whistle. Adela didn't seem to hear

it, so Quill got up and turned the gas cooktop off and poured the hot water into the teapot. "It's a her, actually. Someone named Linda Connelly, from Syracuse. Elm . . . that is, the committee's talking to her this morning." This was a lot easier with her back to Adela, so Quill forced herself to come back and reseat herself at the table. "There's more, Adela, and it's unpleasant, so I want you to be prepared."

Adela bit her lip. She folded her hands in her lap, which for some reason made Quill feel even worse than she felt already. "First, I want you to know I admire you a great deal. I believe in you, too. So does everyone at the Inn, and Marge and Miriam—there are a great many of us."

"I have always had my supporters."

"Yes, you have," Quill said warmly. "Sometimes that isn't enough. There's going to be an investigation into the missing money, of course. I know you've probably anticipated that . . ."

"The what?"

"The money missing from the fete account."

"What are you talking about?"

"Davy hasn't talked to you?"

"Davy Kiddermeister? That youngster that took Myles's job? Talked to me about what?"

"No one's called you?"

"I told you. That man attempted to call, of course. When I arrived home last night, I took the phone off the hook. I haven't come to a final decision, but you may inform that man if you happen to see him, that I have consulted the finest divorce lawyer in the state. I will need more than a written or spoken apology from him. He will have to *crawl*."

Quill wasn't listening. Davy must have run into a delay getting a warrant to investigate the checking account. Which meant he would be at the Henrys' home any minute. She ran her hands through her hair and tugged at it. "How much money is in the account right now?"

"One hundred and eighty-six thousand five hundred and twenty-six dollars."

"No. There isn't. One hundred and eighty-six thousand is missing."

Adela turned perfectly white.

Quill dug her nails into her palms and went on. "Elmer's asked me to look into this, and I'm happy to do what I can."

"Where's the money?"

"We don't know yet. The bank has checked their records, and they say the problem isn't on their end. Marge has hired an expert to support the investigation. She doesn't seem to think much of Mark Anthony's fraud unit . . ."

"Fraud unit?"

"Look. All we need to do is sit down and figure out who could have had access to the checking account. Other than the committee members, I mean."

"Somebody stole that money? It was for the literacy fund!"

"Maybe it isn't stolen. Let's just say we don't know where it is at the moment."

"A banking error. It has to be. I don't trust that little teller Andrea Peterson. She's careless, very careless. Perhaps she put my deposits into another account."

"Mark Anthony is checking into that, too."

"Or those computers! Something is always going wrong with those computers!"

"The investigators will find out, if that's what happened. You know how good Marge's people are."

"Investigators!" Adela's eyes were wild. "There's an investigation?" She began to breathe in a big, gaspy way that alarmed Quill a lot. "Excuse me, I . . ." Adela got to her feet. "The doorbell. There's someone at the doorbell. It's Elmer, undoubtedly." She compressed in a tight, white line. "That fool."

Quill followed her to the front of the house feeling utterly helpless. Adela paused a moment at the front door, adjusted her earrings, smoothed her jacket over her hips, and put her shoulders back.

She opened the door to Davy Kiddermeister, dressed in his uniform and carrying a warrant.

She fainted at Quill's feet.

7

"So where is Adela now?" Marge asked. "In the hospital, or what?"

Marge and Quill sat in the All-American Diner (Fine Food! And Fast!), one of Marge's many holdings in Tompkins County. Meg claimed that Marge's diner partner, Betty Hall, made the best diner food in the northeastern United States. With the increasing popularity of the village as a tourist destination, Marge had redecorated. Instead of vinyl, the restaurant now had pale oak floors, and captain's chairs replaced the old vinyl stools at the counter. The sticky plastic menu was replaced by a chalkboard. Quill was glad the food hadn't changed. She felt like everything else in her universe was upside down.

"In the hospital, for observation. Andy Bishop was great about it. Anyone else would have discharged her, but she's better off under medical supervision, Marge. I mean, she's all alone in that house, and heaven knows what that idiot Carol Ann and her stupid Citizens for Justice are up to. What if they picket her, or something?"

"There's been discussion about picketing."

"You're joking."

"Nope. They had another meeting this morning to decide what to do."

"Where? And how do you know?"

"The showroom at Peterson Automotive's big enough for those fancy cars and a crowd, too. Carol Ann called the meeting there. Just like last night. There's a sign out front, now. It says CITIZENS FOR JUSTICE HEADQUARTERS."

"Did you go to the meeting?"

"Heck, no. They know Elmer's staying up to the farm and they know you and I are tight and they know you think Carol Ann's a terminal disease. No, I sent somebody in undercover."

"You did? Who?"

"Betty. So don't order the special since she's not here to cook it."

"Wow. Betty's undercover." Quill sat back. "That was smart."

"You bet it was," Marge said with an air of satisfaction. "Nothing like having a good spy in place to gather intelligence. So. What's next?"

"What's next is that I'm starving. Then we need to make a list of people who might have had access to that account. But food first."

"You better order something and eat it. What you weigh, a hundred and ten soaking wet?"

"None of your business." Quill looked at the chalkboard. "What do you recommend?"

"The Reuben. The rest of the kitchen's got the sandwich down pat and it doesn't matter if Betts isn't here."

"I'm hungry, so I'll go for the onion rings, too."

"Fries are a better bet." Without looking around, Marge

raised her voice and yelled, "Reubens-with. Two of 'em."
She directed her beady gray gaze back at Quill. "So.
What'd you find out before Adela hit the floor?"

"She doesn't know a thing about the missing money,
I'm sure of that. And I had a chance to talk with her once
she got admitted to the ER. The checkbook hasn't been
out of her sight. She swears up and down that nobody on
the committee even knew where she kept it. She's never
had a meeting at her house, and it's locked in her desk
drawer."

"Elmer had access, then."

"Come on, Marge."

Marge shrugged. "Just pointing out the obvious. What
about deposit slips and things like that? She keep those in
her purse? The account number's on those."

"I didn't think of that."

"Not to mention the bank statements. Those go to the
house, right? And the mailbox is right outside for anybody
to burgle. Thing is, once you got the account number, it's
a lot easier to hack into the system. Knowing Adela, the
password's 'fete' or even '1234.'" Marge waited until the
waitress set the Reubens in front of both of them. "Doesn't
matter who has the checkbook. The real question is who
knows enough about computer hacking to get into the
system."

Quill picked up her sandwich and put it down again.
"I've been thinking about that. Althea Quince claims to
know her way around a computer."

"She does, huh?" Marge put a couple of French fries in
her mouth and thought this over. "Maybe we ought to
check Ms. Quince out. Betty texted me the names of the

87

idiots at that meeting this morning. Althea Quince was there."

"She was?"

"Got there late, and didn't stay long. She had a companion, Betty said. Didn't say who that might be."

"Mr. Quince, probably." Quill ate a couple of French fries, too. "He seems like a very nice man. Quiet." She thought a bit more. "Smart, too. Who else was there?"

Marge pulled her cell phone out of her chinos pocket and tapped at it. "The guys from the *Gazette*. But no TV, like there was last night, and the reporters didn't stay. There still isn't any proof, and past a certain point, no editor is going to run what amounts to a bunch of unsupported allegations over and over again." Marge raised her eyes from her cell phone. "I'd like to get Carol Ann in a small room with a big dog and find out just what the heck she does know."

"Marge!"

"See, my guess is that Carol Ann never got over having to step out of the mayor's race last year. This is part of a power grab. She lost that job as food inspector." A grin flitted across Marge's face and disappeared. "And now she's got nothing going on except a job cashiering at Wegman's over to Syracuse and some loony-tunes diet scam called Nutra-Noshers. Anyhow, once the media figures out this is just Carol Ann after some free press she's going to go begging for coverage."

"Carol Ann has a job as a cashier at Wegman's?" Quill was fascinated by this piece of gossip.

"Not too much that suits her notion of herself in these parts. Job at least keeps the rent paid."

"I thought she owned her own ho . . . never mind. So you think she cooked up this investigation to unseat Adela and the mayor, too?"

"Wouldn't be surprised."

"But the money's gone."

"I think Dina's right. I think Carol Ann lucked into that."

Quill shook her head. "That doesn't make much sense. Somebody tipped her off. I'd sure like to find out who. Unless . . . Do you think she stole the money?"

"Now that would surprise me. Carol Ann's too much of a law-and-order type. Besides, did you see her face when Mark Anthony told us how much was in the account yesterday? She was as surprised as anybody there. I think young Dina had it right. She's a spoiler, Carol Ann is. If the money had been there, she was just going to holler louder, asking for a public accounting, blah, blah, blah. Lot of folks figure where there's smoke there's fire, which is why big lies work so well." Marge sighed heavily. "Tell you what. Unless the bank comes up with some computer error, we might as well look where the smoke's rising."

"You mean the people on the fete committee."

"They're the likeliest to know how much money was floating around. And they knew where the account numbers could be found."

Quill ate some of her sandwich without really tasting it. "Okay. So the only person on the fete committee we don't know a thing about is Althea Quince. "

"So we've got a possible lead."

"Right. A possible lead."

"Or a what d'ya call it? A line of inquiry."

"Fine! A line of inquiry, then. Why did she go off to that meeting this morning? I think that's suspicious, don't you? She'd want to find out what kind of investigation this citizen's committee's going to launch to protect herself."

"Maybe. And maybe she was just nosy."

"Who else did you say was there?"

Marge tapped on the phone. "A bunch of Harland's idiot relatives, but since there's so many of them you have to expect it. Most of the Chamber members, excepting you, me, Miriam, and Dookie. Some little old guy Betts says is at least a hundred and ten with a cane. She's never seen him before."

"A little old . . ." Quill searched her visual memory, which was excellent. "My goodness! Mr. Swenson? What do you suppose he was doing there?"

"Since I don't know him from a hole in the ground I couldn't guess. Who is he?"

"If it's the same man, he's a guest at the Inn. He took the Provencal Suite on a Long-Term Let."

"The only really old people with canes around here are widows," Marge said. "So maybe it is the same guy."

"For heaven's sake, Marge."

"What?!"

"I don't know. I'm just asking for a little respect, that's all. Not for me, for the little old . . . never mind. Anybody else? Anybody suspicious?"

"If you mean former secondhand-rust-bucket drivers flaunting a new Corvette bought with stolen fete money, no. Or if there was, Betts didn't text me about it." Marge clicked her cell phone shut. "Best thing we can hope is that my guy can go through that bank system and trace the money transfer. In the meantime, we got thirty thousand people headed for the fete in two weeks, and nobody to run it . . ." Marge broke off and narrowed her eyes. "Who the heck is that?"

Quill turned around. A small, dark-haired woman was entering the restaurant. She was dressed in an expensive suit—Adolfo, Quill thought—and followed by two much taller men, who stayed a respectful two feet behind. She carried a slim Hermes briefcase that might have cost less than the suit, but not by much. One of the men had an affable expression. He had a ponytail, wore a headband, and in general looked like he'd headed for California twenty years before and gotten lost.

The other was a hunk. Tall, broad-shouldered, dark-haired, and muscular. Mid-thirties, maybe, with an aquiline nose, square jaw, and intelligent brown eyes under level brows. He caught Quill's gaze and winked.

Quill, suddenly mindful of the fact that she was a married woman, looked hastily away from the hunk and again at the short, well-dressed woman preceding him.

She looked around the diner in a calculating way. One eyebrow went up when she sighted Quill and she headed briskly toward the booth. She extended a nicely manicured hand and said, "You must be Sarah Quilliam. Or do you prefer McHale? I'm Linda Connelly."

Quill dropped the remains of her sandwich in her lap, dabbed futilely at the sauerkraut with one hand, and shook Linda's hand with the other. "Hello. You're with the company that we've asked to run the fete."

"That's right. I just came from a meeting with your mayor. He told me you might be here. Call me Linda. Okay if I call you Quill?"

"Certainly."

"This is George McIntyre, our driver, with the headband, and Mickey Greer, my assistant."

The corners of Mickey's eyes crinkled in an attractive smile. He took Quill's hand in a brief, firm clasp.

Linda nodded at Marge. "And you're Mrs. Peterson?"

Marge tore her gaze from Mickey Greer and said, "Schmidt. Marge Schmidt."

Linda nodded. "Yes. Well. We've come to an agreement with your mayor. We're going to run the fete for you."

"That's terrific," Quill said warmly. "Would you like to sit down?"

George smiled. "What we'd like is to sit down and eat a few of those great-looking Reubens. But we don't have time at the moment. We're headed over to the Resort to check in. We wanted to stay at the Inn, right, Linda?"

Linda blinked. Then she smiled. It wasn't a very warm one. "Right. We would have liked to stay at the Inn—we've heard so much about it up in Syracuse, but expenses are going to be on the town's dollar, so we're economizing."

"We'd like to schedule a meeting with you later, though," George said. "Get to know you folks a little better. We were wondering if we might meet with you and the rest of the fete committee tonight? Say about eight o'clock if that's not too late for you? I know you need some time with your little boy. We've got to come up to speed pretty quick, here."

"Eight would be fine," Quill said. "I'll give the other

committee members a call. Would you like to meet at the Inn?"

"Sure," Linda said. "Whatever suits you. We'll see you there." She shook hands with Quill and Marge, wheeled around, and left, trailed by George, who waved a cheery good-bye, and the hunk, who didn't look back.

"Holy cripes," Marge said after they were safely out of hearing.

"She did seem pretty efficient," Quill said. "Somehow you'd expect an event co-coordinator to be warmer."

"Who? Linda Connelly? I meant the guy with her."

Quill rubbed the back of her neck. "Really? Which one?"

Marge pursed her lips. "You know what? If you'd left it at the 'really' I might have bought it. It was the 'which one' that did it. The hunk, of course. I think I better come to that meeting of yours tonight. Keep an eye out for Myles while he's away."

Quill raised both eyebrows. "Oh, yeah? So who's the one that said 'Call me Schmidt' rather than admitting she was married? I think you'd better come to the meeting, too. And bring Harland with you."

Marge made a rude noise.

"I'm glad Elmer found someone so quickly." Quill gazed doubtfully out the window. Linda and her crew were getting into a silver Lexus. George the headband guy got into the driver's seat. Mickey Greer sat next to him. Linda sat in the back. "They certainly knew a great deal about both of us, Marge. Kind of odd, don't you think?"

Marge shrugged. "Probably pumped Elmer. Or maybe they checked you out on the Internet. There are a lot of discussion groups about your paintings. The big thing is they're taking over the fete. It was bad enough when we lost Adela. No offense, Quill, but that thing would have swallowed you up and spit you out. So as long as they handle that, they can be as nosy and rude as they want. It doesn't matter to me. What does matter is where that money went. As far as our investigation goes . . ."

Quill opened her mouth and then shut it. Marge loved snooping. She was pretty good at it. And she herself needed a partner.

". . . There's not much we can do until my guy lets us know where the money went."

"I think we ought to try and talk to Carol Ann."

"Davy will have better luck."

This was true.

"What about Althea Quince?"

"You're reaching."

Quill felt her cheeks go red. "You're right."

"Let things ripen a bit. My tech ought to be getting back to me pretty quick. When she does, I'll call you." She looked at her watch. "I can't sit around here all day gabbing with you. I've got things to do."

"You were the one who asked me to lunch," Quill said, mildly insulted. "Besides, I've got a lot to do, too." She looked at her watch. "Good grief. It's after four already. I'm supposed to be at Bonne Goute to go over the conduct code for the food booth judges. Dina was a peach and faxed everyone their assignments. Well," she said decisively, "I can give them an hour, no more. I've got to get back to the Inn in time for Jack's dinner."

"You think you're going to get out of there in an hour?" Marge hooted.

"Adela always did."

"Adela's Adela. You're . . ."

"I'm what?"

"You're a pushover, that's what you are. Why do you think you've been Chamber secretary all these years? You'll be lucky if you get back before next Tuesday."

"I know how to run a meeting, thank you very much. These people have all been through this before. Well, almost all. Althea Quince is judging the craft jewelry, but that's not my problem, thank goodness. Just the food and the pets. Clare's got this new chef who's going to handle the pies, but I can coach her anytime in the next couple of weeks if she needs extra help. I'll just whip through the conduct requirements, and be out of there by teatime. Of course," Quill added honestly, "I don't quite have Adela's touch, I'll admit that."

Marge grinned, and then sighed. "Poor Adela. It's a mess." She wriggled her shoulders uncomfortably. "I suppose I ought to stop by the hospital and see her. Maybe tomorrow. Bring her a geranium or something."

"We can both go. I promised her I'd keep her up to speed on what's going on." Quill slung her tote over her arm and wriggled out of the booth. She felt a surge of affection and dropped a kiss on the top of Marge's ginger head. "See you tonight. My office. About eight."

8

It was only a few minutes by car from Marge's All-American Diner to Clare Sparrow's culinary academy, but Quill took the opportunity to set her worries about Adela aside and concentrated on getting through her next committee.

The Inn at Hemlock Falls sat directly across the Gorge from La Bonne Goute Culinary Academy. The late (and unlamented) Bernard LeVasque had purchased the twenty acres that lay between Peterson Park and the Resort and built a sprawling complex that included the three-story academy itself, an outbuilding for cars and extra wine storage, and an annex that had ten apartments for staff and visiting chefs.

Everyone not involved in the restaurant business in Hemlock Falls thought the academy was gorgeous. Meg had the same reaction to the architecture that she did to residential kitchens with stainless-steel appliances and acres of granite counters: too shiny, too new, and too generic. Quill, wisely, put this down to Meg's competitive spirit. Marge was outraged at the uninhibited use of investors' dollars. Quill herself admired it, without having the least desire to own it.

The main building was three stories high, with a copper roof, cream clapboard siding, hunter green shutters and window trim, and twenty-foot-wide pine balconies on each story. Two smaller matching buildings were tucked onto the meadow in the back; one held ten apartments for visitors, the chefs, and the instructors; the other was an eight-vehicle garage. The main building held wine cellars, a vast, elaborate tasting room, and a second-floor restaurant with a spectacular view over Hemlock Gorge.

Quill pulled into the first driveway, which led around to the employee parking lot, and sat in her car for a moment, looking at her inn across the way. The air was soft with late afternoon sunlight and the cobblestones glowed like the skin of new peaches. The roses massed at the foot of the sprawling building were a Monet-like blur of soft pink and cream. Her own copper roof was green with the patina of age. The academy looked like a young and vigorous upstart by comparison.

She sighed and went in through the restaurant kitchen to find Madame LeVasque flaying chickens at the fifteen-foot-long, stainless-steel-topped prep table.

"Hello, Dorothy. I didn't expect to see you here."

Madame LeVasque had a nose like a hatchet, iron gray hair tucked neatly at the back of her head, and a very short fuse. She'd mellowed some, since the death of her husband (to no one's surprise) and she greeted Quill with a faint smile. "What do you expect? You people have co-opted all my chefs to be judges for this stupid fete. Somebody's got to keep the kitchen afloat."

"I didn't know you cooked."

"I cook." She whacked at the carcass in front of her and the chicken fell neatly in two. "I just didn't cook when LeVasque was around. Rotten French bum that he was." She jerked her chin toward the doors leading to the academy public rooms. "You'll find all my chefs in the tasting room along with my director. A good few of the townspeople, too. I hope this fete comes off. With Adela out of the picture, you've got some organizing ahead of you."

"True enough."

Quill went ahead into the main part of the building, which had soaring ceilings crisscrossed with redwood beams, and a glass-fronted gift shop that held multiple copies of Bernard's final cookbook *Brilliance in the Kitchen*. The teaching kitchen was at right angles to the tasting room. It had twenty Viking six-burner gas cooktops, five prep sinks, and all the pots, pans, knives, graters, ladles, bowls, and measuring cups amateur chefs could wish for.

She pushed open the great wooden doors of the tasting room, which were carved with grapevines, and went inside.

The air was scented with wine and damp oak. Bernard had imported his wine shelving from his native Brittany and lined the large room with them. Chest-high marble-topped counters formed a U against the tiers of wine bottles. A long oak refectory table occupied the center of the floor with the proposed judges for the fall fete seated around it.

Clare sat at the head of the table wearing her toque.

She jumped up as Quill came in. "Hey! We thought we'd lost you!"

"Sorry I'm late. The time got away from me."

"Seen anything of that crook Adela?" somebody called out.

Quill frowned and scanned the table. She didn't recognize the voice. There were fifteen food-related categories to judge at the fete every year and the judges were usually selected from the town. She waved at her own sous chefs, Elizabeth Chou and Bjarne Bjarneson, who wouldn't have made a crack like that.

Althea Quince waved cheerily at her, her bracelets clanking. Quill doubted that she'd made the comment—but she had been at Brady Beale's squash-Adela-flat meeting that morning, and you just never knew.

Betty Hall sat next to Althea—and as she never said anything aloud, Quill was pretty sure the comment hadn't come from her, and she was on Adela's side, anyway.

Raleigh Brewster, Jim Chen, and Pietro Giancava were all chefs from the academy and familiar to her. That left Dolly Jean Attenborough, president of the Crafty Ladies Art Guild, Brady Beale, who gave her an oily grin, and a tall blond woman of about thirty whom Quill had never seen before.

The blonde stood out like a torch ginger in a bed of sweet peas. She was slender, with a Florida tan, and the kind of white blond hair associated with Swedes. Her eyes were a pale blue—startling in the tanned face—and she stared back at Quill with an "it wasn't me, Mom" expression that would have been funny under other circumstances.

Brady Beale smirked at her. Quill's money was on him. She walked to the end of the table opposite Clare and said pleasantly, "Before we start, let's talk about Adela Henry. I don't believe she took that money. Now, I've always been proud to be part of this fete and I'm proud to be part of it this year, too. Yes, we've run into some irregularities this year. But the fete has an honorable history, and that is totally due to Adela.

"Adela Henry devoted a lot of time, a lot of effort, and a huge amount of expertise to the fete's success for more than twenty years. I checked the records before I came out to see you all today—does anyone know how much money our village has donated to the literacy fund over those years? You'll be amazed. I know I was. One. Million. Dollars. That's an average of fifty thousand dollars a year. Under Adela Henry's stewardship." Quill paused. "I'd like to take a moment, before we go over the code of conduct for the judging, to thank her for her good work. She can't be here today. It looks as though she may not be here for this year's fete. But I know we're all hoping she will be here for the next." Quill shot Clare a quick glance and began to clap. Everybody joined in, except for Brady who, as Quill suspected he would, finally caved to peer pressure and applauded, too. Quill waited until the applause reached a crescendo. She raised her hands and said, "Thank you. I'm going to tell Adela of your good wishes tomorrow when I see her."

Brady nudged Pietro Giancava, who was sitting next to him, and snickered. Pietro sneered at him, dusted his shirtsleeve as if to remove a piece of dirt, and shoved his chair back. Good. So maybe the entire town wasn't out for Adela's blood.

"Now, I'd like to get on to the code of conduct. It's pretty simple. Each of you has the judging standards for your particular food category, and we can talk about those if you have any questions. I know you will all be fair and honest in your assessment of the entries, and that you'll avoid any community pressure that might be brought to bear in the more hotly contested areas. I'd encourage those of you who've participated as judges in the past to offer support to the new guys. Does everyone have the code of conduct sheet? If not, I have some copies in my tote. Everyone's got one? Great." Quill smoothed her own copy on the tabletop and read. "Rule one is pretty self-explanatory. The fete opens at ten on Friday morning, which is the eighth of September. Judges are to check into the Green Room at seven thirty A.M."

"Just for the newbies, the Green Room is the registration tent," Dolly Jean caroled. She jumped up from her seat. "For those of you who don't know me, I'm Dolly Jean Attenborough, president of our very own craft guild. We're known all through upstate New York as the Crafty Ladies." She paused. There was a spatter of handclapping.

Dolly Jean's wispy white hair flared lacelike around her rosy cheeks. She dimpled attractively at the tall blonde with the ocean blue eyes. "Actually, darlin', I know everyone in this room except you."

The blonde looked from side to side, as if Dolly Jean were addressing someone behind her. Then she got to her feet—she really was very tall, Quill thought—and extremely fit, to boot. "I'm Sophie Kilcannon." Her voice was light and pleasant. "This is my first day working at the culinary academy for Chef Sparrow." Then, with a slight note of defiance, she added, "I'm a chef."

Clare stood up. "Forgive me, Sophie. I should have introduced you before this. Everybody? I'd like to introduce Sophie Kilcannon, who comes to the academy from her home in Florida. Sophie has been chef-in-residence for several internationally known clients in Palm Beach, and I'm delighted to welcome her to her new home at Bonne Goute. She will be assisting in cooking classes both in entrées and pastry. She will specialize in fruits and vegetables."

Enthusiastic applause greeted this short speech. Clare sat down again.

"And what are you judging at the fete, Sophie?" Dolly Jean asked.

"I've been recruited to judge pies."

A ripple of amusement (with a dash of commiseration) swept through the audience. Sophie didn't seem to notice.

"How delightful," Dolly Jean breathed. "Several of our Crafty Ladies will be entering the fruit and berry pie competition. You must let me introduce you to them."

Quill cleared her throat. "Thank you, Dolly Jean. That segues nicely into the next item: avoiding charges of favoritism."

~

Almost four hours later, Quill stretched out flat on her office couch and stared up at the tin ceiling. The ceiling was a relic of the 1850s when the Inn had been a young woman's academy and it would have been a high point on any nineteenth-century architecture homes tour, if she'd been interested in running such tours, which she wasn't.

"Can I get you something to eat?" Meg said. She sat behind Quill's desk, playing solitaire on Quill's laptop with one hand, a glass of wine in the other.

"Clare brought out cheese and fruit when nobody would shut up and go home. I'm too tired to eat anything else. What is it about volunteers and meetings, anyway? They just went on and on and *on*."

"At least you got back in time for Jack."

"Five minutes. That was it. He was out of his bath and headed for bed when I finally got here. Doreen gave me what-for." She raised her right arm and looked at her watch. "And five minutes is when Linda Connelly will be here for another meeting. You can flip out from too many meetings, Meg, I'm sure of it. You can go stark staring bonkers." She yawned, suddenly so sleepy that she wasn't sure she could stand up. "I just want to crawl in bed and sleep for . . . oh, my goodness!" She jumped to her feet. "They're going to walk through that door any minute. Mickey Greer and, um . . . what's her name. Linda."

"So?"

"So wait until you see Mickey." Quill grabbed her tote, rummaged through it for her brush, and took out her little hand mirror. "I look like something Clare's cat dragged in." She ran the brush through her hair, whipped on some lip gloss, and hustled Meg out of her office chair.

Meg promptly sat down again, on the couch. "*Who's* coming here again?"

Somebody tapped at the office door and opened it.

Quill assumed a casual pose behind her desk and smiled brightly. "Come in, please, Mr. Greer. And Linda, of course. Welcome . . . oh. It's you, Dina."

"It's me." Dina adjusted her spectacles with one forefinger. "Were you expecting somebody else?"

"Linda Connelly and her assistant are coming by to talk about the fete."

Meg stamped her foot. "Earth to Quill. Who is Linda Connelly and why should I give a hoot?"

"I told you guys about that, didn't I? Elmer found an event organizer to take over Adela's duties while she's, umm . . . in the hospital. He hired her this morning. The organization is called Presentations and it's Linda Connelly, plus two assistants. Two guys. George somebody and Mickey Greer."

Dina's eyes widened. "Is she sort of short in a good suit?"

"I imagine she's short whether or not she's in a good suit," Meg said.

"Oh. My. God." Dina sank onto the couch next to Meg. "If that's the one, she's in the dining room right now, with the hottest guy I've ever seen in my life."

Quill nodded. "That's the one."

Meg glanced at the brush in Quill's hand. "Aha."

"Whoa." Dina shook her head. "Okay. So. I know I told you I was too busy with lab project to take on any fete duties, but I've changed my mind. Any committee this guy is on I want to be on."

Meg rolled her eyes. "How good-looking is this guy, anyway?"

"Sort of Hugh Jackman–ish," Dina said.

"More Robert Downey–ish," Quill said. "Except he's better built."

Meg got up. "I'd better see this guy for myself." She marched out the door, wheeled, marched back, grabbed Quill's brush and ran it through her short dark hair, then wheeled out again.

"I thought you and Justin Alvarez were pretty tight!" Dina yelled after her.

Quill looked at her. "Well, you and Davy Kiddermeister are pretty tight."

"And you're married."

Quill laughed. "True enough. I take it they had dinner in the dining room?"

"Steak frites, Pasta Quilliam, and Hammondsport trout amandine. A glass of wine each. They should be finishing up by now."

"Good." Quill yawned. "I'd like to get this meeting over with. It's been a heck of a day. Is there anything else? Other than the gorgeous guy in the dining room?"

Dina clapped her hand over her mouth. "Oh, dear. Yes, there is. Nate needs you in the Tavern Lounge. You know that little old guy with the cane?"

"Mr. Swenson?" Immediately concerned, Quill got to her feet. "Is he okay? Do we need to call the paramedics?"

"*He's* just peachy keen. We might need the paramedics for the guy he's whacking around, though."

Quill tugged at her hair, which made it fall halfway down her back. "Dina!"

"What? I was just kidding about the paramedics. Mr. Swenson's ninety-eight years old, or so he keeps telling us, and he doesn't pack that much of a wallop." She followed Quill down the short hallway that led to both the Tavern Lounge and the conference room. "I have to say I don't much care for the guy he's walloping, which is why this isn't all *that* urgent."

Quill paused at the doorway leading into the lounge, to assess the situation.

The room had that indefinable atmosphere of a room immediately after a disruption. The patrons seemed to be settling back down to their drinks.

The lounge itself was a well-designed place to have a glass of wine. Quill had round tables made from a reclaimed gym floor and spaced them widely enough so that guests were comfortable talking to each other but didn't feel isolated. The long, highly polished mahogany bar was a relic of the Inn's early days as a genuine tavern, as was the cobblestone fireplace. Over the years, Quill had changed her mind about the walls—initially a teal blue, now a creamy coffee. She'd gone through what she privately called her Georgia O'Keeffe period, and five of her flower studies hung near the French doors leading to the flagstone terrace outside.

This time of night, the lounge was about half full. A few people cast sideways glances at the table nearest the end of the bar, where Jeeter Swenson sat with a middle-aged man and woman at a table for four.

Dina gave her a little nudge. "That's who Mr. Swenson was whacking. The guy in the blue blazer."

Quill walked over and sat down in the fourth chair.

Jeeter was thin and wiry, with a head of bright white hair. Great age had been kind to him; his skin was mottled with age spots, his gray eyes were filmy, and his hands were knobby with arthritis, but there was an alert, merry spitefulness to his expression and he greeted Quill with a wide smile. "The innkeeper," he said with satisfaction. "Mrs. McHale to you, Portly. She's come to throw your portly butt out of here. Didn't you, Mrs. McHale?"

The man next to him nodded, and extended his hand. "Porter Swenson, Mrs. McHale. And this is my wife Melbourne." Porter *was* portly, in a modest way, but he looked very like his father. Melbourne had the figure of a fiercely dedicated dieter. Her carefully applied makeup and unnaturally taut jaw didn't do much to conceal her age, which Quill estimated to be in her mid-sixties.

"Please call me Quill. And no, I haven't come to throw anyone out of anywhere. But I would like to offer assistance if you need it."

Porter rose and put his hand under Quill's elbow. "If you wouldn't mind, could we step over here for a moment?"

Quill glanced at Jeeter, who winked at her. "Go on. Just remember that I'm footing the bill, here. Not him."

Porter drew her to the end of the bar. "I hope you mean that offer of assistance."

"Of course."

He put his hand inside his blazer and pulled out a business card. He was a lawyer, with an office in Syracuse. "You can reach me here, or through Howie here in Hemlock Falls."

"Howie Murchison?"

"Classmate of mine from Cornell. He understands the situation. You can see how it is."

Quill glanced back at Jeeter, who was playfully poking

Melbourne with the tip of his cane. There was a smile on her face, but her eyes glittered in a way that only could be described as homicidal.

"My father's ninety-eight. He is clearly suffering from dementia. I'm going to need your help to get him out of here and into a safer place."

"A safer place? You mean a nursing home or something like that?"

"Something like that."

Melbourne shrieked, grabbed the cane, and threw it on the floor. She took a deep breath, and then called to her husband. "I'm going to sit in the car, Porter. Can you wrap it up, please? I'd like to get back to Syracuse before the damn sun comes up." Then, between gritted teeth, she said, "Good-bye, Dad. You stay well, now."

"Never been better," Jeeter cackled. He bent over and picked up his cane with an effort. He waved it at Melbourne. "Scoot!"

Melbourne scooted.

Jeeter chuckled to himself, and then raised a finger in Nate's direction. "Cup of coffee here, Nate, if you please. Just black."

Porter shook his head in spurious sorrow. "You can see for yourself what we're dealing with here."

What Quill saw was a guy who was taking full advantage of his age to torment a daughter-in-law he didn't like very much. But she said, "He's been seen by a doctor? Your father, I mean?"

Porter's gaze shifted sideways. "Well, the thing is, he's very clever with it. The dementia, I mean. To talk to him, in a clinical setting, you'd never guess that the chandelier's shy a few lightbulbs. And the damn doctors buy it. He's clever, Dad is. Always has been." Porter widened his lips in a grin. His teeth were too white. He smelled like wine and sweat. "Look. It's important, for his sake, that we get him to a . . . a safer environment. And to do that, we're going to need outside verification of what Melbourne and I have seen all along."

Quill raised her eyebrows politely.

"Aggression. Inappropriate behavior in public." Porter rubbed his elbow reflectively. "Assault."

"You think he has dementia because he pokes people with his cane?"

"That's it," he said eagerly. "That's it in a nutshell. Now, if you could just talk to your maids, and the wait-staff, and keep an eye out yourself and report on his behaviors, we will be very, very grateful. We will be happy to reimburse everyone for their time, of course. Handsomely."

Quill stared at him for a long moment. Then she said, "Mr. Swenson checked in a week ago, and we haven't seen any evidence that he's . . . umm . . . demented. Quite the reverse, as a matter of fact. He's made some friends here, including my son and his grandmother—well, his honorary grandmother—and our receptionist Dina Muir."

Porter dropped the smile and stepped in close to her. "So it's going to be like that, is it? You figure the money you're getting for the next three months is more important than my father's health?"

Bullies made Quill lose her temper. Pious bullies were even worse. "It's not like anything, Mr. Swenson. If there's nothing else, I have a meeting to get to."

"I warn you, Mrs. McHale, that if anything happens to my father while he is under your care here at the Inn, you are leaving yourself wide open to legal action. You might think about booking that suite he's in to someone else. The sooner the better."

Quill was standing with her back to the fireplace, facing the door to the Inn proper. She saw with relief that Linda Connelly, Dina, Marge, and Linda's two assistants had come into the lounge. Nate waved them to a table for six by the French doors. She slipped past Porter, with a murmured "You'll excuse me, please," and went to join them.

"What's put your knickers in a twist?" Marge demanded.

"Nothing." Quill scowled at Porter, who'd gone back to his father and was leaning over him. Jeeter glared back up at him, poked him a good one in the shins with his cane, and hobbled out of the lounge. Porter stared after him, and then slammed out of the French doors into the night.

"What was *that* little drama all about?" Linda asked.

"That's Jeeter Swenson," Dina said. "The sweet old guy, that is. The creep is his son, who's a lawyer from Syracuse, and who wants to get his hot little hands on Jeeter's lakeside mansion. It's a gorgeous place, right smack on Seneca Lake and he's trying to get Jeeter into some nursing home and Jeeter doesn't want to go. So Jeeter came here, to get away from them and guess what, they tracked him down and showed up here about an hour ago. It's awful."

"Now's not the time, Dina," Quill said firmly. "We'll discuss this later."

"But it's not right!"

"All he has to do is refuse to go," Linda said, with a clear lack of interest.

"If they get him declared demented, he can refuse all he wants and they'll haul him off like a forgotten teddy bear," Dina said emotionally. "It's all because of what he saw in the lake."

Quill was pretty sure she was going to regret the answer, but she asked, "What did he see in the lake?"

"The Loch Ness Monster," Dina said. "Or more accurately, the Seneca Lake Monster. Of course it's unlikely that there are monsters in Seneca or any other lake, and if anyone knows that, it's me, and I told Jeeter that, but he's got a what d'ycall it. An idée fixe. A harmless one. He is *not* demented." She pushed her spectacles up her nose and added thoughtfully. "Of course, there's more things under heaven and in earth, Horatio and all that, and I've always had my suspicions that there really is a relic of aquatic dinosaurs in Loch Ness, so why not Seneca, too?"

Linda blinked at her. "What?"

"Dina's a graduate student in limnology," Marge said. "That's freshwater pond ecology. I suppose she's more likely to know about aquatic dinosaurs than anyone else around here."

Linda shrugged. "Freshwater pond ecology. Aquatic dinosaurs. Interesting, I guess. I can't see it affecting the fete, however. Let's move on. I'm sure we're all tired after what's been a very long day."

"Sure," Dina muttered, "of course. Sorry."

"Good. So let's get the ball rolling here, shall we?" She swung her briefcase up on the tabletop and opened it up. "I've learned something that distresses me a little, and before we get any further down the road with this project, I'd like to talk it over. It may be that Presentations can't tackle this for you after all." She looked at Quill, Marge, and Dina in turn. "Do any of you know a Carol Ann Spinoza?"

~

"Linda Connelly's going to be very effective, if she doesn't up and quit because she thinks we're all crazy or crooked or both," Quill said to Myles's computer image some hours later. "Between Dina's lake monster and the Citizens for Justice she must think she's fallen in with crazies. What's more important is that Elmer didn't tell her why Adela had to withdraw from the fete when he recruited Presentations. Linda didn't have a clue about the missing money until Carol Ann tracked her down. She's concerned about her company's reputation. She doesn't want to be in the middle of what might turn out to be a case of fraud or theft or whatever."

"Embezzlement," Myles said.

"Right. Embezzlement. Anyhow, Marge and I convinced her that it's all under control, but she's skeptical. She's going to go to another one of those dratted meetings at Brady's to get some idea of what we're up against. I can't blame her, really. No one wants to be associated with a public relations disaster. She wants to talk to Adela, too, of course, even though Elmer's turned over all her fete files, which is going to upset Adela to no end. Anyhow. I'll tackle all that tomorrow . . ." Quill yawned. "What else? Oh! And what shall I do about that horrible Porter Swenson? I mean, I ask you! Isn't there some law against attempting bribery of an innkeeper? Aren't there laws against tormenting the elderly? Although, I suppose to be fair, Jeeter was doing most of the tormenting."

"I don't think I'd be looking on the Internet for a Taser cane to give him, no."

"It'd be great if there were such a cane. I'd Taser that Porter within an inch of his life. I'll talk to Howie tomorrow, too. I can't imagine that he and Porter are buddies, but you never know." Quill yawned again. "Oh, dear. I'm sorry. I think the day is catching up with me. Maybe I'm just getting old, Myles. I used to be able to handle this stuff with one hand tied behind my back."

"Thirty-nine. A dangerous age. I'm sure that's the reason."

Quill bent closer to the screen. "You're not laughing at me, are you?"

"Wouldn't dream of it."

"It was," she admitted, "an unusually odd series of events all in one day."

"Not for Hemlock Falls," Myles murmured.

"What?"

"Get to sleep, dear heart. It will all look better in the morning."

"I doubt it," she said. "But I can always hope."

She told him she loved him. She didn't tell him she missed him. They had an agreement about that. Then she signed off and went to check on Jack.

Quill cracked the door to Jack's bedroom and looked in on her sleeping son. The light fell across his bed. Max the dog lay curled at the foot of the bed, and Jack lay curled on top of Max. Gently, she lifted Jack's solid little body and tucked him properly into bed. Max yawned, scrabbled to his feet, and slouched into the living room to her front door. He cocked one lopsided ear at her.

"You want to go out?"

The tip of Max's tail waved. Quill wasn't sure how old he was; well over ten at least. Their vet, Dr. McKenzie, thought there might be some retriever in his ancestry, and maybe some standard poodle. Whatever his background, Max's coat was a shambly mix of ochres, gray, off-white, and black.

He whuffed a little, which meant he was serious about going out. Doreen's room was right next to hers, and Doreen would be up like a shot if Jack called out, so Quill collected Max's leash and resigned herself to twenty minutes outside before she could get to sleep.

Her rooms were at the west end of the building and it was a short trip down the fire escape to the gardens in back. Max poked around the rosebushes, then, being a modest dog, disappeared around the front corner of the Inn. Quill leaned back against the fire escape and looked up at the sky. The moon was huge and soft, a gigantic plum of a moon nested in wispy silver clouds. The air was soft, peaceful, and quiet until Max barked and howled like a banshee when he discovered Jeeter Swenson's body on the lip of Hemlock Gorge.

9

"I've never seen anything quite like it." Andy Bishop tucked the business end of his stethoscope into the top pocket of his lab coat and shook his head, marveling. "Mr. Swenson's a vigorous old bird. No evidence of a concussion. He has a surprisingly thick skull for his age, and no evidence of a seizure or a heart attack. He may have tripped and fallen and hit his head as he fell. There's a nasty contusion on his right temple."

Quill and Meg sat close together on the couch in the Family Room at the Village Hospital and Clinic. It was three o'clock in the morning, and Jeeter Swenson wasn't dead.

Quill let out a long sigh.

Meg yawned heartily and poked her sister in the side. "Good. Now we can go home."

"Can we see him?" Quill asked.

"Sure. Just don't make it too long. I gave him a little clonazepam, just to help him settle down. He'll be falling asleep pretty quickly."

Meg got to her feet, grumbling a little. Andy's eyes drifted over her rather wistfully. There had been a time, not long in the past, when Quill was sure her volatile sister would make a match of it with the attractive Dr. Bishop, but it hadn't gone anywhere. "We won't be long, Andy. Meg and I are dead on our feet." She paused on the way to the patient rooms down the hall. "Did you call his relatives?"

Andy rubbed his hands over his face. "Yep. I talked to the son, what's his name."

"Porter Swenson."

"Yeah." Andy's grin was cynical. "Didn't seem all that relieved that his dad was going to be okay. Said he'd be by sometime tomorrow. Watch yourself with that guy, Quill. He started asking me all kinds of questions about security at the Inn. You don't want to find yourself in the middle of a lawsuit."

Quill nodded.

Hospital rooms diminish everybody, and Jeeter was no exception. He looked smaller, paler, and infinitely fragile. A neat bandage circled his head. He lay back against the propped-up frame of the hospital bed, eyes closed, his skin a grayish yellow. An IV drip was attached to one skinny arm. Meg caught Quill by the elbow and whispered, "Maybe we ought to let the poor guy sleep."

Jeeter's eyes popped open. Quill was glad to see that the malicious sparkle was still there. "It's mine host," he rasped. He cleared his throat with an effort. "Hostess, I should say. The hostess with the most-ess."

"We just stopped by to make sure you're all right," Quill said quietly. "We'll be back to see you in the morning."

"Hell, I'll be out of here by morning." He cackled.

"Nothing wrong with me that a good slug of Scotch wouldn't cure. Doc says he'll be happy to prescribe it once I'm back in my room." He patted the bed. "Take a load off, honey."

Quill sat at the very edge of the mattress. Meg wandered around the room, which was small, spotless, and smelled like Pine-Sol. "Meg and I are really glad you aren't hurt."

"Me, too. Gonna make it to a hundred and seventeen, you know. Can't let a little thing like a fall set me back."

"You fell?"

His eyes clouded. He worked his lips. "I must've, I guess."

"Were you out for a walk last night?"

He yawned. "I was out to meet somebody. On account of the note."

Meg and Quill looked at each other. "The note?" Meg said. "What note?"

"From those guys. You know, the guys against the conspiracy."

"The Citizens for Justice?" Quill said, astonished. "You got a note from Carol Ann Spinoza?"

"She the one who smells like shampoo? Nah. Not her." Jeeter's eyes began to close and he fought it. "Nope. Nope. Nope. The other . . ." His eyes closed and his mouth dropped open. Quill's heart turned over. Asleep, he looked as vulnerable as her own child.

Meg drew the thin blanket up over his chest. "We'd better let him rest," she whispered. "And we'd better find that note."

~

"If there's a note, it's either at the bottom of the river or in the old guy's pockets," Doreen said over coffee and brioche at ten o'clock the next morning. "I figgered you two might of missed something last night when you searched his room, so I got housekeeping to go over it with a fine-tooth comb. Nothing."

"We should have looked at his laptop," Meg said.

The three of them sat in the dining room at the table nearest the kitchen doors. Outside, it was another fine August day. Quill almost never tired of the sight of the water cascading over the falls; today she watched the plumes of green water without really seeing them. She shook her head. "The laptop would have been a real invasion of his right to privacy. I'm okay with checking out his room. I mean, housekeeping is in there every day to clean. But I'm not okay with taking it further."

Doreen scratched her head. Her hair was iron gray and made an exuberant cloud around her head as she charged through her day. Her eyes were black and birdy and she looked like an inquisitive chicken when she cocked her head at Quill. "What exactly did this note say, anyways?"

Meg shrugged. "Meet me outside by the waterfall at midnight, or something like it, I guess."

"Was he attacked, like?"

"Davy thinks so." Quill took another sip of coffee, which was very good. "Davy went over to question him this morning and he talked to the admitting physician, too. There's no evidence of a physical assault. Jeeter's being cagey. Says he must have 'gotten dizzy-like' which is no surprise for a healthy ninety-eight-year-old. But there are grass stains on the knees of Jeeter's chinos and a mud smear on his back. Davey thinks he was pushed to his knees and hit his head on a rock. The question is why?"

Meg spread her hands wide in a "haven't got a clue" gesture.

Doreen said, "T'cha." Then, ominously, "I don't like this. I don't like this at all. Secret notes. Late-night meetings. Adela Henry accused of thievin'. Vigilante groups meetin' all over the place. I tell you what I'm going to do and that's make sure young Jack isn't alone for a minute."

"Jack's never alone for a minute," Meg said. "When you aren't with him, Quill is, and when Quill isn't, I am."

"Yeah, well, that goes in spades until this all here is cleared up." Doreen stood up and brushed the crumbs from her capri pants. "That Dina's watching him now, and she doesn't have the sense God gave a goose. So I'm off. You tell me when you're through detecting. Until then, I don't want to hear a word about it."

She marched off through the foyer that led to reception. Meg sighed. "I can relate to that. What do you think?"

"I think," Quill said darkly, "that none of this stuff started bubbling up until Althea Quince and her husband took the Long-Term Let and moved to Hemlock Falls for three months."

Meg pointed her chin at the foyer. "And the lady herself enters, stage right. You can ask her, 'why?' "

Quill turned around in her chair. Althea and her husband were poised at the main entrance to the dining room.

The dominant color in today's scarves was grape. She must have spent part of the morning at the Hemlock Hall of Beauty; her hair was a vivid, purple-y red that made an alarming frame for the amethyst necklace, bracelets, and earrings. Nolan Quince stood behind her, one hand on her shoulder. Nolan had a dusty look to him: grayish hair that had once been blond, pale gray eyes that held an intelligent twinkle, indoor skin that hadn't seen much of the sun.

"You two look pretty cozy over there," Althea Quince said in a cheery voice. "We could use some company. Mind if we join you?"

Quill murmured "of course" and signaled Kathleen for two more setups at the table. Althea settled herself with a rustle and a scent of Chanel No. 5. Nolan held her chair for her, and then sat down quietly beside her.

"We had a wonderful breakfast this morning, just wonderful," Althea boomed. "French toast filled with this marvelous cheesy sort of thing." She patted Meg's hand. "Your reputation is well deserved, my dear."

"Thank you," Meg said.

"Which isn't to say that I'm not just a little peckish at the moment. Marvelous word that, 'peckish.' The inference is that I eat like a bird, which, of course, isn't true." She patted her substantial frame.

"Birds eat several times their own weight during the day," Nolan observed. "So I think the simile is quite apt, my dear." He looked up at Kathleen. "We'll both have a little cheese, and perhaps some fruit."

Althea lowered her voice several decibels. "We heard about poor Mr. Swenson. Is he going to be all right?"

Quill nodded. "Thank goodness."

"The question I have," Althea said, "is this. What in

the world was that poor man doing out on the edge of the gorge at one o'clock in the morning?" Her eyes, a pale but penetrating blue, swept the table. "Trying to escape that dreadful son? I don't mean to be more intrusive than is seemly, dear Quill . . ."

A warm, skeptical chuckle escaped Nolan.

". . . Nolan knows me too well," Althea said with a fond smile. "I am always intrusive. But what I have decided is this: perhaps we should take some measures to look out for Mr. Swenson. Quietly, to be sure, so that he doesn't feel oppressed by our attentions." She grinned companionably at them.

"I am a little worried about him," Quill said. "But I don't see how . . ."

"We'll put him on a fete committee, of course," Althea said. "Nothing strenuous. Do you think the Crafty Ladies might welcome a new member? They're sponsoring one of those booths where you shoot at things."

"Decoys," Nolan said. Kathleen placed a plate of fruit and cheese in front of him and another in front of his wife. Nolan paused to look over the grapes. "Quite nice decoys, as a matter of fact. Ducks, geese, elk, and whatnot. I believe they are all made by the Crafty Ladies themselves."

"Perfect," Althea said. She scooped up a cheese made of ewe's milk and popped it in her mouth. "Yum! Anyhow, I ran into that Dolly Jean whosis yesterday at a meeting and she and Jeeter were getting along like a house afire. When I heard what had happened to him this morning, the idea came to me just like that." She snapped her fingers. "If you think he's up to it, I can give Dolly Jean a call.

Those ladies spend all their waking hours in meetings. He won't have an unprotected minute."

There was only one meeting Quill knew of where Dolly Jean, Althea, and Jeeter had all been in attendance. "The meeting out at Peterson Automotive?"

"The very one." Althea picked up a clutch of grapes. She nudged her husband. "That Carol Ann Spinoza is a piece of work. Spite, malice, all wrapped up in one squeaky-clean package. Amazing." She put three grapes into her mouth at once and said thickly, "But I'll be damned if I think she's the one behind the theft of the funds. Too law and order, although sometimes those zealots are the worst offenders. I mean, think of all the shenanigans some padres get up to. What do you think, Quill. Should I keep it up?"

Quill felt as if she were in a force-ten gale, losing everything she was wearing minute by minute. "Keep it up?"

"The undercover work, of course." Althea finished the last of her cheese and grabbed the remaining slices on her husband's plate. "Adela didn't take that money. Somebody did. You've got a bent for detection. So do I. So I thought I'd help."

"Thank you," Quill said, feebly.

"You don't mind my butting in, do you? This is a lovely village, and Nolan and I are having a lovely summer, but there are just so many novels I can read by the waterfall. I'm going to go nuts if I don't have something interesting to do. And most detectives can use a sidekick. I'm a great sidekick, aren't I, Nolan?"

Nolan kissed her on the cheek. "The very best, my dear." He leaned back in his chair. "But Quill may need some assurances from you before she can commit to using your help . . ."

"Of course!" Althea said. Then, with an air of mild uncertainty, she asked, "What sort of assurances?"

Nolan's face was as bland as ever, but Quill had the distinct impression he was amused. "Our innkeeper suspects that you may have something to do with the embezzlement."

"Me!"

Quill felt herself turn bright red.

Althea looked insulted. Then she looked thoughtful. Then she grinned. "I can see that, I guess. If the situation were reversed, I suppose I'd have my suspicions, too. The stranger from out of town. Nobody knows a thing about her. But I'm just a mom, Quill, and a grandmother, too. I can show you pictures. Honestly. I didn't embezzle a thing. Never have. Never will."

Nolan looked at Quill. Meg gave her ankle a sharp kick under the table. Quill, who was thinking that the best place for a crook who didn't want to be discovered was in the middle of the investigation, said, "Sure." Then, after a long moment, she added, "I mean, I can use all the help I can get."

"Partners in the pursuit of crime, then! Hurrah! I love it!" Beaming, she swallowed the last of her coffee and said, "So. What shall we do next?"

"Hm. As far as what next . . . well, did you discover anything suspicious at the Citizens for Justice meeting?"

"Just that Betty Hall is undercover, too. This village," Althea continued sunnily, "is chock-full of undercover agents."

"Oh." Quill didn't look at her sister, who was two seconds away from falling off her chair from laughter. "Yes. Well. Marge thought that maybe . . ."

Althea beamed at Meg. "It *is* amusing, when you think about it, Meg. I couldn't agree with you more. Everyone running around playing detective? It'd be useful if we could all get together, don't you think? Pool our resources? Perhaps we should add Betty Hall to Detection Unlimited, too."

"Oh, dear." Meg rubbed her napkin over her face and tossed it on the table. "Althea, I'm really glad you are on board with Undercover Bosses, or whatever you guys are going to call yourselves. It takes me off the hook and I can get back to my kitchen." She patted Quill on the back. "Go get 'em, Sherlock." She paused, halfway through the swinging doors. "So what are you going to do next?"

"There's a meeting of the Justice people this morning at Peterson Automotive," Quill said. "Linda Connelly is going to be there to assure herself that we aren't going to get a raft of bad PR for the fete. Elmer thought I should go, too, to run interference." She glanced at her watch. "It's at noon, which is smart of Carol Ann, I guess, since it's everyone's lunch hour. I have to meet with the Furry Friends exhibitors in the afternoon but that shouldn't take too long. Maybe Althea and I can sit down and make up a plan after that."

"Over one of Meg's superb dinners, perhaps? Excellent!" Althea said. Then, with an air of hope. "I thought perhaps I might go to the Justice meeting in disguise?"

Quill looked at Althea's fire-red hair. "Disguise?"

"I'm going to cozy up to Carol Ann, but I don't think

she'll talk to me if I appear as myself. She already knows that I'm staying here at the Inn and loving it." Althea waved her forefinger. "Mark my words. That woman knows more than she's saying. Do you think I should get her on tape? There's time enough for me to run out and buy a recorder at Nickerson's Hardware. I wonder if they carry wigs."

Quill rubbed her temples. She was getting a headache. "Sure, Althea. Whatever you think best." The cell phone in her pocket vibrated. "Excuse me while I get this, please." She pulled out her phone and read the text. "I'm needed in the office. Would you like to ride with me to the meeting? I can meet you back here at quarter to twelve."

"Thank you, my dear. But undercover is undercover. I will wend my way on my own."

Quill left Nolan and Althea with their heads together and found Dina behind the mahogany registration desk.

"You look pretty cheerful." Dina commented. "What's up?"

"Althea Quince would cheer up a wake."

"So she's off your suspect list?"

Quill shook her head. "It's too soon to take anyone off the suspect list. But she's slipped down a couple of notches, that's for sure." She chuckled at the thought of the nearly six-foot, purple-haired Althea in disguise.

"Hm. Too bad your cheeriness is doomed."

"It is, huh. Why?"

"It's a delegation, they said. Although is it a delegation if it's only two people? Anyhow, it's Harvey Bozzel and Dolly Jean Attenborough and I put them in your office since Harvey looked like he was going to burst into tears any minute and who wants a weeping ad guy in the foyer? Bad for business."

"Do you know what they want? It's not about Adela, is it?"

"In a way. I think they're, like, totally pissed off at Linda Connelly."

Quill slipped behind the registration desk, tapped at her closed office door, and opened it. Harvey sat at one end of the couch and Dolly Jean sat at the other. Harvey looked tearful. Dolly Jean looked mad.

They demanded that the fete committee fire Linda Connelly.

"She's rude, bossy, and cold," Dolly Jean said indignantly. "Not that Adela, poor soul, isn't bossy, too, but my goodness, there's got to be a limit."

Harvey smoothed his hair. It was blond, carefully gelled, and cut to show off his cheekbones. "There's the expense, too. If I'd known that the village was willing to pay for a consultant, I would have pointed out that I've had considerable experience in running events of this sort."

"Of course you have," Dolly Jean said. "It's outrageous, what the steering committee went ahead and did. Just trampled all over the expertise of our very own people without a hey-howdy to anyone else. Anyhow. That's why we're here. There are a lot of us who are very unhappy about this. You're head of the steering committee. So we've come to you." She fanned her cheeks with her hand, wafting a scent of lavender into the air. "You've got to fix this, Quill. Harvey and I have formed a committee . . . Save Our Fete . . . and we've elected you to the chair."

Quill declined the honor, figuring that would make a total of six committees she was on, and she didn't want to be on one. She thanked Dolly Jean for her concern. She commiserated with Harvey over the fact that a contract had been signed, and the village would have to pay Linda Connelly to go away. She wondered exactly what toes Linda Connelly had stepped on, but was smart enough not to ask. "But I will," she promised, as she coaxed Dolly Jean and Harvey to the office door, "speak to Elmer about making her a little more sensitive to village concerns."

"You do that," Dolly Jean said crossly. "Or somebody's going to throw the woman right over the lip of Hemlock Gorge. Do you know what she did? No, don't you push me out the door until I've finished, Sarah McHale. You sit right back down and listen to me."

10

Peterson Automotive was on the outskirts of the village on Route 15, a mere fifteen minutes from the Inn. Quill, with uncharacteristic firmness, coaxed Dolly Jean and Harvey out of her office at ten minutes to twelve and got into her Honda. She put her cell phone on speaker, put the car into gear, and called Elmer.

"It's more a matter of Linda's style, than anything else," Quill said, after she'd summed up the delegation's list of vague, but loudly expressed complaints. "Harvey's very upset that we didn't ask him to take over the fete, so his feelings are hurt. Dolly Jean is . . . well."

"Bossy," Elmer said. "That woman's like a bulldozer. She's one of them that's always right even when she's dead flat wrong, which is most of the time. Bossy, that's the word."

"Linda and Dolly Jean do seem to have clashed over decision making," Quill admitted. "The placement of the Crafty Ladies booth, in particular. Dolly Jean wants it moved closer to the entrance."

"Hah," Elmer scoffed. "She tries to pull that one every

year, so that she can rake in more of the tourist dollars. Adela never had any problem with her."

Quill didn't say that when it came to bossiness, she'd put her money on Adela any day. "Yes, well, Dolly Jean's position is that if we hired Linda, we can fire Linda and put Harvey in her place."

"Harvey's a worse pushover than you are," Elmer said. "That's not gonna work. Here's what I think you should do, Quill."

Quill was getting pretty tired of hearing she was a pushover. "No. Whatever it is you think I should do, I'm not doing it."

"All you got to do is sit down with Linda Connelly and put her in the picture."

"She's already in the picture."

"Tell her not to give Dolly Jean squat."

"You tell her. And you can tell Dolly Jean and Harvey that, too. I sent them over to you, Elmer, and I'm just calling to give you a heads-up."

"I'm busy," Elmer said promptly and hung up before she could hang up on him.

Quill muttered to herself, looked up, and realized that she had almost driven past Peterson Automotive.

Car dealerships were like airports, she thought as she slowed to pull into the lot. Since they were purpose-built, there wasn't a lot to distinguish one from the other, although George Peterson, who'd owned the dealership before his death, had done his best to make his building stand out. George was fond of balloons, and there were always dozens bobbing gently around the eaves of the sprawling one-story building. Brady—a third cousin, if Quill had her Peterson genealogy right—hadn't seen any reason to change that. Bright globes of orange, red, purple, and green drifted above her head when she walked into the main showroom. The place smelled like new cars and hot Hemlockians.

New cars had been moved out of the way to accommodate several dozen metal folding chairs. Quill was glad to see that only about half of them were filled. Carol Ann stood near the glass-fronted offices in the back, in earnest conversation with Brady.

Quill took a seat in an empty row at the back and waited for something to happen.

Brady, arms folded, his chin sunk on his thin chest, listened attentively as Carol Ann spoke intensely into his ear. Two of his orange-suited mechanics, clearly bored, stood with their backs against the wall next to an overhead door marked SERVICE. Two women Quill recognized from the Crafty Ladies group bent over a desk and carefully inked in signs that read JUSTICE FOR ALL and PUT ADELA BEHIND BARS.

Harvey Bozzel sat slumped in a corner, biting his thumbnail. He looked up, saw Quill, and scowled. Dookie Shuttleworth and his gentle wife Kate sat quietly side by side, hands folded. Dookie saw Quill, winked, and mouthed *we're undercover.*

"All in all," said a voice in Quill's ear, "it doesn't look like a real activist bunch. May I sit down?"

Quill turned slightly. "Hi, Linda." She tried not to look as if she were looking for Mickey Greer. "Are you alone today?"

"For this? Not for long. I sent the boys out for some R and R. We just came off a pretty intense gig. But they'll be along."

"A wedding? The intense gig, I mean."

"Yeah. Something like that." She sighed. "You suppose this cockamamie demonstration is going anywhere? Or can you and I sneak out for a glass of wine? I had a run-in with a couple of your folks this morning. You're part of the fete committee, right? So I should let you know what's going on."

"That's really more Elmer's bailiwick than mine."

"I tried to see him this morning. He's not taking my calls."

She had an interesting face, Quill thought. Very strong features: decided chin, straight dark brows, and smooth olive skin. There was something a little unsettling about it.

Linda brushed at her cheeks. "I managed to grab breakfast this morning. Did I leave some of it on my face?"

"What? Oh. No." Quill blushed slightly. "You have very interesting lines. I sketch a little, is all."

Linda looked at her. "You sketch a little? Even I know who Quilliam was. That's quite a compliment. Thank you. But don't even think about it. I'd rather not have pictures of me floating around."

Quill, stung by the past tense, subsided into confusion.

The silence stretched on and became uncomfortable. To break it, she asked, "So was the gig before this one actually a wedding? The big ones can get really intense. The last one we held at the Inn . . ." She trailed off. The last wedding at the Inn had ended in murder. "So," she began again. "How do things look for the fete?"

"Fine," Linda said shortly. "Good. It looks like something's going to happen, here at last. Spinoza's marching up to the front."

"That's probably what's going to happen. A march, I mean. You see those signs? My guess is that Carol Ann is going to organize a demonstration down Main Street." Then, since the enthusiasm in the room was tepid, at best, she said, "Or try to, anyway."

"'We Want the Truth!'" Linda read aloud. "'Where's Our Money! Hang the Henrys!'" She raised her eyebrows. "This is a demonstration? There's like, twenty people here. That's not much of a demonstration."

"Carol Ann scares people," Quill admitted. Then, mendaciously, "She has her good points, of course."

"That so? Looks like a cheerleader, to me. But just in case . . ." She slipped her cell phone out of her tote and tapped at it.

Carol Ann bounced on her toes, clapped her hands together, and shouted, "People! People!"

The conversation in the room, desultory at best, died away completely.

"Thank you!" Carol Ann put her hands on her hips. "We are gathered here today to rip open the secrets of this town and expose the corruption . . ."

"Excuse me?" Linda Connelly got to her feet. She was small, but somehow, threatening. "I'd like to say something to you folks before you make decisions you might regret later on. I'm here to organize your fete. My name's Linda Connelly. My company's called Presentations. I had a chance to go over the numbers last night and I'm astonished at the success the fete's brought to this town over the years. The revenues from that week are doing a lot to keep your small businesses afloat. If you want to jeopardize that, that's fine with me. I'm from out of town. I'll do my job and be out of here in a couple of weeks. I don't care. But you should. All of you. You're dealing with an issue that's going to attract the wrong kind of media attention. Nobody likes crooks. And these days, people *really* have it in for crooks committing crimes involving money. You guys can make a big deal of this if you want, but it's going to cost you. Not just this year, but next year and the year after that. Get some common sense. Get real, and ditch this idea. If you don't . . ." She turned her hands out, palm upward. "Makes no difference to me. But it's going to make a lot of difference to you." She swept her gaze around the room. To Quill's unease, Mickey Greer and George had appeared out of nowhere. George crowded Brady against his office door. Mickey Greer had his eye on Carol Ann.

Nobody said anything. Carol Ann was a study in suppressed rage. After a long moment, the two ladies who'd been making signs headed for the door. A couple of people slumped down into their seats and looked furtive. Brady slipped into his office and shut the door. Finally, the room emptied in twos and threes except for Carol Ann herself.

Linda's hard gaze swept the room again, with a detached, calculated air. "Good," she said. She grasped Quill's elbow and pulled her out of the chair. "You ready? Why don't I follow you to Bonne Goute? You've got the

Furry Friends meeting there, or whatever the hell these people are calling it and I've got to drop off a couple hundred pounds of cat food for the pet booths. There's a restaurant there, right? We'll get some lunch." She put her hand on the small of Quill's back and propelled her out the door.

11

"What do you mean, strong-arm tactics?" Linda Connelly asked Quill.

Her tone was more curious than upset. They sat in Viandes, the second-floor restaurant at Bonne Goute. It was an attractive space, with maple floors, and huge glass doors that overlooked the gorge and the waterfall. The doors were open to the soft afternoon, and the rush of the water was pleasing. It was late, for lunch, well after one o'clock, and Linda and Quill were the only diners in the room.

Clare's menu was classic bistro, focusing on small plates and tapas. The academy was a teaching institution and not primarily designed for the retail restaurant trade, but Viandes's food was excellent. Quill was especially fond of Clare's summer soups. Today's was chilled cucumber and shrimp with a graceful swirl of crème fraiche on top. She stirred the cream into her soup, and then put her spoon down.

Linda prodded her. "Did you hear me say anything threatening to those people?"

"No. No. Of course not. Not physically threatening."

She reconsidered this. George had loomed over Brady Beale in an uncomfortably nasty way.

"I just threatened their wallets." Linda took an efficient bite of her avocado chicken sandwich. "That usually gets people where they live. If not, there are other paths to follow. But everyone left, except Spinoza, and she can hardly wage war on her own."

"Carol Ann's pretty resourceful. Linda, I know Presentations has a lot of experience with this sort of thing, so I certainly don't want to second-guess you, but . . ."

"Then don't." Linda finished her sandwich and flipped open her phone. She stared at the screen for a moment, tapped at it, then said, "I've got five minutes before I have to leave for Syracuse and talk to the media people about TV coverage. Clare was supposed to join us here. She's fifteen minutes late. I don't wait more than ten and I'm not going to chase her down. Will you give her a message for me? I'm redesigning the parking area—there were a lot of complaints about delays and jams last year."

"There were," Quill admitted. "But how did you know that?"

"All in Adela's files. The woman wasn't bad at running a function. If she turns out not to be an embezzler, I could use her in my business. Anyhow, I'm going to use that green space behind the academy apartments for parking. We'll use school buses for shuttles. I've got bulldozers coming in to level a couple of the rises flat. Tell her that. I'm off. I'll dump the kitty food by the back kitchen, okay? You get someone to haul it inside." Linda swung her briefcase over her shoulder and left the room just as Clare came in.

"Was that the woman from Presentations?" Clare sat down across from her. "I thought we had a meeting scheduled."

Quill looked at her watch. "She said she never waits more than ten minutes for a meeting."

"Is that so," Clare said indignantly. "There was a snafu for a food order I had to straighten out and then I couldn't find Bismarck and I wanted to bring him to the exhibitor's meeting downstairs. But you guys were having lunch here, so I didn't think it'd matter if I wasn't spot on time. I'm really sorry. I should have sent a message."

"You don't have to apologize to me," Quill said absently. Through the open windows, she could hear a dull rumbling. She couldn't identify it. "Did you find Bismarck?"

"That cat," Clare said fondly. "He could be anywhere." She bent forward to look at Quill more closely. "Anything the matter?"

Heavy machinery. That was the sound coming through the open windows. "Well, no. On the other hand, maybe yes. Does Linda seem a little high-handed to you?"

"Oh, I don't know. Maybe a little. I'm the wrong person to ask. Any chef would be. We're all petty dictators in our kitchens. Which wrecks us for judging normal human behavior. Did Linda tell you why she called the meeting?"

"Yes. The fete is going to need the field beyond the apartments for parking."

"Madame won't do it. Says it ruins the grass. Apparently they tried that last year."

"Uh-oh."

"Uh-oh? What's that sup . . ." A shriek cut her off in midsentence. Clare jumped to her feet, knocking over her

137

chair. "That's Madame!" A second shriek split the air, louder than the first. "It's coming from outside, isn't it?" Clare turned around in a complete circle, searching for the source of the noise.

Quill was already outside on the upper deck, looking down at the bulldozers cutting through Madame LeVasque's nice neat lawn. Madame LeVasque herself stamped around the parking lot, waving the boning knife and shouting.

"Oh, my God," Clare said slowly. "I suppose I better get down there." She didn't move. Madame LeVasque had her cell phone in one hand. She yelled into it. Quill couldn't make out much of the conversation over the roar of the machinery, but she was pretty sure she heard the word "cops."

Clare nudged her. "You'll come with me? You're good at defusing this kind of thing."

"I would, Clare. Honestly. But I've got all the Furry Friends waiting for me downstairs."

"Most of the Furry Friends are out in the parking lot watching the show."

This was true. At least most of the pets were on leashes. Nadine Peterson's poodle danced excitedly on its hind legs, barking furiously. As a matter of fact, all of the dogs were barking furiously including, Quill was dismayed to see, Max himself, who was out for his usual unsupervised afternoon constitutional.

"You'd better catch Max before he's run over by a bulldozer," Clare said.

"Tell you what. Why don't you catch Max and I'll go downstairs and get everybody back inside." In the distance, Quill heard the wail of a sheriff's cruiser. "That's Davy, headed this way, or one of his deputies. He'll get things under control."

"Maybe we can leave?" Clare said hopefully. "We could head out the back door and up to the Tavern Lounge. We could sit on the terrace and drink wine. We could pretend we were out-of-towners who wouldn't dream of settling in a lunatic asylum like Hemlock Falls."

"I'm not hearing that!" Quill stuck her fingers in her ears, said "la-la-la-la" very loudly, and walked downstairs to find Dolly Jean standing triumphantly in the middle of the kitchen.

"I told you Linda Connelly was trouble! And your hair's falling all over your face." Dolly Jean's little pink mouth pursed disapprovingly. "Although if you ask me, this whole fete's falling down, too. What a mess. That idiot consultant." She caressed the little Yorkshire terrier in her lap. The glittery bow in the terrier's topknot matched Dolly Jean's glittery earrings. "Frieda agrees with me, don't you, Frieda." Frieda gave her mistress a disbelieving look and yawned. "It's five minutes before two. I told everyone outside to get in here because I want this meeting to start on time." She settled the dog on her lap.

Quill wound her hair up on the top of her head and re-fastened the clip. She spread her worksheets out on the marble pastry slab. The exhibitors in the Furry Friends competition trailed in from the outside and milled around the kitchen.

There wasn't enough seating for everyone, which she figured was a small and significant mercy. People didn't like to stand up too long, and they could whip through the meeting and go home. Dolly Jean had copped one of the few folding chairs and had the look of somebody ready to stay awhile, but Quill was through being a pushover and a wimp. She'd throw Dolly Jean out with the rest of them when the time came.

Outside, the roar of the bulldozers flattening the field mostly drowned out the outraged shrieks of Madame LeVasque. Davy Kiddermeister's black-and-white police cruiser, blue lights flashing, drew into the employee parking lot. Davy got out, hitched his uniform trousers a little higher on his hips, and went over to talk to Madame LeVasque. Mayor Henry stamped up and down the path circling the field with short, agitated strides. He looked confused.

Inside, most of the exhibitors in the Furry Friends competition, human and non, clustered at windows, looking out at the bulldozers.

The noise level in the kitchen was tolerable, which was pretty amazing. Quill had made a point of insisting the animals be brought to the meeting in crates. The only owners who had complied were the chickens and the birds. All the other animals were on laps or leashes, and she was pretty sure the amnesty currently in effect wasn't going to last. All it would take would be one dog lunging at one cat for bedlam to break loose. The faster she could get through this meeting, the faster she could go home and hide under the bed with Jack. Clare had scooped up Max and then left to look for Bismarck, and as soon as she returned, the meeting could begin.

"Where is this Linda Connelly, anyway, Quill?" Harvey Bozzel demanded. He watched one of the bulldozers make a second run at a particularly recalcitrant hummock. "She can't just order destruction of this size and disappear." He smoothed his Akita's ears. Quill thought the little dog was quite handsome, with black-and-tan German shepherd markings and a compact little body. Dolly Jean's Yorkie was handsome, too. She was very glad she didn't have to judge this contest.

"I don't know where Linda Connelly is. She's not answering her cell phone. I think she's gone to Syracuse."

Harvey and Dolly Jean exchanged meaningful looks. "Derelict. Quite derelict," Dolly Jean said. "I make a motion that Harvey Bozzel be named managing director of this fete and that we fire Linda Connelly."

"Second," Harvey said.

"You can't second a motion to put yourself in charge, Harvey," Quill said firmly. "And anyway, this meeting is an informational one, for the exhibitors. We don't have the, um . . . jurisdiction or whatever to fire Linda or to make Harvey director. So if you guys don't mind, we'll just tackle any questions you might have about the rules for the pet show."

Dolly Jean's hand shot up.

Quill resisted the temptation to tug at her hair. She'd just have to bundle it up again. "Can we hang on a bit, Dolly Jean? The meeting doesn't officially start until two, and it's not quite that now. Besides, not everyone's here yet."

"Who's missing?" Dolly Jean demanded. "There's fifteen dogs entered in Man's Best Friend and I count fifteen dogs right here in this room. The chickens are over by the coolers and the parakeets and whatnot are, too. Wait." Using her forefinger, she counted around the room. "Cat. We're missing a cat."

"It's Bismarck," Quill said. "Clare's gone to look for him."

Outside, the drone of the bulldozers stopped.

"Glory be," Harvey said. He walked away from the window and settled himself on a stool at the prep table. "The noise was driving me mad."

"What's happening?" Dolly Jean asked without moving.

"Go look for yourself."

Dolly Jean smirked. "You've got your eye on my chair, Harvey Bozzel. I'm not moving an inch. What's going on out there?"

"Madame's lying down in front of the bulldozer. The guy from the *Gazette* is taking pictures."

Quill looked at her watch. "Okay, everybody. It's two o'clock. I'm sorry Clare's not here, but I can fill her in later. Let's get started."

Reluctantly, people began drifting back from the windows.

"First, you'll all be delighted to know that the veterinarian from Summersville, Dr. Austin McKenzie, has graciously consented to judge the Furry Friends competition again this year."

"That old fart," Dolly Jean said. "He told me Frieda was too fat."

"Frieda is too fat," Nadine Peterson said. She had a handsome Scotch terrier on leash whose black coat shone with glossy health. "I told you before, Dolly Jean, you can't raise a prizewinning dog on table scraps." She eyed

Dolly Jean's plump figure. "Especially your kind of table scraps."

Dolly Jean jumped out of her chair in a fury. Harvey took two steps sideways and sat down in her chair.

"Stop," Quill said. "Both of you, right now. And you, Harvey, give Dolly Jean her chair back."

Harvey glowered, but he got up and moved away from the chair. Dolly Jean smirked more widely than ever and sat back down.

The silence in the room was respectful.

"My goodness, Quill," Nadine Peterson said. "Having a child certainly has stiffened your backbone."

"I guess I should say thank you. Okay. You should all have copies of the exhibitor's code of conduct, the class standards, and . . ."

"I'm late! Again! I'm sorry!" Clare rushed into the kitchen. "But I can't find Bismarck anywhere."

"Did you check up at the Inn?" somebody called out. "He's there more than he is here."

"I think he prefers Meg's cooking," Nadine Peterson said, a little maliciously.

"He's not at the Inn," Clare said. "He's not at the Croh Bar, and he's not anywhere down by the river that I could see."

"He's kind of hard to miss," somebody from the back said. "That's one whopping big cat."

This was true. Bismarck was a Maine coon cat, and an outsized member of that hefty breed. Quill was willing to bet he weighed forty pounds at least.

"And he don't blend into the shrubbery, neither. That cat is *orange*."

"Marmalade," Dolly Jean corrected. She really had an infuriating air of being right all the time. It was worse when she was.

"Well, let's hope he ain't in a *jam*," the wit snapped back. A roar of laughter greeted this sally.

Clare touched Quill's shoulder and said in an undertone, "I know it's silly, but I'm really worried. You know how he likes to walk down the middle of the street."

"Everybody in town watches out for him. On the other hand . . . you don't think . . ." Involuntarily, Quill's gaze went to the windows.

"The bulldozers!" Clare turned perfectly white. "No! Oh, no!"

~

"Is Bismarck dead?" Jack asked with rather ghoulish expectancy.

It was late afternoon. The lowering sun turned his bronze hair to rose-colored fire. Quill, Clare, and most of the participants in the Furry Friends pet show had been searching for Bismarck for hours, with no success.

Quill tightened her arms around Jack and buried her nose in his neck. He smelled like soap and little boy. They sat in the Inn's gazebo, overlooking the gorge.

Below them, Doreen, Meg, Elizabeth Chou, and Kathleen Kiddermeister searched along the pebbled shores of the stream. Max the dog padded along behind them, his nose to the ground.

"Bismarck isn't dead, darling. He just went off on an adventure and forgot what time it is."

"Cats can't tell time."

144

"You're right. Not like humans do. But Max knows when dinnertime is, doesn't he?"

Jack nodded yes.

"And when it's time for you to get up in the morning."

"He *does*!" Jack said with delight.

"Bismarck tells time like that, too."

Jack digested this. "He wasn't where the bulldozers were."

"No."

"And he wasn't in his basket at Auntie Clare's."

"Not there, either."

"And he wasn't here! So where is he?"

"I don't know, darling."

"Maybe he's lost."

"That's possible," Quill admitted. "But if he is, he'll be found. Look at all the people looking for him. Everybody in town is helping out."

"Everybody in town," Jack repeated, in satisfaction.

Quill wasn't sure what to do if, in fact, poor Bismarck wasn't found, or worse yet, was found horribly flattened by some roadside. Five was too young to talk about death, wasn't it? Too young to lose a pet.

"Bismarck!" With a shout of joy, Jack jumped out of her lap and scrambled down the gazebo steps to the lawn. Bismarck, his orange fur matted with some oily substance, blinked his great yellow eyes at them. You could have heard his purr in Syracuse. Jack picked the cat up by the middle, staggered a few feet, dropped him, and then raced to the lip of the Gorge.

"No farther!" Quill shouted. "Stop!"

Jack screeched to a halt and shouted down the slope to

the river: "Auntie Meg! Gramma! Bismarck remembered what time it was. He's here! He's here!"

Marveling, Quill left the gazebo and knelt by the cat. His fur was sticky with black goo. She tickled him under the chin, and then petted him. She raised the palm of her hand to her nose and sniffed. "Motor oil?" she said aloud.

"Yes, ma'am."

Startled, she looked up to see Davy Kiddermeister standing a few feet away. His hands were covered with motor oil. She dug into the pocket of her skirt, and handed him two of the wipes she carried with her at all times, now that she was a mother.

"Thanks." Davy cleaned his hands, and then shoved the wipes in his pocket.

Quill scrambled to her feet. "I'm so glad you found him, Davy! Where was he? I swear that cat has used up all of his nine lives, as well as some of mine."

"He was over at Peterson Automotive, in the trunk of Linda Connelly's car."

"In the trunk of her *car*? Good grief! How did he end up there?"

"I don't know yet, Quill. Just like I don't know why he was with the body of Linda Connelly."

12

"Linda Connelly was shot in the back of the head," Quill said. "It was a horrible way to die. They haven't found the gun." She shuddered. "Good Lord, Myles. I thought I'd never have to deal with murder again."

Myles rubbed his hand across his mouth. The computer transmission was spotty. His face kept fragmenting. "I don't need to remind you . . ."

". . . That I'm not investigating this murder. The sheriff's department is. Right. You're right."

He was on a ship somewhere; the walls in back of him were an institutional gray and the space was compact. She hoped it wasn't a submarine.

"But I'm dealing with the consequences of murder. Everyone's in shock. The arrangements for the fete are in total disarray, and there's talk of canceling it, although with all the out-of-town dealers coming in, I don't see how that can happen." Quill stopped herself. "I'm babbling. One thing at a time. Jack's fine. I'm fine. Poor Linda Connelly is not so fine."

"Who found the body?"

"Brady Beale. No, that's not strictly accurate. One of

Brady Beale's mechanics was walking by Linda's car. Did I tell you it was parked with the other Lexuses Brady has for sale in his parking lot? There was even a price sticker on the window, so she could have gone undiscovered for *days*. Anyway, Bismarck howled, poor thing. Would he have been running out of oxygen? That's a horrible thought, so I won't think about it. We think he jumped into the car in the parking lot at Bonne Goute when Linda delivered the cat food. There was some spilled in the bottom of the trunk. He's fine now, poor kitty. Doreen had some stuff that got the grease off him quicker than quick. Clare's so scared she lost him for good, I think she's going to put a harness on him and attach him to her wrist with a lock. Anyhow, this mechanic got the trunk popped, and out popped Bismarck."

"They called Kiddermeister?"

"The state police, actually. So the awful Lieutenant Harker's back in the picture for the time being. Anyhow, the scene-of-the-crime people took the body away to do all the forensics. Andy Bishop talked to the coroner, and the preliminary cause of death is the gunshot wound. The time of death is between one o'clock, when I saw her last, and six o'clock, when the mechanic heard Bismarck crying. Closer than that, we don't know."

"There's no 'we' in this scenario, Quill."

"I know, Myles. I know."

"What about the goons?"

"The goons?" Quill blinked at him. "You mean George McIntyre and Mickey Greer? They'd been swimming, of all things. Linda gave them the afternoon off. She said they'd been working pretty hard lately and they deserved it. She said she was headed toward Syracuse. But she went back to Peterson's instead. What in the world for?"

"Could you do me a favor?"

"Of course, Myles. Anything."

"You are not, and I repeat not, to get involved in this thing any further than this. Because you love me. Because I love you. Because we both love Jack."

Quill nodded.

"But I'd like to know a little more about the goons."

"They aren't goons, Myles. They seem like perfectly decent guys."

"I just need their names. Is it Mickey Michael Greer? And it's George McIntyre with no middle name? Do you think you can find out for me?"

"Sure. If I can't, Marge certainly can. Elmer should have had Presentations sign an employment contract, and the names might be on there. I'll start with that."

"Maybe on the website, too." Myles bent forward to take a note. "Listen, dear heart. I might not be able to use this communications channel for the next couple of days. We'll keep in touch by e-mail. All right?"

So she wouldn't see him or hear him for how long? Too long. However long it was, it was too long.

She told him she loved him. She didn't tell him she missed him.

She went to bed and dreamed she was lost in a vast subterranean room that had mysteriously appeared underneath the Inn.

She woke to the scent of peanut butter. She had slept hard and she woke hard, as if fighting through a swirl of gauzy drapes.

"Mommy!"

She shot out of bed, stumbled over a furry body (Max) and grabbed a solidly warm one (Jack). She righted herself and rubbed the sleep out of her eyes. The soft light of an August dawn flooded her bedroom.

"I'm so glad you're awake, too!" Jack said sunnily. His smile was angelic. It was also smeared with peanut butter. "I brought you breakfast!" He thrust his fist out.

She cradled it in the palm of her hand and coaxed his fingers open. "Peanut butter. Thank you so much! But you remember what we learned about peanut butter?"

Jack wrinkled his forehead in thought, and then shook his head.

"We put it in a dish." She hoisted him onto her hip, and then caught sight of her bedside alarm. "Jack! It's five thirty in the morning."

He sighed happily and snuggled his cheek under her chin. "Isn't it nice?"

The early start to her morning meant that Doreen would be grouchy for the rest of the day—she was no fan of early hours, either, but it also meant that she was at her office desk before seven.

"Which," she said aloud to the empty room when she got to her desk, "is a good thing." She'd plow through the stack of messages and mail that Dina had left for her and seize the day by the neck and shake it.

The pink While You Were Out slips were on the top of the pile, with Dina's neat notes attached. She'd return the calls from the hospital first.

Jeeter Swenson wanted to come back to the Inn. She

was glad the old man was feeling better. Mike the grounds-keeper could pick him up.

Adela was scheduled for discharge. Quill frowned at that one, and read Dina's note. *Pls pick her up since she is not speaking to that man.* She'd assign Mike to that duty, too.

There were a total of twenty-six messages about the fete. Dina had separated them into three piles labeled A, B, and C. There were a number of sticky notes attached to the piles, and a longer note that read:

> **Pile A:** demands for payment for various fete invoices
> **Pile B:** questions about fete booths and stuff????
> **Pile C:** who killed Linda Connelly????
> **BTW:** Elmer said the committee voted you in as fete
>   director.

There was a smiley face at the end of the note.

Another committee? Worse yet, the committee that managed all the other committees?

There was a hissing sound in the office. Startled, Quill realized she was making it.

She called Elmer's cell. He didn't pick up. Quill didn't bother to sound pleasant. She wasn't feeling pleasant. "My office, Mayor. Nine o'clock. Be here." She called Dookie, who always answered his phone no matter what the hour, and he said, of course, he would be there and so would Mrs. Shuttleworth and they both felt Quill would make a fine fete director.

As for Althea Quince, Quill was pretty sure she'd find

her where she was every morning; on the terrace off the Tavern Lounge.

Quill stacked the pink slips up and scrawled a note to Dina: *RE: All inquiries: fete director to be announced soon. P.S. I'm not doing it!!!!*

She set those aside.

There was a stack of mail, too.

Quill sat and looked at it. There was a time, in the past, when it was agony to go through the mail, mostly because of the unpaid invoices she had to juggle. That wasn't true anymore. The Inn was doing well thanks to the thousands of tourists who'd discovered the glories of upstate New York.

The top letter was an enthusiastic "thank you!" from a party of four guests who had loved their stay and wanted to come back in September. The letter after that was an offer to feature the Inn in a cable TV special about best travel destinations. The letter under that was from a law firm in Syracuse called Beasley and Caldecott:

To: Sarah Quilliam-McHale
Owner/Operator/INN AT HEMLOCK FALLS, LLC
One Hemlock Lane
Hemlock Falls NY 14555-1255

Dear Madam:

This is to inform you of pending litigation in the matter of Porter Swenson v. the Inn at Hemlock Falls, LLC

Sincerely,
E. Caldecott, Esq.

A copy of a summons and complaint was attached. It was undated, which meant, Quill knew, that Porter Swenson wanted to rattle her cage, as opposed to actually haul her into court. And it was Porter behind it, not poor Jeeter himself, and since in her opinion and in the opinion of everyone else who had ever met him, Jeeter was of perfectly sound mind, she wasn't all that worried. But she'd have to see Howie Murchison, who handled all the legal affairs of the Inn, and sooner would be better than later.

Dina had attached a sticky note to the letter. *Sorry! (What a jerk!!!!)* and added a smiley face.

Quill looked at her desk clock: it was seven fifteen and she wanted to go straight back to bed.

She waited until seven thirty to call Elmer and leave a message that the emergency meeting of the fete committee would be at his office, not hers. The mayor's office was on the second floor of the municipal building, steps away from the sheriff's office and the jail and a block from Howie Murchison's law offices. With luck, the committee would beg Adela to come back and run the fete, and she would be free to talk to Davy Kiddermeister about Linda Connelly and the missing funds, and to Howie Murchison about Porter Swenson's litigious threats. If the innkeeping gods were on her side today, she could be back home for lunch with Jack.

Great. She'd go downstairs, find Althea at breakfast, and tell her that if she didn't support Quill's motion to reinstate Adela, she, Althea, would be a wonderful candidate to run the fete.

So why did she have the feeling things were out of control?

~

She grabbed her tote and went to find Althea, who was, as she expected, breakfasting with Nolan on the terrace of the Tavern Lounge. The sun was up and the air smelled like fresh grass. Mike the groundskeeper had placed tubs of Martha Washington geraniums on the flagstones, and the brilliant pink blossoms were cheering. Despite the murder, the lawsuit, and the imminent arrival of tens of thousands of tourists in Hemlock Falls to attend a director-less fete, Quill's mood was optimistic.

"So we're meeting with the mayor at nine this morning," she said to Althea, who had readily agreed that Adela was irreplaceable, "and you're going to back me up when I tell them I am not, not, not taking charge of this fete."

"Absolutely."

"Would you like to ride down with me?"

"Certainly, my dear. But do you really think the committee will bring Adela back? That silly Citizens for Justice league has petered out, but feeling in town seems to be running pretty high. That hundred grand is still gone-zo."

"The steering committee doesn't have any option. We have to bring Adela back. So we'll settle that, and then we can walk down to the jail and talk to Sheriff Kiddermeister about the progress of the investigation into the missing money. I have a feeling we're going to find it's all a giant mistake . . . Marge put her computer tech onto it yesterday, and I'll just bet she's gotten some solid results."

"The heck with the missing money," Althea boomed. "What about the murder? That's a far bigger opportunity for some real investigation."

She'd abandoned her purple scarves for bright yellow and orange this morning. Quill fought the urge to have a word with her about her hair color and won. The clash of colors had a certain raffish charm.

"Well, any murder would be, of course, but this one's a matter for the state police, don't you think? I can't imagine that anyone from Hemlock Falls killed Linda Connelly. She'd been here less than two days." Quill cleared her throat in a deprecatory way. "The cases I've been able to solve in the past were mostly due to the fact that I know the village very well."

"Hometown advantage," Althea said. "There's a lot to be said for that. So you don't think this a little local murder? I bet it is. She managed to lethally annoy almost everyone she ran into in the two days she was here. I can think of three people who wouldn't mind caving her head in with a tire iron right off the bat."

The couple at the table next to them got up abruptly and left the terrace.

"Althea, my love," Nolan said. "You might lower the decibel level a trifle."

"Emptying the room again, am I?" Althea grinned. "Too bad. Back to the murder. Look at how obnoxious the woman was. She was right on the money in her speech to those justice league idiots but she could have delivered the bad news in a much less brutal way. Did you see the look Spinoza gave her? If looks could kill, Connelly would have keeled over on the spot. Brady Beale was spitting nails, too."

"I didn't see you there," Quill said, surprised.

"I told you I meant to go in undercover. I was in disguise."

"You were?"

Althea, clearly delighted, examined her fingernails with an insincere air of unconcern. Quill grabbed her hand and stared. "Is that grease under your fingernails?"

"Motor oil."

Quill thought back to the scene at the car dealer's. "Oh, my goodness. You were one of the mechanics?"

"I was, indeed." She sipped her coffee, delicately. "It's my height, you know. It's a terrific advantage in crowds. Not as much when a disguise is needed. Sherlock Holmes was tall, too. But he was better at crouching than I am. The old knees aren't what they used to be."

Quill took a deep breath. "Tell me you weren't . . . that you didn't . . ."

"Discover the body? I did. You may place the continued health and well-being of that gigantic cat directly at my door."

"But." Quill didn't know which question to ask first. "What did you do there all day? The meeting broke up around twelve thirty, didn't it?"

"Did a couple of lube jobs and rotated a set of tires. Figured I should hang around and see that the organization had really petered out. I don't trust that Brady Beale as far as I could pitch him, and Spinoza's just as sneaky. Pilfering those funds isn't something Spinoza's up for, although I've been wrong before, haven't I, Nolan?"

"Not often, my love."

"But Brady's another story. I just wanted to get a peek at the history on his laptop—see if he'd visited any bank sites lately."

"Did you? Get a peek at his laptop, I mean?"

"In a manner of speaking. With all the brouhaha over the body, I didn't have a chance to do my peeking on-site." She glanced down at her tote, which she'd parked under her feet. "So I brought it back with me."

"You stole Brady Beale's computer?"

"Borrowed it," Althea corrected with a minatory air. "I would have looked at it last night, but I'm afraid the long day caught up with me. I'm ashamed to say I fell asleep."

"We neither of us are as young as we used to be," Nolan murmured.

Quill stared at Althea's tote. It was made of straw, with yarn butterflies stitched on the side. She could make out the faint outline of a thin, laptop-sized rectangle. "You borrowed Brady Beale's laptop?"

"I did."

Quill felt a little light-headed.

Althea checked her watch, which was a big stainless-steel item totally in keeping with her dress and demeanor. "I've got five minutes to nine. Shall we scamper on down to the mayor's office?"

"Yes," Quill said dazedly. "Sure." She picked up her tote and slung it over her shoulder. "My car's just out back."

Althea gave Nolan a hearty kiss on the cheek, swallowed the last of her cherry turnover in two large bites, and followed Quill across the terrace to her car. "You may be wondering how I obtained a job as a mechanic at Peterson Automotive."

"I am." Quill opened the passenger side door of her

Honda. Althea swung in with surprising grace for a woman her size.

"I called Marge Schmidt for assistance. That is one capable lady. She carries the business insurance for just about everyone in Hemlock Falls. The woman's a gold mine of information. One of the mechanics is a kid just out of high school . . . a Peterson, as a matter of fact. Zeke Peterson. I assume that it's short for Ezekiel, who was one of the minor prophets, if I am not mistaken."

"They're everywhere," Quill said. "Petersons, not prophets. There's a billion of them in Hemlock Falls." She started the Honda and pulled onto the drive that led into Main Street.

"So I called the kid. Said I was from the New York state lottery and he had to go to Syracuse to pick up his winnings. Then I showed up at Peterson Automotive in Zeke's place."

"How did you know Zeke Peterson bought lottery tickets?"

"All nineteen-year-old grease monkeys buy lottery tickets. Just like they all drink beer."

Quill didn't bother to challenge this. After all, Althea's ploy had worked. "He went all the way to Syracuse for nothing? Poor kid."

Althea looked at her, amused. "Aren't you the bleeding heart, though? No, no. Don't get ruffled. I'm just as bad. I left a couple hundred in cash in the kid's mailbox in an ordinary number ten white envelope."

The parking lot in the municipal building was almost full, which meant that Howie Murchison was holding traffic court. Quill pulled into a parking space next to a black-and-white police cruiser. She was very aware of the stolen laptop in Althea's possession. Howie could probably handle the letter over the lawsuit and defend Althea against a stolen property charge with one hand tied behind his back. And she'd decided that she really wanted a look at Brady's computer.

"Look at all this! Town court, mayor's office, sheriff's office all in one place," Althea said. "And every building on Main Street seems to be made of cobblestone. This is just great."

"We aren't very large as a village, really. Just under four thousand people. It's the tourists that drive the economy here." Quill put the Honda into park and sat there, scanning the parking lot.

"You don't look as sprightly as you might, girlfriend. We're going to go into the mayor's office, vote to reinstate Adela as chair of the fete, and get cracking on our murder, aren't we?"

"Maybe. That's Harvey Bozzel's Nissan there, right next to Dolly Jean's Taurus, which is right next to Carol Ann's Escalade. I don't think they're all here for traffic court. They're here to try to bully Elmer."

"Today's traffic court?"

"Third Thursday of the month. Like clockwork."

"But all these people mean Adela's doomed?"

"Doomed is the word, I think. Me, too, if I end up getting elected head of the steering committee. I'll tell you something, if they try to stick me with the job, I. Am. Not. Doing. It. Got that?"

Althea nodded vigorously.

Quill sighed and got out of the car. "Hang on. There's Marge's pickup truck. If she's at this meeting, it's because she's found something out about the money. Maybe Adela's not toast after all."

An outside staircase on the east end of the building led directly to the mayor's office. Quill nudged Althea in its direction. "Would you mind going up and seeing if she's there? If not, I'll give her a call. Don't bother with your tote. I'll bring it up."

Althea bounded up the staircase, her scarves floating gaily in the breeze. She disappeared inside, then re-emerged, and gave Quill a thumbs-up.

Quill waved her back in, then ducked into the Honda and stashed the laptop under the driver's seat. She grabbed her tote as well as Althea's and went up the stairs.

The door opened into a tiny reception area, with a ficus in a wood pot and two molded plastic chairs. A door leading to Elmer's office sported a brass plaque that read: THE HONORABLE MAYOR OF THE VILLAGE OF HEMLOCK FALLS. A large black plastic sign beneath it had ELMER B. HENRY in etched white letters. The door was partway open. Carol Ann's sweetly precise tones wafted nastily through the opening. "What do you mean, Miami? How come that money got routed through Miami? Miami's full of drug smugglers and Colombian dope fiends. On the other hand, I wouldn't be at all surprised to find Adela Henry got mixed up with them."

"That's ridiculous!" Elmer shouted. "You lay off my wife!"

Althea and Quill entered the mayor's office together. It was a large room, running the length of the south end of the municipal building. Elmer's desk sat in the middle, in front of four double-hung windows that looked out over Maple Street. The American flag, the flag of New York State, and a banner with the village emblem ranged on either side.

At the far end of the room, a round conference table seated up to a dozen people. Elmer sat with his back against the wall. Carol Ann paced up and down the indoor-outdoor carpeting, waving her arms. Dolly Jean and Harvey were huddled together in the far corner. Dookie sat on Elmer's right. Marge sat on Elmer's left. She was scowling. She looked past Carol Ann as Quill came in. "'Bout time you got here."

"It's just on nine," Althea said. "We're not late. You're early." She pulled out a chair and sat down with a noisy crash. "So. What's going on?"

"My tech guy found the money. It's in the Cayman Islands. Transferred electronically through a Miami bank two days ago."

Quill sat down with a sigh of relief. "Thank goodness. I mean, I'm sorry the money got moved, but I'm sure glad you found it. Now we can ask Adela to come back."

"So Adela can just put it back and it's business as usual?" Dolly Jean said disapprovingly. "That doesn't seem right. You can say all you want to say about bygones being bygones, but I ask you."

"Adela didn't take it," Marge said bluntly. "Unless she made a trip to Florida recently?"

"We were planning on a trip in November to see my cousins," Elmer said. "But we haven't been near the place this year."

Marge tapped her file emphatically. "My tech guy went through both the Henrys' computers and he couldn't find a thing linking them with any Miami bank. Unless you think Elmer's a lot smarter than I know him to be, they're in the clear."

Elmer looked as if he were trying to work Marge's statement into a compliment. He gave it up and glared at Carol Ann. "See! I told you it was all a mistake."

"You got hacked," Harvey said with a knowing air. "Happens all the time."

"Like you'd know anything about it," Marge said rudely. "But yeah. The account got hacked."

"I don't believe a word of it," Carol Ann snarled.

"You're not important," Althea said, without a particle of malice. "The important thing is the cops. What'd your local guy do, Marge, turn this over to the state fraud unit?"

"He had to. The experts are up in Albany."

"And let's hope they remain there." Althea reached out one long arm and plucked the file away from Marge. "May I?" She flipped through the contents, shaking her head all the while. "Wow. Wow. This mean anything to you, Marge?"

Marge reached up and grabbed it back. "Mean anything to you, Mrs. Quince?"

"Not a thing!" Althea said cheerfully. "But if this proves Adela's innocence, I say, go for it."

"We haven't heard from the fraud unit," Carol Ann

said. "I don't trust anybody in your pay, Marge Schmidt. You'd just as soon bribe somebody as look at them. I may not be Mrs. Richer Than God like some people, but I'm somebody in this town. I say we wait for the fraud unit to report back to us."

Althea made a rude noise. "Phooey. It'll take the fraud unit twenty years to get back to you on this one, and I've got a fiver in my pocket that they'll tell you exactly what Marge just did." She slapped a five-dollar bill down on the table with a flourish. Nobody picked it up. She waved the file at them. "There's not enough evidence to hang a cat in here, much less Adela Henry. I'll tell you what you do. You put in a claim on your village insurance policy for the hundred thou or so and cross your fingers that your agent doesn't hang you out to dry."

"The insurance!" Elmer said. "Thank the good Lord. I forgot about the insurance. Reverend, it's a miracle."

"Perhaps not for Mrs. Schmidt-Peterson," Dookie said mildly.

Althea gave a shout of laughter. "No kidding! You carry the town policy, Marge?" One look at Marge's expression confirmed it. "Well, damn. Sorry about that. Your loss ratio is going to stink this year." She slapped Marge on the shoulder. "And you did it to yourself. It's true, isn't it? No good deed goes unpunished."

Quill bit her lip . . . Pique, rue, and a certain amount of humor warred in Marge's face. She wanted to make a grab for her sketch pad but didn't dare.

Althea re-draped her scarves over her shoulder. "Have we got all the fete committee members here? We do? Reverend Shuttleworth? Would you care to second any motion I'm going to make to reinstate Mrs. Henry to the position of chairperson of the fall fete?"

"I would indeed, Mrs. Quince."

Quill felt as if a ten-ton weight had been lifted from her shoulders. She raised her hand. "I'd be more than happy to second that motion as well."

13

"That's a happy ending there," Althea said, when they had left the meeting and were once more in the parking lot. She and Quill both watched as Carol Ann peeled onto Maple with an angry squeal of tires. "Carol Ann's little cabal's been squashed and the fete will go on as planned with Adela in charge. Very satisfying."

"But why?" Quill said.

"Do you mean why was the fete's bank account targeted? Who knows? These big-time hackers plant roaming bugs in the management information systems of all the big banks if they can. One of the hazards of doing business in the twenty-first century."

"The Hemlock Falls Savings and Loan isn't a big bank. It's a little local bank. And why just that account? Mark Anthony Jefferson hasn't said anything about any other money being stolen, has he?"

Althea shrugged. "Not that I know of, no. You don't know these hackers, Quill. There's a lot of different ways to raid a system. You'll probably never know why. It's done. Let's forget it. We've got a murder to solve."

"I think the two crimes are linked."

"How could they be?!" She cocked her head and sucked her lower lip, deep in thought. "I'll tell what's going on. You're an artist. You look at objects, people, things, whatever, and you see a pattern that nobody else can see. You put it on canvas and wham! Suddenly everyone else sees it, too. This is different. This is real people doing real stuff and real stuff is random."

"Maybe," Quill said doubtfully. "I don't trust coincidence, myself."

"Happens all the time. Your guys are doing the right thing sending this off to the fraud unit. You should be happy this is settled. The town gets its money back. Adela's back on point with the fete. Case closed. On to the next one—the mysterious murder of your event coordinator. Shall we go talk to cops now? See what we can shake out of them? Or maybe we can go out to Peterson Automotive so I can sneak that laptop back into Brady's office."

"I don't think that's a good idea at all," Quill said earnestly. "Maybe we could put the investigation on hold for today? I really have to see Howie Murchison about a legal matter. Why don't you and Nolan take the day off? Maybe go on one of the winery tours. You've been so involved with helping with the fete, you two haven't had any vacation at all. Nolan is just a dear man. I hate to say it, Althea, but you've been leaving him alone an awful lot, lately."

Althea raised her head and inhaled the fresh spring air. "You know, you're right. It's a lovely day and Nolan would love a drive. No need to take me up to the Inn. I'll walk on down to the coffee shop and give Nolan a call. He can swoop down and carry me off to a wine tasting. We'll make a nice afternoon of it. You go see what you can coax out of Davy Kiddermeister. Might be a lot easier with me somewhere else, anyway. It's in that direction? Balzac Café?"

"Just one block down and turn right."

Quill waited until Althea disappeared down the block, locked the Honda, and then walked around to the rear of the municipal building to the sheriff's office. Davy's cruiser was parked in its reserved spot. She hoped Davy was in and not tied up in traffic court.

The main entrance was a heavy metal fire door. A tiny window, heavily barred, let a small amount of light into the office proper. Quill dragged the door open and went in.

She always felt a stab of nostalgia in the place. It wasn't that much different from other sheriff's offices throughout upstate and central New York, but it was where she'd first met Myles, all those years ago. The floor was industrial-grade vinyl and smelled like Pine-Sol. The dispatcher's desk was up front. Behind it, past a hip-high wooden barrier that reminded her of a baby guard, was Myles's old steel desk, with Davy in Myles's chair instead of Myles himself.

"Hey, Davy."

"Hey, Quill.

"Where's your dispatcher?"

"Early lunch. You heard about Marge's computer tech?"

"The fete account got hacked by a hacker or hackers unknown. Yes, I heard about it. Do you think that's what really happened?"

"Why not? Hacking's got the fastest rising crime rate in the nation. No reason why it can't happen here. Case isn't closed, but as far as I'm concerned, it'll wrap when the fraud unit in Albany gets back to me. Nothing else for either one of us to do except wait." He propped his feet up on the desk and grinned at her. "Now, there wouldn't be any other reason why you're here, would there?"

She knew that look. "Myles called you, didn't he?"

"Not called, no. I got a pretty pointed e-mail, though."

A metal folding chair stood next to the gate in the wooden barricade. Quill grabbed the chair and sat down. "He probably told you he was interested in the name of Linda Connelly's associates."

"That he did. He said he shouldn't have asked you to check the names out. He also said . . ."

Quill held her hand up. "I can guess what he said. I'm not investigating this murder."

"Good."

"But I'd just like the answers to a couple of questions."

"Why?"

"I'm not sure." She thought of Marge's comment—was it only two days ago?—something funny's going on in the village. "I've just come from a meeting of the fete committee. Adela's back in."

"Good." He slapped the manila file folder that lay in front of him. "Marge e-mailed a copy of her tech guy's report to me this morning, first thing. I sent it on to Albany. I don't really understand this stuff, to tell you the truth, but Marge said Adela's probably in the clear. Unless Albany tells me I have enough to push the case further, it's going in the pending dismissal file. I figure I'll hear from them, oh, maybe next year sometime at the earliest."

"But Adela's still under a cloud."

"Yeah. Sorry about that."

"And there's a dead woman in the morgue somewhere in Syracuse."

"No connection to the fete's missing money?"

"Uh-huh," Quill said skeptically. "The state troopers are on this one, right?"

"It's just inside their jurisdiction, yeah."

"And that means Lieutenant Harker."

Davy made a sound like "t'cha." Then, "That jerk, yeah."

"Is he copying you in on the investigation?"

"Yeah, but only because . . ." Davy's cheeks turned bright red.

"Because he's got a couple of suspects from Hemlock Falls. Who?"

"You know Harker."

"I sure do. Mean as a snake and twice as treacherous. Let me help, Davy. Between the two of us, we know almost everybody in town. We can track things down Harker never takes the time to do, or, if you'll forgive me, the intelligence to contemplate. The sooner the real killer's found, the better. Then Harker's out of everybody's hair."

Davy sighed. "All right. There's stuff you can do that I can't. My hands are tied a lot of the time, and there's no question you can help. But just on the QT, okay? I like my job; I want to keep it." He swiveled in his chair and tapped at his keyboard. "Harker made notes of possible motives, which is stupid, because motive isn't evidence. Motive doesn't mean squat in court and motive isn't going to . . . anyway . . . here we go. This is Harker's idea of who to look at. Harvey Bozzel: revenge, thought he should have the vic's job." He looked up at Quill. "The vic meaning Ms. Connelly."

"I know that, for Pete's sake."

"Dolly Jean Attenborough: motive is also revenge. Thought Harvey should have vic's job. Carol Ann Spinoza, ditto; Michael Allan Ryan Greer, wanted to take over the company."

"That's Harker's suspect list? Harvey, Dolly Jean, Carol Ann, and Greer? The only one who makes any sense at all is Greer, but that's mainly because we don't know him from a hole in the ground." And, she added to herself, he looks dangerous.

"This will make you feel better. He's redlined Louis Bergdorf."

"Louis Bergdorf? Who's he?"

"Mechanic who found the body."

"The mechanic who found the body. Oh, dear."

"For once, Harker seems to have his head screwed on straight. Somebody called Zeke Peterson with a cocka-mamie story about a lottery win and the kid hared off to Syracuse. This mechanic showed up in his place, disappeared, and hasn't been heard from again. Not only that, Brady Beale claims the guy took off with his laptop and forty thousand dollars' worth of tools."

"Forty thousand dollars' worth of tools?" She rubbed her forehead. She was getting a headache. What in the world would Althea want with forty thousand dollars' worth of automotive tools? And where the heck would she keep them?

"Yep. He's already filed a claim with his insurance company."

"Oh." Of course Althea didn't have forty thousand dollars' worth of tools. Those tools were in Brady's active imagination. Then she said, "I'll bet he has, the little weasel." Then, "He's insured through Schmidt Realty and Casualty, I'll bet. Poor Marge."

"My money's on this Louis character," Davy said, who hadn't listened to a word she'd said. "It's nice and straightforward, like most crimes. Guy cons the Peterson kid out of town so he can rob the garage and Linda Connelly walks in on it. Bam. There you are."

Quill shook her head. "This whole Louis Bergdorf thing is a no-go, Davy."

"You're kidding! It makes total sense. The vic shows up at the dealership, tries to stop the perp from swiping the tools, and bang, Bergdorf shoots her in the head and stows her in the trunk of her car."

"But why would Althea . . . I mean Bergdorf stick around to discover the body? Why not just take off?"

"If crooks were smart, they'd be on Wall Street."

"There *are* crooks on Wall . . . never mind. Trust me, Davy, there is no Louis Bergdorf."

Davy swung his feet to the floor and stood up. He loomed over her. "Whatever you know, you'd better tell me, Quill."

"Sit down, Davy. Please." She held his gaze until he sank back into his chair. "Thank you. All I can tell you is this: Louis Bergdorf is going to make Lt. Harker look like a big fat idiot."

"Yeah?"

"Yeah. So if you insist, I'll tell you who Louis Bergdorf really is and why Louis Bergdorf was at Brady's car dealership but I really wish you'd leave it alone. Believe me, it has nothing to do with the murder."

"Not good enough, Quill."

"Okay, then let me tell you something I couldn't know unless I know the identity of Louis Bergdorf. Zeke Peterson found a number ten office envelope with two hundred dollars in his mailbox when he got back from his futile trip to collect his lottery winnings."

"Dammit, Quill!"

"I know he's a fellow law enforcement officer and all that—but Harker is . . . ugh. And trust me, he's going to look pretty foolish. Let the Bergdorf thing ride, Davy. If Harker does discover who Bergdorf is, he'll have egg all over his face."

Davy thought about this for a minute.

"And there is nothing, nothing criminal involved at all. Who has Brady's insurance policy? Marge, right?"

"She does, sure."

"Then I'll let her know the tools claim is bogus." She thought about the laptop. She wanted a look at that laptop and she'd return it to the dealership herself after she had a chance to go through it. "And I'll bet you five bucks Brady misplaced his laptop and it isn't even stolen. Or maybe he lent it to somebody and forgot that he did. Look, hasn't Harker done a background search on Linda Connelly?"

"Sure. She's a successful event planner from Syracuse. Former Xerox employee. All kinds of recommendations from her clients. Doesn't appear to have any enemies in her background. Not the homicidal type, anyway."

"Think about this for a minute. I've met the woman, remember? She's here less than two days, and she manages to offend half of the people in town. Just look at your suspect list. A successful event planner rides to the rescue of a little town swamped with one of the biggest events of its year and she incites half the village to homicidal thoughts? It doesn't make sense. When you think event planner, what do you think? Cheerful, friendly. A real . . . people person, if you don't mind the cliché. This woman is cold as ice and has a pair of thugs in tow. She's no event planner, Davy. And she ends up in the trunk of her car at Brady Beale's place? She'd already been out to the dealership once that day. Why did she go back there?"

She didn't add what she was thinking. It was all speculation, and Davy hated speculation. What if Brady Beale had hacked into the fete bank account and set up Adela's departure? He'd shown up at the steering committee meeting almost immediately and volunteered to take over. But they'd hired Linda Connelly instead, and somehow, some way, Linda had interfered with Brady's plans.

What were Brady's plans? And how did Linda Connelly manage to interfere with them?

"So you don't think Linda Connelly's an event planner, despite a ton of references from her former clients and a résumé a yard long?" Davy shook his head in exasperation. "If she isn't, what is she?"

"I don't know." Quill got up and slung her tote over her shoulder. "But I'm going to do my best to find out."

14

Outside, it was getting hot and the sun was unusually fierce. It had been a dry summer, so far, and Quill wondered vaguely if the dryness had to do with the heat or the other way around. She was pretty sure there was a hat of some kind in her Honda. She wanted to sit outside and make an orderly list of questions. And then make a little map with connecting lines, to show the relationship of all the unknowns. She was very curious about what might be on Brady's laptop—she might need Marge and Marge's computer wizard for that. She needed a list and the peace and quiet to make one.

Peterson Park was only two blocks away. It would be a good place to sit and figure out what her next steps should be. By then, justice court should be over, and she could turn the letter from the Syracuse law firm over to Howie.

She wished Myles were home. Too many things were up in the air.

She was sure of one thing, though. As much as she liked Althea Quince, there were too many questions about that overly resourceful lady. She made Quill uneasy. Was she going to regret diverting Davy from investigating the fictitious Louis Whatsis? But what possible reason could Althea have for whacking Linda Connelly over the head? And why stick around to discover the body?

She opened the rear hatch of her car and stood contemplating the chaos inside. An extra car seat for Jack, in case something went wrong with the car seat up front. Three pairs of shorts, two jackets, and a fuzzy hat. A Game Boy, a portable crib, a portable stroller. A cooler, packed with snacks in foil and juice boxes. All Jack's.

"Hello, Quill. Having a yard sale?" Howie Murchison hailed her as he crossed the parking lot. He had his judge's robe over one arm and his briefcase in one hand. "If you are, you can toss this in the mix." He flapped the robe.

She turned with a smile. "This is a lucky surprise! I was going to look you up later today. Tough day in justice court?"

"Not bad, actually. And I got through the docket before lunch. That's even better." He stood beside her and gazed into the depths of her backseat. "It seems to me, when I was younger, and married, and my kids were Jack's age, that we made do with far less stuff."

"I seem to recall that when I was Jack's age, my mother made do with less stuff, too." She rummaged through the detritus. "Aha." She emerged with a John Deere billed hat. "Perfect."

"I'd say something gallant, like the green of the hat matches your eyes, but they're not green, are they?" He moved closer and peered at her. "More tea-colored. I thought all redheads were green-eyed." He brushed a strand of hair from her cheek.

"Then you must have flunked Logic 101." Surprised at

her tart retort, she apologized. "It's just that you don't usually flirt with me, Howie."

"I don't, do I? I'm off my game. I'll tell you why if you join me for lunch?" He held up his hand, palm out, as if taking an oath. "I promise, no flirting."

She hesitated. "Well, okay. I wanted to talk with you about something anyway, so over lunch would be nice. Shall we walk down to the Croh Bar?"

"My local spot," Howie said with satisfaction. "Miriam's, too. You think we'd get tired of it, but we never do. It's the endless fascination of small-town life, I suppose. Sooner or later, everything and everyone seems to pass through the Croh Bar."

They didn't have to wait for a booth. In just a few days, the place would be crowded with tourists from the fete, although, Quill thought, not as crowded as the other restaurants in the village. With its orange-patterned indoor-outdoor carpeting, red vinyl stools, and battered pine bar, the Croh Bar had been a village institution for years. Marge and her partner Betty Hall bought it when Norm Pasquale retired to Florida, and, with that instinct for business that made her the richest woman in Tompkins County, Marge had updated the tattered bar in exactly the same materials, only new. It smelled like it had since 1932; old wood polish, warm beer, and aging carpet.

Betty herself took their order. She greeted Quill with a friendly blow on the shoulder, ignored Howie, and cocked her head with weary expectancy. "Special's mac 'n' cheese."

"I'll have that," Quill said. Betty's macaroni and cheese

was made with heavy cream, top-of-the-line Cheddar, and panko bread crumbs.

"Cobb salad for me," Howie said. He slapped his middle, which bulged gently over his belt.

"You're dieting, Howie?"

"Setting up for the big day, most like," Betty said. "Ha-ha." She clumped away.

"What big day?"

Howie wore wire-rimmed spectacles, primarily, Miriam said, so he could peer sternly over them at the petitioners in his court. He took them off, polished them nervously, and put them on again. "I don't know how she does it."

"Who? Betty? Does what?"

"Guesses. I've been thinking about asking Miriam to marry me. You know. I've been divorced for what, fifteen years now, and I'll be retiring from the bench, soon. I'm thinking maybe it's time."

"Why, Howie! How wonderful."

"Yeah." He stroked his chin. "Think she'll say yes?"

"I have no idea. Well, actually, I think she'd be thrilled, but I certainly can't speak for her."

"You two are pretty good friends."

"We are, but if you think I'm going to run interference for you, you can forget it. You'd better ask her before Betty lets the cat out of the bag."

"You and Myles are pretty happy."

"Very."

"I'm thinking we could be happy, too."

"I'm sure of it."

"So. You wouldn't want to maybe sound her out a bit before I made a fool of myself?"

"That would be no. If she turns you down, you can handle it. And if this is why you wanted to buy me lunch, you can forget it. We'll go Dutch. Although, I'll be happy to pick up the tab if you don't mind answering a few questions."

"My advice is worth exactly what you pay for it."

She picked up the menu. "Good. Then I want exactly six dollars and ninety-eight cents' worth. I think I'm about to get sued." She pulled the letter from her tote and handed it over.

Howie read it with the absorbed, focused attention that made him so good at his profession. Then he read it again.

"Saber rattling," he said. "You notice the summons and complaint is marked 'draft.' And the cause of action is pretty weak. This assumes that you have an obligation, under the Innkeeper's Act to exercise greater care and control over your guests than you actually do. As the law is written now, at least."

"Should I retain you and Justin to handle it?"

"I think that'd be a good idea." He folded the letter and tucked it into his suit jacket pocket. "I'll ask Justin to write a formal response."

"Porter says he knows you."

"He does. We were at Cornell together. He called at my office a few weeks ago. Wanted to retain us to handle a competency hearing for Jeeter."

"You turned him down?"

"Yep."

"Because Jeeter Swenson isn't demented."

"Any healthy ninety-eight-year-old has some dementia, Quill. It's a normal part of the aging process. And further than that, I'm not willing to go."

"Because you don't like Porter Swenson?"

"All lawyers take an oath . . . aw, hell." He grinned suddenly. "Because I don't like the son of a B. There's lawyers around that'll take the case. As a matter of fact he found some."

"Do you know the firm?"

"Not at all. I think they're from Savannah and opened a satellite office up here, but I'm not even sure of that."

"Why is Porter so anxious to put his father in some nursing home? If Jeeter were a danger to himself or to other people, I guess I can see it. But he handles himself awfully well, Howie, except for that bit about the Loch Ness Monster, but I know forty-year-olds who believe in the Loch Ness Monster."

Howie looked momentarily bemused, and then shook his head, as if to get rid of flies. "Family law. It's a swamp."

Betty slapped Quill's mac and cheese down on the table, and held Howie's salad out of reach. "Does that mean you're not going to handle the Henrys' divorce?"

Howie scratched his chin. "What are my options, here? Can I get my lunch? Or are you going to dump it on my head? Come on, Betty. I'll talk about anything you like. The Rochester Rhinos. The weather. Meg's dumping poor Justin for some slick out-of-towner. But not my profession."

"Meg did what?" Quill asked.

Betty turned on her heel and walked off. Howie pressed his lips together and looked stubborn. Quill took the bread plate and scraped half her mac and cheese onto it. "Here. Have some of mine."

"I didn't want the damn salad anyway. I'm not a rabbit."

"Miriam will love you with or without your little tummy," Quill assured him. "Can I ask you something?"

"If it's about Elmer and Adela . . ."

"No, no. It's about Meg. She didn't dump Justin, did she? She wouldn't."

"Oh. That." Howie sighed. "Relationships. You know what? Maybe I'll wait a bit to pop the question. Miriam and I are getting along fine just as we are."

"But what about Meg?"

"A smart man stays completely out of his friend's relationships issues. You're going to have to talk to Meg yourself."

~

Quill finished what was left of her lunch more quickly than she wanted to, and headed back up the hill to the Inn. She found Meg at the prep sink in her kitchen. She was dressed for the weather in shorts, a T-shirt that stated *I'm Not Doin' It!* on the back, and one of the kitchen's long cotton aprons. Her socks were a temperamental orange.

"You dumped Justin Alvarez for this guy Greer? You've known him what . . . for an hour and a half?" Quill kept her voice down. The lunch hour was in full swing, and Meg's kitchen was bustling.

"NYB, Quill." Meg held a colander of fresh peas. She pushed them around with her forefinger, and then ran the colander under the tap.

"What? What? Oh! Not my business. Well, it is my business. You're my sister." Furiously, Quill grabbed the clip out of her hair, and then rewound her hair on the top of her head. The activity gave her enough time to keep her temper in check. "You know, you go through men like a bag of Oreos on movie night."

"Oreos are a fake food, did you know that? Chemicals. Pure chemicals."

"Whatever." Then, very gently, "Don't you want a sort of settled relationship, Meggie?"

Meg didn't look up from the peas. "I had one. He died. End of story."

"But that was fifteen years ago."

Meg bit her lip. She and her husband had been very young and married only six months when he'd been killed in a horrific car accident. They hadn't time to emerge from love's heady, irreplaceable beginnings to the more sober realities of a long-term relationship. If her sister was going to measure each new lover against the long-ago image of her young husband, she was never going to find heart's ease.

Quill kept her voice gentle. "I'll shut up about Justin. I'm sorry you had to break his heart." She grabbed a handful of pods and began to shuck peas back into the stainless-steel bowl. "I guess you know what you're doing."

"I guess I do. So. What's up with the fete?"

Quill grabbed a second handful of pea pods. "Adela seems to be in the clear, so the steering committee is sending a delegation to her home this afternoon to ask her to reconsider her resignation."

"No kidding. That's great news. What happened? Did

Marge's computer whiz discover that Adela'd been set up?"

"The official word is that the account was hacked by any one of those computer bandits that lurk in the cyber sphere."

"Those crafty devils." Meg combined Quill's shucked peas with the ones in the colander and rinsed them. "Do you believe that?"

"Do you?"

"It seems kind of . . . serendipitous to me."

"Serendipitous for whom?"

"Carol Ann, of course."

"I don't see how Carol Ann could have taken the money. Marge says the money's in some offshore account in the Caymans and Carol Ann can barely manage her e-mail. Plus, she's all about law and order. It just doesn't fit, Meg."

"Damn. I keep thinking somehow, someway, she'll disappear forever. Well, at least you're off the hook for the fete. I hope so anyhow. Who's in the delegation to coax Adela back on board? Not Elmer. She's still as mad as fire at him."

"No. Harvey, Dolly Jean, and Dookie."

"Dookie will swing it. He's the sweetest man I know. So what's next? How are you and the Amazing Althea doing on solving our recent murder?"

"Althea swiped Brady Beale's laptop."

Meg's eyes got big. "She did? Why?"

"She says that Brady's the likeliest one to steal the money because he wanted to move the fete to Summersville and he wanted to embarrass Adela. That made sense to me. She was also on the spot, or very nearly, when

Linda Connelly was killed. Did you know she discovered the body? Do you know how frequently the murderer is the one who discovers the body?"

Meg rolled her eyes. "I refuse, absolutely, categorically, and unequivocally to believe that Althea Quince murdered anybody. She's practically seventy years old, for Pete's sake. Did Howie buy you a couple of vodkas for lunch? Because tipsiness is the only explanation for this lunatic speculation."

"You're probably right. But just in case, I wanted to take a look at Brady's computer myself. So I swiped the laptop from Althea."

Meg pounded the top of the prep table. "Whoa! Way to go, Sis! Now what are you going to do?"

"I can't trust Althea."

"You never did trust her. I don't know why. I think she's a hoot."

"And I think Linda Connelly's a fake."

Meg handed the peas to Elizabeth Chou, who distributed them over four plates containing the basics of Meg's spring salad: new lettuce, goat cheese, hothouse tomatoes, and chives. "Linda Connelly's a fake what?"

"A fake event planner."

"A fake event planner? Why? Who'd want to be a fake event planner?"

"I don't think it's the event planning part so much as the fact that it got her here."

"To do what?" Meg chuckled. "Rob the fete?" Her mouth dropped open. "Oh. My. God. You're serious. I'd just like to point out that somebody has already robbed the fete."

183

"How many people are we expecting?"

"Thirty thousand, this year."

"And how much are tickets?"

"Twenty bucks at the gate."

"And we get about ten thousand of those paying cash at the gate. So you do the math."

"I can't," Meg said frankly. "You do it."

"Okay. It's . . ." Quill rubbed her nose. "Give me that scratch pad."

"That's not a scratch pad, that's my notes for a new recipe."

Quill snatched the pad and the pencil attached to it. "It's two hundred thousand dollars. In cash."

Meg grabbed the scratch pad back. "Wow," she said in a small voice. "So maybe Brady Beale robbed the fete and Linda Connelly was in on it so she could help him rob more of it, and they had some kind of falling out."

"You betcha."

"So now what?"

"Now I find Marge so I can get into that purloined laptop. There's something else, Meg. That hottie you dumped good old honorable Justin Alvarez for? I'll bet he's a crook, too."

Meg's face darkened. "Hang on a minute. Have you bounced this crazy idea off anyone else?"

"It's not a crazy idea."

"It's not," Meg admitted. "But you have zero proof. Zero. You're theorizing ahead of the facts. Wait! Wait! Did I say facts? There aren't any!!" She glanced at the pot rack, where her trusty, much-dented eight-inch sauté pan hung invitingly close. "I've never thrown that thing at you but I maybe, just maybe, am ready to break the habit of a lifetime."

Quill backed a prudent six feet away. Meg's aim was lousy, but there was no sense in taking a chance. "Listen. Are you really going out with Mickey Greer?"

"It's Thursday," Meg said, as if this explained everything.

"So you're out of here at two o'clock. It's almost that now. Where are you two going?"

"We were planning on hiking Buttermilk Falls."

"Meg! That's where you and Justin had your first date."

Meg looked thoughtful. "I guess you're right. Maybe that's what set him off."

"Set who off? Justin? You know what? I don't want to know anymore. Not right now. Honestly, I don't think you ought to cross the street with this guy, much less hike forty miles from civilization."

"Buttermilk Gorge is practically a suburb of Ithaca."

"And besides, what the heck is this guy doing going out on a date when his boss is lying murdered in the Tompkins County Morgue?"

"I needed a little downtime. Your sheriff said it would be okay." The voice was very male and very deep.

Quill whirled. The double doors to the dining room swung closed behind Mickey Greer. He wasn't exceptionally tall, perhaps an inch or two under six feet. He wasn't conventionally handsome, either. His mouth was too wide, his nose too aquiline. His eyes were deep set; the whites very clear, the pupils dark. He wore jeans and a denim shirt. The sleeves were rolled halfway up, revealing heavily muscled forearms. The combination of all of these things made him devastatingly attractive.

"Your sister said she was in need of a little downtime, too." He paused. "Do you have a problem with that?"

"Of course not," Quill said. "I mean, not with Meg needing some time off. But Ms. Connelly's death must be very upsetting for you?"

"Naturally," Mickey said, with a reassuring air. "Very upsetting. Not to mention the fact that I'm out of a job." He grinned attractively. "Your Lieutenant Harker seems to think that my taking over the company is a motive for knocking her off myself. She was great at it. There's no way I could take over from her. No way that I'd even want to. I'm very sorry she's gone. George is taking it harder than I thought. But he's worked with her longer than I have. I wasn't close to Linda. We'd only worked a few events together. But her death was a shock, certainly." He smiled, devastatingly. "I'm lucky your sister agreed to spend a little time with me. I need to clear my head."

Elizabeth Chou waved her whisk. "I can go with him, Meg. If you're too tied up."

"I've got it covered, thanks." Meg untied her apron and tossed it on the floor. "I'm just going to run upstairs and get my gear. Give me two seconds."

"In the meantime, Mickey," Quill suggested. "Why don't we sit in the dining room? Would you like something to eat?"

"Why not?" He stepped to one side and pushed the doors open. "After you."

"Elizabeth, could you bring Mr. Greer something light? He won't want to eat too much if he's hiking in this heat. Bring me something, too, if you would. Howie Murchison ate most of my lunch."

Mickey followed her out of the kitchen. The dining room was almost empty.

"Looks like business isn't too hot," Mickey said.

"It's a weekday in late summer and a lot of families are home getting their kids ready for school next week," Quill said. "In a week or two, when people start coming into town for the fete, we'll have a line all the way down to Main Street. Why don't we sit here?" She indicated the small table for four that was her habitual spot.

Mickey sat with his back to the wall. He glanced around the room once, but Quill had the feeling that he could make his way through it blindfolded if he had to.

"Is there any progress on the investigation?"

He turned his palms up in a "who knows?" gesture. "Not enough to satisfy me. George, either. You know anything about this state trooper? Name's Harker."

"Yes," Quill said with feeling. "I do. None of it good, I'm afraid." Then because even a justified criticism of a resident of Tompkins County seemed disloyal, she added, "But his resources are excellent."

Elizabeth pushed her way out the kitchen doors with her hip. She carried a tray with a half carafe of red wine, a plate of spring salad, a plate of country pâté with cornichons, mustard, pearl onions, and cheese, and a basket of Meg's sourdough bread. She arranged all of this carefully in front of Mickey Greer, shook out his napkin, and stood there with a sappy smile on her face.

Quill cleared her throat. "Maybe you could bring me a spring salad, Elizabeth?"

"Oh! Sure! Whatever."

Quill waited until Elizabeth bounced back with her salad and bounced away again. Mickey Greer attacked his lunch in a methodical way, a man who saw food as fuel and not much else. "How long have you worked for Presentations?"

"Four months, give or take."

"What did you do before that?"

He smiled. "This and that. I was in the navy for a while. I mustered on out with pretty good retirement benefits."

Quill was good at determining ages. Mickey Greer was in his early forties, no older than that.

"You must have joined up at a pretty young age."

The look he gave her was opaque. "Right out of high school. Why all the questions? You think I had something to do with Linda's murder?"

Quill felt just like an interrogator on *NCIS*. "I don't know. Did you?" The tough-guy effect was probably marred by the fact she was blushing, but she pressed on. "Where were you and George yesterday?"

"We went down to Seneca Lake for a swim." He swallowed the last of the pâté and bit into a roll. "Linda told us to take the afternoon off, so we did." Then, in a genuinely appreciative tone, he said, "It's beautiful country around here."

"Do you know what her plans were? Why did she go back to the car dealership? Did she and Brady Beale know each other before she got to Hemlock Falls?"

Mickey shoved his plate to one side and tipped his chair against the back wall. "Okay, Ms. McHale. You want to play detective? It's fine by me. As far as I know, she went back to Peterson Automotive because what's his name, Brady, wanted more space for his exhibit. She had to shove a couple of other booths around to accommodate him. There's a lot of back and forth with these things."

This was true. As a matter of fact, "back and forth" was an understatement. Booth placement was a hotly contended issue at the fete. "Did she actually talk to Brady?"

He shrugged. "You'll have to ask him."

"What time did you and George get back?"

"Aaahh. Let's see. We ate at some diner in Geneva. An Italian place."

"Nona Maria's?"

"That's it. We must have left there about seven? I've got a credit card receipt if you'd like to take a look." He looked beyond her shoulder. "There's your sister. Thanks for the food."

Quill turned in her chair and watched Mickey saunter across the room. Meg wore shorts. Very short shorts. Meg had excellent legs, and her Uggs hiking boots somehow served to make them look even better. Quill bit back the first comment she wanted to make (too snide) and the second (too maternal). In the end, she just waved and watched her sister leave with one of the scariest guys she'd ever met.

15

". . . And that includes that idiot from the winery case five years ago," she said to Marge half an hour later.

"I remember that one," Marge said nostalgically. "That's the first time you and I ever did a B and E together."

"B and . . . ? Breaking and entering. Yes. Well. We're probably breaking more laws by hacking into Brady's computer."

"And why are we doing this again?"

They sat in Marge's office on Main Street. Outside, a group of ladies from the Fireman's Auxiliary were filling the sidewalk planters with bright red geraniums and English ivy. Members from the Hemlock Falls Church of the Word of God attached hanging planters filled with purple petunias and asparagus fern from the wrought-iron lampposts. In two weeks, at the start of the fete, the old village would be looking its very best.

"Because Althea Quince took it and she was going to hack it, too."

"What'd she expect to find?"

"Initially, I think she expected e-mails from Carol Ann to Brady, planning more mischief. Then, I think she suspected Brady of being involved in the theft of the fete funds."

"No flies on that lady," Marge grunted. "Althea, I mean. Okay. Let's see here." She flipped open the laptop. "You do know that if this is password protected, we're going to have a problem."

"I thought maybe your computer guy can handle it."

"She can. It can take a while though." Marge tapped the power button and the laptop began to boot up. "Brady's not the brightest bulb in the chandelier so maybe we might get lucky."

The screen pulsed with light. The little box requiring user name and password identification glowed at them.

Marge input 'Brady' and then '1234' with an air of resignation. "Doubt this'll work. Nope. Shoot. I'll give Caitlyn a call, ask her to come in and pick it up."

"Hang on a second." Quill pulled the laptop in front of her. She examined the case, turned the computer over, and carefully peeled off a piece of tape from the underside. She set the laptop back in front of Marge. "Try this." She read off a string of letters and numbers and Marge typed them in.

"We're in!" Marge said as the laptop chimed "Welcome." "I told you Brady's not going to win any awards for smart."

"This tape with his password on it has been peeled off from somewhere else. I'll bet Althea found it under a desk drawer or something. We need so many passwords to function these days, I do it, too. Write them down and put them somewhere in my office."

"You're not going to win any awards for smart, either." Marge went straight to the site history and began to scroll down. "'Hot Chicks in Cool Coops,'" she read aloud. "'Wild, Wet Women.'" She made a face. "Jeez. And I buy cars from this guy? I'm going to switch over to his e-mail account. What do you think? Should I try 'old' or 'sent'? I'll try sent. Aha. Ah-*ha*!" She started to chuckle.

Quill couldn't see the screen from her position across the desk. "What? Did you find something?"

"E-mails from Carol Ann to Brady and back again. Hoo. Carol Ann sure has it in for you!" Marge scowled suddenly. "And for me. The little witch. But if you ask me . . ." Marge tapped rapidly, scrolling through the e-mails. "That whole protest crud is pretty well pooped out. Take a look for yourself. Carol Ann sent this after the steering committee meeting this morning."

From: carolann@spinoza.com
To: bpeter@petersonmotors.com
Re: village disgrace

So the money's disappeared into somebody's pocket (you can bet I know who!!!!) and as usual the Quilliam/Schmidt faction has shown once again who runs this town. I don't know why you won't march on opening day. We could rip this town wide open!!! But if you're going to be a poopyhead, there's not a darn thing I can do about it. You will be sorry!!!! It's not over till it's over!!!!

"Bluff and bluster," Marge said. "You can set Althea's mind at rest about any funny business at the fete."

"What do you suppose she meant, 'it's not over till it's over'?"

"Who knows? Who cares? Brady runs with the grumblers and malcontents and if he's not able to get his people out to demonstrate, Carol Ann will be out there all on her lonesome."

"And she thinks she knows who has the money?"

Marge's face darkened. "Me."

"You?"

"Grabbed me by the collar after the meeting"—Marge cracked her knuckles and smiled in a sinister way—"or tried to. Anyhow, yeah. She thinks I took the money in cahoots with Adela. She's just grabbing at straws. That's her style and always has been." She bent over the laptop again.

"Maybe we should return this to Brady," Quill said. "He's got all his business accounts on there."

"Along with the wholesale price of a pickup truck Harland wants to buy. Give me a second while I look for it."

"Marge, I don't think that's quite fair of you."

She raised one hand. "Yeah, yeah, yeah." Then with a very different tone in her voice. "What the hell is this?"

Quill bent sideways to look at the screen.

"That's the new girl at Bonne Goute, isn't it? Sophie something."

"Yes," Quill said soberly. "Yes, it is. Sophie Kilcannon."

There were dozens of pictures of the tall blonde. About half of them were on the beach somewhere, with Sophie in a very brief bikini. The others had been taken with a long-distance lens. Sophie in her apartment at Bonne Goute, reading in her living room. Sophie getting ready to shower. Sophie getting out of a Ford Escort that had seen better days. It was clear she had no idea someone was taking pictures of her.

Quill rubbed her arms. "This is creepy. And bad. Really bad."

"You got any idea where that beach is?" Marge scrolled back to the photos of Sophie on the beach. She was smiling, her blond hair caught up in a billed cap, her sunglasses in one hand.

"The days are long gone where I could wear a bathing suit like that," Quill said wistfully.

"I never could wear a suit like that." Marge rapped the desk. "Focus, please. Those big buildings behind the beach. That look at all familiar to you?"

"Miami, maybe?" Quill hazarded. "Didn't Clare say she recruited Sophie from Miami? It looks like somewhere in the US, at least. It's not tropical enough to be Hawaii and it's too tropical for the west coast."

"Harland and I have been looking at Florida property," Marge said. "We've been thinking about getting out of these winters. That's Miami, for sure." She clicked rapidly through the photos once again, then shut down the laptop and closed the cover. "Now what do we do?"

"What possible reason could Brady Beale have to take sneaky photos of Sophie Kilcannon?"

Marge snorted. "You're kidding, right? Do I need to remind you of the crud on that guy's browser? Hot Chicks in Cool . . ."

Quill held her hand up. "Ugh."

"The guy's a voyeur, at best. At worst—well. Maybe we don't want to know the worst."

"I should take this to Davy." Quill reached for the computer.

Marge pulled it out of reach. "And what, have Brady charge us with petty larceny? Of course, you could tell him that Althea Quince was really the one who stole it, so we can get her into trouble, too. No, here's what we do. We go talk to this Sophie Kilcannon. And then," Marge cracked her knuckles. "We have a couple of Harland's linebacker cousins have a talk with old Brady."

16

Quill and Marge left the office at close to four o'clock. Quill suggested they drive separately up to the academy, "because," she said to Marge, "this is when I spend time with Jack. We can make this quick, can't we? I took a blood oath that I wouldn't let anything interfere with Jack's afternoons. I spend little enough time with him as it is."

Marge paused in the process of snapping on her seat belt. "Tell you what. I'll tell Sophie I took the laptop. You go on home."

"No, no. I can't let you do that." Quill looked at her shrewdly. "And you don't want to, anyway. It wouldn't be fair. I started this mess—well, Althea started this mess—and I've got to see it through. Just let me give Doreen a call to tell her I'm going to be late." She speed dialed Doreen, who went "t-cha!" then talked to Jack, who didn't seem distressed at all that he might not see his mother until bedtime.

"He's a well-balanced kid," Marge said stoutly. "And that Doreen may be a little crusty tempered with adults, but she's a wizard with kids. I'd be proud of any kid of mine that wasn't clingy. Of course," she added, "it may be his mamma that's clingy."

"Any more words of wisdom you want to share?" Quill asked crossly. She put the car into gear and reversed into the street, narrowly missing a flat of begonias. Alice Nickerson, who was putting the last of a pot of baby's breath into a planter, waved her trowel and shouted. Quill was pretty sure she wasn't telling her to have a nice day.

The drive to the academy was short, less than two miles from Marge's office, which was at the heart of downtown. They passed Peterson Park, where the grandstands for the fete were already going up.

"Slow down a bit," Marge ordered. Quill, who hadn't been going faster than thirty, slowed even more, to the frustration of the two cars behind her. "Ignore the horns. Look! See that purple blob where the entrance sign is going up?"

"Adela!"

"Hot damn!"

Quill raised her right hand and Marge slapped it. "I'm so relieved, Marge. Dookie must have talked her into coming back on board."

"My money's on Dolly Jean Attenborough," Marge said cynically. "She's been pushing to have Harvey take over. I'd like to see the day Adela took a backseat to Harvey."

Quill speeded up, just as the car behind her began to pass. The driver shouted out the window. It was Nadine Peterson. Quill decided to wait a few weeks before she got her hair trimmed at the Hemlock Hall of Beauty.

"Slow down, darn it. You almost went past it."

"Do you think I should pull into the annex or the employee parking lot?"

"Where's Sophie likeliest to be?"

"The kitchen, I would think, at this time of day. Oh, my goodness. She's jogging in the field. Look, Marge." Quill braked at the edge of the field. "How beautiful."

Sophie raced around the edge of the field, effortlessly avoiding the piles of dirt and gravel put there by yesterday's bulldozers. The grass was the deep rich green of late summer. The trees were touched with russet. The sunlight was silver gold. Sophie herself was a slim, vibrant figure, her long legs flashing in a graceful rhythm.

"Now I suppose we have to wait while you do one of those sketches of yours," Marge said with rough affection.

"No," Quill said absently, "no sketch."

"Really? You just said it looks beautiful. Don't you want to draw it or something?"

"She's happy. You can't draw plain old happy, Marge. I can't anyway. There has to be some tension."

"Wait until we tell her Brady Beale's been playing Peeping Tom. She's not going to be happy about that."

Sophie raised a hand in greeting as she flashed around the back of the field, and then slowed down as it became obvious that Quill and Marge were waiting for her. She wiped her face with the back of her hand and jogged up to them.

"Hi. You're Meg Quilliam's sister, aren't you? And?" She looked at Marge with an inquiring smile.

"Marge Schmidt."

"Of course. You're married to that nice dairy farmer, Harland Peterson." She wiped her palms on her jogging shorts and shook Marge's hand. "It's nice to meet you. And nice to see you, Quill. Clare's in class right now, but if there's anything I can help you with, just ask."

"Actually, it's you we came to see. I'm sorry to interrupt your run, but Marge and I have something to tell you. It'd be better if we could find a place to talk."

"That's okay. Why don't we go to my place?" She grinned happily. Her eyes were very blue in her tanned face. "Doesn't that have a great ring to it? My place." She stretched her arms wide, as if to embrace the field itself. "And isn't this a gorgeous spot! I can't believe I lucked into this job. This place is paradise."

Marge snorted. "That's true enough. It's even got the snake. You want a ride up to the annex?"

"Ah . . . sure." She checked the pedometer on her wrist. "I only logged six miles, though. If this is important, that's enough for today, I guess."

"Six miles? Heck," Marge said, "that's enough for a week. And yeah, it's important. Hop in."

Quill pulled into the driveway that led to the annex and parked in front. It was a pleasant building, constructed in the same style as the three-story academy. Sophie led them through the foyer, which was carpeted in an unobtrusive hunter green, and down the hallway. "I have one of the middle apartments, so there are only windows on the one side. They all have sliding glass doors out to the field, though, so I don't feel too claustrophobic." She unlocked the door and stepped back to let them precede her. "Come in. Can I get you some tea? Or something cold to drink?"

"Not right now, thank you." Quill had been in the annex

apartments before. They were equipped like a pleasant, middle-grade hotel; durable wall-to-wall carpeting, unpretentious furniture in dark wood; a small, efficient kitchen with a four-burner electric stove and an apartment-sized refrigerator. A Mason jar of daffodils sat on the bookcase. A five-string guitar was propped in the corner. Sophie had made the place less anonymous with pictures of sailboats, collections of seashells, and movie posters. The posters were of American movies in a variety of foreign languages. After a moment, Quill realized that all the posters were of an old James Cameron movie, *Terminator 2*, with a middle-aged Arnold Schwarzenegger and a young Linda Hamilton. Quill walked over and looked at them closely. "What an interesting collection."

Sophie giggled. It was a delightful sound and infectious. She shoved her hair back with both hands. "Yeah. That's from Bombay, the one there's from Tokyo, and the others are from Amsterdam, and Paris and Rome. I try and pick one up whatever country I'm in. I loved Arnold Schwarzenegger from the neck down. Gorgeous, just gorgeous. Of course, in real life, he's old as the hills, not to mention that from the neck up he's a complete and utter doughhead. Some men should just shut up and pose, don't you think?"

Quill bit her lip so she wouldn't laugh.

"You sure travel a lot," Marge said warily.

"Well, yeah, of course." Sophie blinked. Her eyes were very blue. "I mean before I got this gig here, I was a chef for hire. On yachts. You know, have sauté pan, will travel."

"That must have been a lot of fun," Quill said a little wistfully.

"Well, it depends," Sophie said judiciously. "I was cool with the bigger boats, but not so much on the small ones. Anything under sixty feet I spent most of my time in the galley tossing my cookies."

"You get seasick?"

"It kind of monkey wrenched my career plans," Sophie admitted. "So when I ran into Clare Sparrow at the Miami Food Fair last November, I asked her to let me know if she had ever had an opening. To tell you the truth, I didn't think I had the stuff to get a job here—I mean Bonne Goute is famous and I haven't been cooking all that long. But here I am!" She looked from Quill to Marge and back again, her face glowing. "So. Before we talk about stuff, can you give me five minutes to shower and change?"

Quill made an effort not to look at her watch. "Sure."

"Just have a seat then. I'll be right out." She disappeared into the bedroom and moments later, Quill heard the shower go on.

Quill sat down on the couch and rested the tote with the laptop in it at her feet. The couch was positioned so that Sophie could look out onto the field, and beyond that, the trees of Peterson Park. Marge wandered around the apartment, stopping at the bookshelf. "Lot of books about cooking here."

"That's not surprising."

"Lot of books about sailing ships, too. Oh, my Lord."

"What?"

"The girl's a lefty. She's left of Attila the Hun. Look at these books on social justice."

"You don't mean Attila the Hun. You mean left of a

humanist's humanist. I can't think of a role model for humanism at the moment, but it'd be to the left of that."

Sophie emerged from the bedroom, dressed in white shorts, sandals, and a baggy T-shirt that read *Port of Palm Beach* on the back and *There's nothing better than messing about in boats* on the front. She grabbed a bottle of water from her refrigerator and sat down next to Quill. "Okay, guys. Shoot. You said something about a snake in my Eden? Now what does that mean?" She turned pale. "Oh, my goodness. Oh, my goodness." She pulled on her lower lip, sighed, and said in a very small voice, "Clare sent you here to fire me, didn't she? I knew it was too good to last. I just knew it. I mean, I'm really sorry about the pasta." Then, with an air of painful honesty, "I wasn't at the time. I admit it. I was just so ticked off at the guy that I didn't stop to think."

"Of course Clare didn't send us to fire you," Quill said. "If Clare were going to fire you, she'd do it herself."

"She would?"

"Of course she would." Then, more kindly, she said, "We're friends, but the businesses aren't connected at all."

"Of course they aren't." She bit furiously at her thumbnail. "It's just that I still can't believe I'm here. I wake up every morning thinking Clare's going to knock on my door and say it was all a mistake. You know all the other chefs have these homogenously fabulous résumés. Jim Chen was a sous chef at Arnaud's in New Orleans. Raleigh Brewster's been written up in *Bon Appétit* like a billion times. I'm nobody compared to them. But I'm *not* getting fired." Sophie beamed. "Well, yahoo and hooray! Then, carry on, ladies."

"What is it about the pasta?" Marge said.

"It sort of ended up in a guy's lap. It wasn't anything, really."

"About the pasta . . ." Marge said stubbornly.

She waved her hand airily. "Nothing. Nothing. The nice thing about Clare is that she doesn't lose her temper like a lot of chefs. I mean she does, but there's not a lot of yelling and screaming. More like, icy annoyance. What time is it?"

"Six o'clock," Quill said. Jack would be eating his dinner now. Without her.

"Since I'm not fired, then I'm due back in the kitchen in thirty minutes. Is there something I can help you with?"

Quill picked up the laptop with a grimace. "Do you know Brady Beale?"

"Nope."

"Did you buy a car at Peterson Automotive recently?"

"Nope. I don't have a car. I don't drive. I have a bicycle."

"You didn't go to any of the Citizens for Justice meetings at the auto dealership, did you?"

"You mean that protest group run by Carol Ann Spinoza? Heck, no." With a certain amount of admiration, she added, "You don't meet all that many sociopaths in the traveling chef business. More than a few filthy-rich capitalists that deserve to be keelhauled for greed, of course, but you have to be relatively sane to make big bucks these days. That Carol Ann's a case study for somebody."

"And what's wrong with capitalism, young lady?" Marge asked in a dangerous way.

"That's *exactly* what my parents want to know!"

Sophie said delightedly. "I've got a few books you might like to read, Marge. But." She swiveled that very bright blue gaze back to Quill. "That's not what you've come about."

"No." Reluctantly, she opened up the laptop, booted it up, and handed the laptop to Sophie. "These were apparently taken by Brady Beale."

"Ick." Sophie clicked rapidly through the photos. "Ick. Ick. Ick. Where the heck did the little bugger get these pictures of me in Miami?"

"Trade show?" Quill hazarded. "I know he was there for an international car show recently."

Sophie shuddered. "Ugh." She looked thoughtful. "The big question, of course, is why me?"

Marge and Quill glanced at each other. Sophie couldn't be that oblivious to the way she looked in a bikini.

"I'm awfully sorry," Quill said. "We came to you as soon as we came across them . . . what are you doing?"

Sophie tapped rapidly at the keyboard. "Seeing what else the little peckerwood has in here." She paused and demanded sharply, "Who's this?" She pivoted the laptop. The photo file was in slide-show format, and a series of pictures showed a small dark-haired woman walking briskly along the streets of a crowded city. She wore dark glasses, a gray hoodie, and cargo pants. The people around her were Asian. Chinese, Quill thought, rather than Korean or Japanese. There were a lot of palm trees, and the streets were broad.

"Linda Connelly," Quill said. "Where is she, do you suppose?"

"Singapore," Sophie said. She caught their looks of

surprise. "I was there earlier this year. A hedge-fund banker with twenty of his closest friends. Big boat, thank goodness, although I was a little urpy in the bay. You say this woman calls herself Linda Connelly?"

"The village hired her to manage the fete in Adela Henry's, ummm . . . absence. But she was killed yesterday afternoon. Didn't you hear about it?"

"Sure. Sure I heard about it. Who didn't?" Sophie stared at the screen, and then began biting her other thumb.

"Do you know her?"

Sophie looked up, and for a moment, Quill saw what the girl would look like in twenty years. "No," she said after a long moment. "I don't know her. Not personally, thank goodness." She clicked the photo file closed. "As far as this creep Brady Beale . . ." She shook her head. "All I can say is what I said before. Ick. Thanks for the heads-up. I guess I'd better keep my drapes drawn from here on in."

"I think you should do more than that. I'd like to take this to Sheriff Kiddermeister. I was hoping that you'd swear out a complaint. We should be able to get Brady arrested. Or at least make him stop."

"It's not that big a deal."

"It's a very big deal." Quill touched Sophie's shoulder. "This is a total invasion of your privacy. And if he's stalking you, he may be stalking other women."

"Gosh. I doubt that."

"If you're afraid of reprisals," Marge said, "all I can say is you don't need to worry about a thing. One way or another, we got resources."

Quill shook her head. "Really, Marge. We've got

enough on our plates as a village without jumping into vigilantism. The best possible thing is for us to take Sophie to Davy Kiddermeister and let the law take care of it the right way."

"Did this Peterson let you use his laptop? I mean, how did you guys get hold of it?"

"It fell into our hands in a roundabout way," Quill said vaguely. "The person that borrowed it from Brady's office intended to put it back."

"And you borrowed it from the original thief?" Sophie raised her eyebrows. "Sounds to me like there'd be a whole lot of hoopla falling on you guys if I went down and made a complaint."

Quill shook her head. "We can handle that. Your safety's more important."

"Oh, I can take care of myself." Sophie looked perfectly blank. "Let me think about this. Okay. I've got a great solution. You guys are gonna love it. We wipe this baby down so there's no fingerprints, and we stick it in a ditch outside or somewhere, and one of us calls the sheriff's office in a very anonymous way and tells him where it is. We maybe put a sticky note on it, to send the sheriff right to the place where my photos are."

"An anonymous sticky note?"

"Sure."

"The forensics," Marge said heavily. "They can trace anything these days."

"Phooey," Sophie said. "No government office I ever heard of is going to waste department resources on anything more than a fingerprint check. Nope. I say sneak this into evidence."

"We could do that, I suppose," Quill said unwillingly. "I'm not big on being sneaky."

"She would have jumped on this before she had her kid," Marge said to Sophie. "She got a lot more law-abiding since she became a mother. Quill, I think young Sophie's got the right idea. We drop this off to Davy, un-obtrusive-like. We'll let the law take its course." She cracked her knuckles for the third time that day. "In the meantime, I'll give Harland's linebacker nephews a heads-up."

"Sounds like a plan," Sophie said cheerfully. "When the sheriff comes to interview me, I'll swear whatever I need to swear and peckerwood can hire a defense lawyer." She looked brightly from Marge to Quill. "So where shall we put it?"

"My diner," Marge said. "I'll let Betts find it and make the call. In the meantime, young lady, keep your curtains closed."

"I've got a better idea." Sophie's slim fingers grasped the laptop. "Leave it with me. I'll put it in the tasting room, and then 'find' it in front of a couple of the other chefs. I'll suggest we call the cops and there you are. Keep you guys out of it altogether. Now, I'm really sorry, but I've got to get back to work. And I still have to dry my hair! If Clare didn't fire me over the pasta thing, she'll sure as heck fire me if I miss my shift."

Something about the way Sophie hung on to the laptop bothered Quill. That, and her comment about not knowing Linda Connelly personally.

Ever since Jack's second birthday, (in self defense) Quill had gotten really good at being stern. She often thought her life as an innkeeper would have been easier if she'd learned it a lot earlier. "Sophie," she said. "What's going on? What do you know about Linda Connelly?"

"I don't know a thing about Linda Connelly." She scowled. "What's it to you, anyway?"

"We're looking into her death," Marge said breezily. "We do that."

"You do what?"

"Quill here's by way of being one of the best detectives in Hemlock Falls."

"I didn't know there were any detectives in Hemlock Falls."

"There aren't," Quill said. "I mean, over the years we've had the occasional . . ."

"Corpse!" Marge said cheerfully.

". . . At the Inn and once or twice I've stumbled over the solution to the murder . . ."

"And we're going to solve this one, too." Marge settled comfortably back against the couch. "Soon as we get this yahoo Brady Beale and his snoopy camera off the streets."

Sophie carefully unwound the towel from around her head, shook out her wet hair, then folded the towel neatly and set it on the coffee table. "Wow." Then, "You were trained in police work, is that it?" She glanced at Marge. "Or maybe you were in the military? I'll bet you would have been a great Marine."

"No formal training, no," Quill said.

"Just nosy," Marge added. "And I was never a Marine, thank you very much."

Sophie got up and walked up and down the living room, as if sitting still were a penance. Quill was struck again by her sheer vitality. Maybe a sketch would work, after all. She felt in her skirt pocket for her charcoal sticks, to reassure herself they were there. "From what we've discovered so far, we're pretty sure Linda Connelly isn't her real name."

"That's for sure," Sophie muttered.

"And I don't think . . ." She looked at Marge. "Well, we don't think that she's even a legitimate events co-coordinator."

"You'd be right about that, too."

"So after we settle Brady's hash, we're going to check out her so-called company in Syracuse," Marge said.

"We are?" Quill said. "But the police have already done that."

"Harker," Marge said in derision.

"You've got a point."

"Only logical to follow up and see if the Linda Connelly her clients knew is the same one that's dead as a doornail in the Tompkins County Morgue. Right after we finish up here. Figured we'd tell people we're doing background checks for an insurance claim."

"I suppose you're right." Quill sighed. She wished she didn't have so many sidekicks. First Althea, who was going to get them all in hot water over the purloined laptop, and now Marge, who was a little too enthusiastic about impersonating people. She looked at her watch again. Jack was in his bath now, looking adorable, and she was missing all of it.

"Look, you guys. You can't do this." Sophie stopped striding and put her hands behind her back, reminding Quill of a lecturer at a podium.

"Linda Connelly isn't her real name. You're right. And she's not an events co-coordinator—at least, not the kind of events you want here in your beautiful little village.

"She's Russian. And what she does for a living is kill people."

17

Quill gaped at Sophie. "Linda Connelly's an assassin?"

"Was," Marge said. She looked delighted. "She's gone toes, remember."

"Yes," Sophie said tightly. She pointed at the laptop. "If the woman we just saw on the streets of Singapore is the woman who ended up in the trunk of a rented Lexus at Peterson Automotive, then that's Natalia Petroskova. A hired assassin. A good one. Although not good enough, since she seems to be dead."

Marge pounded the couch in excitement. "Oh, my Lord. What do you suppose we ought to do now, Quill?"

Sophie's face turned bright pink. "What do you do now? Are you crazy? You go straight home and forget that I said one word about this. That's what you do now!"

"Absolutely," Quill said. She scrambled to her feet. "As a matter of fact, this is us, leaving. Come on, Marge."

"Now wait a second. Just hang on." Marge was no slouch in the stern-looks department. Her gun-turret glare had reduced more than one investment banker to jelly. She turned it on Sophie. "How the heck do you know all this, missy?"

"That doesn't matter."

"Of course it matters. How do we know you aren't making all this up?"

"You don't."

"Then I don't see one good reason why Quill and I here shouldn't go on looking for Linda Connelly's murderer."

"Oh, I do," Quill said fervently. "For heaven's sake, Marge. I'm a mother, now."

"Look." Sophie folded her arms across her chest, as if defending herself. "You want to ask yourself—why does Brady Beale have pictures of both me and this Linda Connelly on his computer? I don't have a clue as to why he was mixed up with a Russian assassin, but my guess is he was keeping tabs on me."

"Why would he be keeping tabs on you?" Marge demanded.

Sophie hunched her shoulders. "The kind of career I had, going all over the world in these yachts, well, it's perfect for undercover work. You can see that. And I was the chef. Nobody on a yacht pays attention to the chef. Well, they do, but it's either to yell at them that the food sucks, or fall all over them because the food's fabulous. Who's going to think your chef's a spy? So I got talked into doing a couple of jobs for the government, much against my personal preference." She looked very cross. "Much!"

"Were you coerced?" Quill asked gently.

"Huh? Coerced? Yes, I darn well was. But not in the way you mean, I think. I led a perfectly blameless life up until I got mixed up with this stuff." She blinked away a tear.

"I'm so sorry," Quill said.

"Yeah, well. You'll be a lot sorrier if you insist on getting mixed up in this thing. Honestly. This isn't a little local murder. You've got nasty Russians involved in God knows what. Stay out of it."

"You seem to know more about this kind of international crime stuff than we do," Marge said in a coaxing way. "Maybe you'd want to give us a hand here."

"No, no, and no." She took a shaky breath. "I am going up to the academy kitchen now and I'm going to do such a fabulous job that Clare Sparrow will get down on her knees and thank the food gods that she hired me. And you guys?" She slapped the laptop closed and handed it over to Quill. "You guys go straight home and lock your doors."

~

"Do you believe a word of what that youngster had to say?" Marge demanded once they were in Quill's Honda and headed back into town.

"She's not that much younger than I am," Quill said, nettled.

"A bit of a drama queen, though."

"Maybe."

"Thing is, is she stark staring bonkers?"

"No, I don't think she's crazy. And we aren't, either. As far as this case in concerned, I'm done. It's over. There's no way either one of us is getting mixed up with assassins."

"You know who could check on this for us."

"Of course I know," Quill said testily. "Unfortunately, I won't be talking to Myles tonight. He's out of touch for a few days."

"You must have some way of getting a message to him if there's an emergency."

"I do."

"Well, if a dead assassin in Hemlock Falls isn't enough of an emergency, I don't know what is."

"True enough."

It was close to seven o'clock and the sun was gone, leaving a peacock's tail of burnished pink and gold against the pale blue sky.

"Your truck's at your office, Marge? I'll drop you off there."

"Yeah. But Jack's headed off to bed by now, isn't he?"

"Yes," Quill said reluctantly.

"And Harland's over to an Agway meeting tonight. Won't be back till after nine."

"So?"

"So I think we should catch some dinner at the Croh Bar and talk about this."

"I had lunch at the Croh Bar today already."

"What, you don't like the food? Come on, Quill. We're here already. There's the entrance into the back parking lot. Pull in."

Quill pulled in, parked, and followed Marge into the Croh Bar.

The bar itself was to the immediate left of the entrance, crowded with the regulars. Quill waved to Howie and Miriam. Justin Alvarez, Howie's junior partner, and

Meg's latest dumpee, sat next to them, looking down in the mouth.

There were a few faces she didn't know; some of the vendors at the fete came into town early to make sure of their booths' location during the setup period. At the farthest end of the bar, slumped benignly over a beer, was Linda Connelly's driver, George McIntyre. Quill clutched at Marge's arm. "Marge!"

"What?!"

"Meg! She went out on a date with Mickey Greer this afternoon. Oh, my God. I've got to get back up to the Inn."

Marge pulled her firmly into an empty booth. "Call her."

"Call her! My sister's on a date with an assassin's assistant and you want me to call her?"

"She's in the kitchen, you doofus. If she was missing or dead, you would have heard about it by now. Go on. Call her."

"She doesn't answer her cell when she's cooking."

"Then call Dina. Get a grip."

Quill speed dialed her sister. She didn't pick up. Then she speed dialed Dina, who did. "It's me, Dina. Where's Meg?"

"In the kitchen."

"Where's that guy, Mickey Greer? He's not in the kitchen, too, is he?" If her sister were feeding him, she was going to race right back up to the Inn, grab her son, her sister, and Doreen, and move back to the house she shared with Myles.

"Haven't seen him. Meg came back here around five. She was all alone. And in a bit of a snit."

Quill took a deep breath. "Thank God. Listen, I absolutely have to talk to Meg. Would you go tell her to call me? Right this minute."

"Is anything wrong?"

"Yes, but it's under control. Or it will be when I hear from Meg." Quill closed her cell phone and tapped the table impatiently.

"I ordered us a half carafe of wine," Marge said, "and I got you corn cakes. Betty's started to use egg whites in the batter. I'm seriously thinking of franchising them." She reached over and closed her hand over Quill's restless fingers. "Not like you to lose your head."

Marge was one of her oldest friends, but she didn't have any children. She'd married Harland at fifty-six. She didn't think she could explain to her how having a child changed the entire way you looked at the universe.

Quill's cell phone chimed. "Meg?"

"Of course it's me. What do you want? I'm in the middle of dinner, here."

"How busy are you?"

"Busy enough. Not too bad."

"Is Bjarne on?"

"Yes, but I was thinking of sending him home. After this seating, it's going to get light."

"Could you turn the kitchen over to him, please, and come down to the Croh Bar? I have to talk to you."

"You sound a little frantic, Sis. Everything okay?"

"Everything's *not* okay."

Marge wrested the phone out her hand. "It's me, Marge. Your sister's got her knickers in a twist, but things are hopping. You eat yet? No? You want to try Betty's cornmeal cakes? Good. See you in five." She handed the phone back to Quill. "Wine's headed this way. Have a glass. Have two."

Meg was at the booth in seven minutes, not five, and by that time, Quill had called Doreen, reassured herself that Jack was safely asleep, and started on her second glass of a very good Finger Lakes Riesling.

Meg slid into the booth just as Betty placed the cornmeal cakes on the table. She was flushed with sunburn. "So what's up?"

Quill hesitated. She wasn't sure how to plunge into this. "How was your hike?"

Meg paused, a corn cake halfway to her mouth. "How was my hike? That's what you hauled me down here for?" She bit the corn cake in half and chewed it. "If you order me another plate of these, I won't be mad at you. My hike was fine, thank you very much."

"We got some news about the murder," Marge said, "and it's going to knock your socks off."

"Let's start with the photos of Sophie," Quill said. She pulled the computer out of her tote and booted it up.

Between them, she and Marge managed to give Meg a reasonably coherent account of the events of the past hour.

"You'd better check the battery on that laptop," Meg said after a long moment of silence.

Quill took a restorative sip of wine. "That's all you've got to say?"

"Of course that's not all I have to say. Give me a minute. This is a lot to take in all at once." She ran her hands through her hair, making it stand up in spikes all over her head. "First off, you believe what Sophie told you?"

Marge nodded. "That's what I said. Half of me thinks the kid is smoking funny cigarettes."

Meg kept her eyes on her sister. "Quill's very good at reading people, partly because of her artist's eyes, and partly because she's got all this intuitive intelligence as opposed to the regular kind."

Quill rolled her eyes.

"So what do you think, Sis?"

"She's telling the truth."

Meg expelled her breath in a long sigh. "Dang. And you're wondering if I learned anything about Mickey this afternoon that's going to help the case."

"There's no case," Quill said flatly. "I mean, there is, but we're staying out of it. Out, out, out."

Marge signaled one of the young waitresses for a second carafe of wine. "So did you find anything out about the guy when you went hiking this afternoon?" Then, in response to Quill's exasperated look, she said, "Just asking. No harm in asking. So what kind of a guy is he?"

Meg's cheeks were redder than could be accounted for by sunburn. "A jerk."

"You came back early," Quill said. "And alone, according to Dina. Shall I take a wild guess that he didn't have hiking at Buttermilk Falls in mind?"

"Oh, we got to Buttermilk Falls. It's not all that long a hike, not if you're in reasonable shape, so after we mogged around there for a bit, Mickey said he wanted to show me the navy yard at Dresden. He's a former SEAL, he says, although I'll bet you a second bottle of this Riesling that they drummed him out of the navy."

"Dresden?" Quill peered into her empty wineglass. Two glasses of wine on a weeknight might be one too many. "As in Dresden, Germany? He wanted to go overseas with you?"

"She means the Naval Research Station in Dresden, New York," Marge said. "Right? Down on Seneca Lake. They did a lot of underwater weapons testing there in World War Two. There's still a naval depot there, right smack on the lake. But it's all buttoned up." She squinted with the effort of memory, and then said slowly, "You know what? Brady Beale's grandpa worked at the depot. I'm sure of it. I'm *damn* sure of it."

"Whatever," Meg said irritably. "Anyhow, turns out it wasn't the navy yard that attracted Bozo so much as the barge that was tied up at the dock. Nice and private, Bozo said." Meg rubbed her upper arms and winced. She wore a fitted T-shirt with elbow-length sleeves.

"Meg!" Quill reached over and gently shoved her sister's sleeves up. "Bruises!" she said. There was an ugly scratch on her wrist, too.

"Lordy!" Marge said. She touched Meg's arm, clearly shocked. "I hope you bruised the son of a B right back."

"Did better than that," Meg said with a smile. "I pushed the son of a B into the lake and took off in the car we came in on." She slapped her hand flat on the table. "Haven't seen him since. And I hope I never see him again."

"Might be a while." Marge chuckled. "That's some long way to thumb. Although looking like he does, some dumb female's already picked him up."

"Well, this dumb female is feeling pretty stupid." Meg

shook her head and sighed. "I never ever say this, Quill, unless it's absolutely screamingly necessary, but you were right. I'm way too prone to fall for a pretty face."

"Hey." An unfamiliar voice made all three of them look up. George, the wandering Californian. "Hey there."

George looked as if he'd spent most of the afternoon sipping beer at the bar. His graying ponytail dripped over his shoulder. He had a pleasant, if vacuous grin. He pointed an unsteady finger at Meg. "Hey," he said, for the third time. "I thought you and Mick were out gettin' it on."

"Beat it," Marge said.

George raised both hands in a placatory gesture. He scratched his head vigorously. Then he put a gentle hand on Quill's shoulder and eased himself next to her in the booth. "Just wanted to find out where Mick is," he said apologetically. "We got to decide what to do now that Linda's passed on."

The three women looked at him in silence. Quill was the first one to break it. "Have you and Mick known each other a long time, George? Is it McIntyre?"

George chuckled. "Yep, that's me! George McIntyre." He held out his hand and solemnly shook hands with each of them in turn. "As for how long we've known each other? Coupla weeks. Linda took me on as a driver when she got this gig. Said she wasn't planning to spend her time hoofing it around the sticks, and she was soaking you pretty good for the fee."

"And Mick?" Quill said politely. "How long have you known him?"

"Oh, he's worked for Linda much longer than me.

Coupla months, at least. Anyway, he said he had a hot date this afternoon with cutie over here . . ." He grinned at Meg. "And that he'd catch up with me later."

"You could try Seneca Lake," Meg said sweetly. "Last time I saw him, he was striking out for dry land."

George blinked. "That a fact. Well, now. The thing is, I was kind of countin' on him meeting me here. I got a couple of days' pay coming. I figure with Linda dead and all, the gig's up. Ha-ha. Ha-ha. The gig's up, get it?"

The silence that greeted this remark would have hushed a more sensitive man.

"Soooo." George shuffled his feet uneasily. "I guess I'll be seeing you around." He got out of the booth, ducked his head at them, in a confused gesture of farewell, and shuffled off.

Marge went "t'cha" and tapped a number into her cell phone. Quill heard a telephone ring at the front of the bar. "Bertie? How long has that character with the ponytail been soaking up my booze? Since when? He pay anything on account? Well, get some money from him and throw him out." She snapped her phone shut. "Doesn't look to me like the guy's any part of this conspiracy. But you never know. He's gonna stiff me on the bar tab, looks like, so I can have Davy pull him in. Make sure he sticks around."

"I don't know that you have to arrest the poor guy," Quill said doubtfully. "I tell you what. They were all booked into the Marriott, weren't they? I'll give Seth at the front desk a call. He can let us know if George is going to check out." She turned to her sister. "As for you, Meggie."

"I'm fine. Just totally pissed off."

"As long as nobody's hurt, least said, soonest mended." Marge straightened up, much like a deer—or given her sturdiness, Quill thought, an elk—that scented a disturbance in the woods. "What's going on up there?"

The Croh Bar was equipped with four large windows that faced Main Street. The windows were always covered with wooden blinds, whose slats didn't completely shut out the light from outside. Quill caught the red orange flash of emergency vehicle lights.

She sat on the side of the booth that faced the front door. There was a slight commotion in the crowd around the bar. "Oh, dear. I hope nobody's sick up there."

Marge shoved herself out of the booth. "Either that, or one of the underage Peterson kids got served. Damn. That new bartender of mine hasn't got the sense God gave a goose. Lets that bozo George run a tab and now this."

Quill saw who was thrusting his way down the aisle and bit her lip. "I don't think it's that."

Anson Harker shoved his way through the press of bodies at the door. He was dressed in New York state trooper beige and carried his Stetson. There was a fellow trooper on his right. Davy Kiddermeister trailed unhappily in their wake.

Harker's reptilian gaze slid over Quill and came to rest on her sister.

Quill had come up against Harker only four times in the last fifteen years, and each time she grew to loathe him a little more. Her marriage to Myles had stopped the "accidental" brushing of his hands against her breast, and the press of hips against her thighs, but the man carried his sliminess of character like a bad smell. He was a competent cop, which made things worse.

"Margaret Quilliam?" he said.

Meg glared at him. "You know who I am, Lieutenant. What's up?"

"I'd like you to tell me your whereabouts this afternoon."

Quill's breath was short. She got out of the booth, grabbed Marge, and whispered, "Get Howie! Quick!"

Meg shrugged. "I went to Buttermilk Falls with a friend of mine, and then on to Dresden."

"Would that friend be Michael Ryan Greer?"

"Mickey Greer, yes. What of it?"

"And where was Mr. Greer last when you saw him?"

Meg grinned. "Taking an unexpected swim in Seneca Lake, why?"

Howie, Miriam, and Justin Alvarez followed Marge back through the crowd to the booth.

Harker snarled back at her. "About what time would that be?"

"That's enough, Lieutenant," Justin Alvarez said. Justin was tall, taller than Myles, who was six-two in his stocking feet. He was slender and fit.

"What's enough, counselor?"

"About four fifteen," Meg said loudly. "That's when I saw Greer last, the skunk." The sweep of sunburn on her cheeks looked very bright against her pale skin. "What's this all about?"

"Margaret Quilliam, you are under arrest for the murder of Michael Greer. You have the right to remain silent . . ."

18

"So Mickey Greer was shot in the back of the head, just like his boss. I've never heard the like. And they had enough evidence to arrest Meg?" Althea Quince said at breakfast the next morning. "Do they think your sister murdered Linda Connelly, too? I've never heard of anything so absurd."

Quill shivered. She was exhausted and the morning was cool. She'd stayed with Meg until her sister had been led off to the county jail overnight, and had gotten back to the Inn at three in the morning. Jack had gotten her up at five and she'd joined Althea and Nolan for breakfast on the terrace at seven thirty. Meg's arraignment was scheduled for two o'clock Monday afternoon at the Tompkins County Courthouse. Howie and Justin would be there, too, but they were already discussing retaining a law firm specializing in criminal defense. Howie had told her to be prepared to put up bail of a half a million dollars or more. Today was Saturday. She had two and a half days to do it. She'd already put a call in to their business manager, John Raintree, about raising the cash from a second mortgage on the Inn.

It may have been her distress over Quill's predicament and Meg's arrest, but Althea showed her age this morning. Her colorful scarves—pink and gray—drooped dispiritedly in the light breeze. Even her purple red hair looked dim.

"You're cold, Quill. You shouldn't be sitting out with us without a sweater. Nolan, darling, put your jacket around the poor thing. Or better yet, go up to my room and bring down that nice wool shawl of mine."

Nolan nodded gravely. "I'll be back in a moment."

"And you have to eat, Quill. Here. Have some of this wonderful oatmeal. Now. What is it you wanted to see me about?"

"You wanted to see me," Quill reminded her gently. "You left a message with Dina last night. It was marked urgent."

There wasn't much that she could do this morning about Meg, except wait and worry, so she had gone down to her office and made a stab at trying to conduct business as usual. She had a couple of fete committee meetings this morning, but her first task was always to return any phone calls from the day before. Althea's message was on the top of the list.

Althea blinked worriedly at her. "I did? Oh, my. In all this to-do over these awful murders, I'm afraid I . . . Oh! Of course!" She leaned forward and whispered urgently. "Carol Ann has stolen the laptop."

"The laptop," Quill repeated. "Oh, good grief. The laptop. I forgot all about the laptop."

"Nolan came to pick me up yesterday after the meeting with the fete steering committee, remember? And I talked about sneaking it back into the dealership?" She veered off on a tangent with a pleased expression. "By the way— did you know that Adela Henry agreed to come back to manage the fete? Everyone is so relieved! In any event, I confessed my little peccadillo to Nolan . . . there you are, Nolan, dear. That was quick. Thank you so much for fetching the shawl. I was just telling Quill about my appropriation of that computer." She took the shawl from her husband and draped it carefully around Quill's shoulders. Quill snuggled gratefully into the warmth.

"My wife the petty thief," Nolan said with fond disapproval. "Or rather, not so petty. I take it the thing was a rather sophisticated piece of equipment. Quite expensive."

Althea waved her hand in a grand dismissive gesture. Her silver bangles clanked. "I don't do things by *halves*, Nolan. Anyhow. Yesterday, Nolan and I agreed that we should go back to the car dealership and pretend to look at one of those new foreign imports, as if we were thinking about buying one, you see, and then Nolan was going to sneak into Brady's office and leave the laptop under his desk. But when I went to get the thing out of my tote . . ." She glanced from side to side. There was no one else out on the patio. It was too cold. "It was gone! Gone! Now, I ask myself. Who could have taken the thing? Who would have the nerve to go into a person's private tote without so much as a by-your-leave and steal a computer?"

Quill cleared her throat and began to eat the oatmeal. It was very good, even if it was cold.

"I thought back to our meeting, which was the very last time I could remember seeing it. Would the Reverend

Shuttleworth do such a thing? Never. Would the mayor? Why would he even think about it? Who was the only person there other than you and I who even knew Brady was corresponding with Carol Ann?"

"Carol Ann?" Quill asked hollowly.

"Exactly. She stole that computer right out of my bag. What a guttersnipe."

"It does solve one problem, Althea," Nolan said. "You've removed yourself from the suspicious eyes of the law."

"As if that mattered," Althea said with magnificent indifference. "At any rate, I thought you should know about this, Quill. Although the machinations of the Citizens for Justice are small potatoes compared to what you're facing at the moment. Your poor sister! Is there anything at all I can do?"

"As a matter of fact, there is." Quill's brain had been moving sluggishly until she remembered the computer.

Fact: Brady Beale had been a diver in the Navy before he'd taken over his uncle's car dealership.

Fact: Linda Connelly was really a Russian spy named Natalia Petroskova. Well, perhaps it wasn't a fact, since the information had come from somebody Quill didn't know very well . . . but she'd be willing to bet a substantial sum that it was true.

Fact: Brady Beale was a member of the Foreign Imports Export Association, an organization with a recent trade show in Miami. He had photos of Sophie—who claimed to be a former spy—and Natalia/Linda, who may be a spy, too, on his computer.

Fact: the Navy Depot in Dresden New York had been

an underwater weapons testing site in World War II. And Brady Beale's grandfather had worked there.

Fact: Brady Beale's laptop had surveillance photos of Linda Connelly/Natalia Petrovska.

Fact: Linda Connelly had been found shot to death in Brady's parking lot.

Fact: Mickey Greer's body had been found floating in the waters of Seneca Lake at the naval depot. He, too, had been shot to death.

. . . And then there was Jeeter Swenson's monster in the lake.

"Quill? Are you all right, my dear?"

Quill shook herself, and then drank an entire cup of coffee in one swallow. "I'm fine, Althea. Better than fine. Yes, there is something you can do for me, if you would. I have two meetings this morning, both on fete business. Could you take them for me?"

"I'd be delighted."

Quill grabbed a cloth napkin and scribbled the meeting times and places on it. "The first one is with the people planning the booth sites. Don't let anyone change their booth location without checking with Adela first. The Crafty Ladies and the Craft Guild are both aiming for the same spot, and they can get mean. The second is with the firm putting up the temporary fence. You'll have to walk the site with them to make sure they know where the fencing is to go this year. Adela should have the site map."

"Say no more. I've had a lot of experience with setting up food expos. This should be—not to make a bad pun—a piece of cake."

Quill gave her a quick hug, draped the borrowed shawl over her chair, and hurried into the Tavern Lounge.

Jeeter Swenson sat at the bar, sipping coffee, chatting amiably with Nate. He raised his coffee cup in a shaky salute. "Mine innkeeper." He began to struggle off his stool.

"Please," Quill said. "Don't disturb yourself. I'll sit with you a moment, shall I?" She settled next to him.

His smile lit up his face. He turned to Nate and rapped authoritatively on the bar top. "Nate, my friend, a cup of coffee for my lady friend. And don't spare the cream."

Nate wiggled his eyebrows at Quill and set a fresh cup of coffee in front of her.

"Thank you for sending the Inn van to pick me up from the hospital," he said. "That fella Mike said it was free of charge. You aren't going to bill me for it, are you?"

"All part of the service."

"This is a good Inn," Jeeter said with satisfaction.

"Thank you." Quill thought a moment, and then said, "But you must miss your own home, some?"

"My lake house. Lake mansion, more like, if what that young snip of a Realtor says is so. Can't b'elive the price of real estate these days. That no-good son of mine, now he'd sure like to get his hands on it."

"So I understand. Perhaps it's because the view of the lake is so wonderful?"

"The view. I'll tell you about the view. I don't need much sleep anymore, you know. You know how old I am? Go on, Guess."

"Ninety-eight," Quill said with a smile.

"That's right, Ninety-eight damn years old. Anyways, at ninety-eight you don't sleep so much, and along of a moonlit night, you know what you can see in that lake?"

"Something wonderful?"

"Monsters! Just like that what d'ya call it. Loch Ness."

"Just like?" Quill hazarded. "Some people think the Loch Ness Monster is a relic of a dinosaur. With a long, snaky neck and a small head."

"Nah. This here's more like a seal."

"A seal. With a small, round black head?"

"And big googly eyes. Yes, ma'am."

Wet suit and swim goggles, Quill thought. *I knew it.*

"Breathes like a monster, too," Jeeter offered. He made a wheezy sound, taking deep breaths. "Like this: *a-huh, a-huh.*"

Scuba tanks.

Jeeter began to topple sideways. Quill caught him and righted him on the barstool. "Nate," she said. "Give Mr. Swenson anything he asks for today. On the house."

"On the house!" Jeeter echoed. "Hee!"

"Will do, Boss." Nate looked concerned, although it was a little difficult to discern it through his big brown beard. "Sorry to hear about Meg. If there's anything I can do . . ."

Quill took a deep breath of her own. "I'm going to run upstairs for a minute and then I'm going to see Davy Kiddermeister, and then by God, I'm going to bring Meg home."

She ran up the stairs to her rooms on the third floor, too impatient to wait for the elevator. When she'd left to go downstairs at seven fifteen, Doreen had Jack dressed and ready for his day at preschool, so she let herself into an empty apartment.

Housekeeping hadn't been in yet. Both beds were unmade. Jack's juice cup and the remains of his yogurt sat on the kitchen sink. Her tote was where she'd dropped it when she'd come in exhausted at three that morning, on the leather couch that faced the French windows to her little balcony.

Quill grabbed her tote and plunged into it. The laptop was evidence that Brady Beale knew Linda Connelly in another time, in another place, and, if Sophie Kilcannon were to be believed, another, more horrible personality altogether as an assassin. She hoped the battery wasn't dead, but if it was, she could run down to Walmart and buy another power cord. And that would be proof enough to begin a conversation with Davy and that awful Harker about much more sinister doings in the village than a guy making an unwanted pass at her sister.

The laptop wasn't there.

Frantic, Quill dumped the contents of the tote on to the couch. Wallet, tissues, change purse, hairbrush, compact, note pad, pens, pencil.

No laptop.

Quill sat down and took three long, deep breaths. She'd had the laptop at the Croh Bar. She and Marge had shown the photos of Linda Connelly to Meg. Then George Whosis—McIntyre, that was his name—had shown up to hassle Meg. And sat right down next to Quill. He'd even pretended to bend down to scratch his leg.

"Dammit!" Quill rarely swore.

She grabbed her address book out of the heap of junk

on the couch and found Seth Norman's name under the "M"s for Marriott. She glanced at the time on her cell phone; after eight. He should be on duty by now.

He was.

She extracted Seth's promise to let her know the minute George emerged from his room, and then grabbed her keys.

Everything depended on Davy Kiddermeister now.

~

"I just don't think I can help you, Quill."

Quill sat in the visitor's chair at Davy's desk. She was so tired she wanted to cry. She was so mad she wanted to spit. The rational part of her brain, the part that knew she was being unreasonable because of her fear for her sister, was well and truly shoved aside. "I can't believe this. You know where Meg is. She's in jail, David. She's alone and miserable and scared to death."

Davy attempted a smile. "Heck. I bet you five bucks she's in the kitchen showing the deputies how to improve their meat loaf."

Quill bit her lip, to keep from screaming at him.

"Okay, so you say you have good information that this Linda Connelly's a what?"

"A Russian agent."

"And you won't tell me who told you this."

"I'd be happy to tell you. But that person will deny that person said it." She pointed at his landline. "Call Marge. She'll verify what I said. She was there."

"You know as well as I do that at the moment, this is just unsubstantiated hearsay." He held his hand up at her

232

sharp intake of breath. "It's unsubstantiated if this person denies this person says it." He rubbed his cheeks with both hands. "Can't you give me a hint? I can go lean on the person. Say I'm acting on information received."

Quill thought of Sophie's incredible athleticism. She'd have Davy for lunch. She shook her head. "Will you go with me to talk to Brady Beale?"

"In what capacity? We're not the Gestapo, here."

"He killed both of them. Linda, or Natalia or whatever her name is. And Mickey Greer, too. Goodness knows if that's *his* real name. And if Brady Beale didn't do it, McIntyre did." Quill shoved her hands through her hair. She felt frantic. "What about the laptop that George McIntyre stole from me? Can't you go and arrest him for taking it out of my purse?"

"The one you stole from Brady Beale?"

"I didn't . . . never mind. Yes, the one I stole from Brady Beale."

Davy rubbed both hands over his face. "Brady rescinded the theft report after Marge demanded receipts for the supposed forty thousand dollars' worth of tools. There's no way I can even show up at McIntyre's hotel room pretending I'm acting on information received about a theft when there's no reported theft. What did you expect to find on it, anyway?"

"We thought Carol Ann was planning something more than usually malevolent. We also thought Brady might be behind the theft of the fete funds and it turns out we were probably right. But we need that laptop to prove it."

"Carol Ann seems pretty harmless, compared to this bunch. Assuming what you're telling me is true." For a minute, he looked totally overwhelmed. "You let Myles know about this?"

"I sent an emergency message, last night. I can't tell you how it works exactly, because I don't know myself. The message will get to him, but it'll take a while. It'll be at least twenty-four hours before I can talk to him and only because I used the code word for extreme emergency. I probably wrecked some huge mission."

"If this woman was a spy, or something, the state investigation should turn it up."

Quill said, "Ha."

"Okay. So maybe we need the Feds."

"Maybe? Maybe? Of course we need the Feds."

"But," Davy said patiently, "I need more to go on than somebody told you she was a Russian agent. And what's a Russian agent doing in Hemlock Falls anyway? Did this person tell you anything about that?"

"I told you. I think it has something to do with the naval underwater weapons research center."

"And I told you. The navy doesn't do weapons testing there anymore."

Quill kicked the metal desk. "Dammit, David."

Davy looked shocked, whether at her language or her abuse of his desk, she didn't know.

"You know the rules. Bring me something, anything other than guesses and hearsay, and cockamamie theories and I'll go the mile for you, Quill, I really will. Look, I'll go up to the Marriott and talk to McIntyre, okay? I'll think of something. But I'll tell you right now, the staties have already talked to him. He couldn't have killed Michael Greer—he was in Marge's bar almost the entire afternoon.

We've got six solid citizens that will testify to that, not to mention an unpaid bar bill. As far as Linda Connelly— you know she was killed sometime between four and six that afternoon. Michael Greer swore up and down that he and McIntyre were diving in Seneca Lake all that afternoon."

"Both of them could have killed Linda Connelly?" Quill said hopefully. "And then lied about where they were? And then McIntyre killed Greer to keep him quiet? Somehow."

"You're really reaching, here. McIntyre's not our killer, Quill. Unless he can be in two places at once."

Quill bit her lip and stared at him without really seeing him. "I don't want my sister in that jail another minute. You want something? I'll bring you something. Just wait."

I'll bring you Sophie Kilcannon.

19

Quill drove up to Bonne Goute. It was Saturday. The academy would be in full swing with classes, wine tastings, and tours.

The public parking lot in front was jammed with cars, vans, and buses. Quill drove around to the back, parked, and let herself into the kitchen. Raleigh Brewster was at the twelve-burner stove, sautéing shallots. She looked up with a friendly smile. "Hello, Quill."

"Where's Clare?"

"In the classroom. Teaching a busload of retired teachers how to make an omelet."

"You can do eggs, right?"

"Do eggs? Of course I can . . ."

Quill grabbed her. "I need you to take over that class. I've got to talk to Clare."

Raleigh was in her mid-forties. She had two teenaged daughters, and was one of the calmest people Quill knew. She set the sauté pan aside. "Is everything okay?" Her pleasant face was concerned. "You look like you could use a nice cup of tea. Let me fix you something."

"I need you now, Raleigh."

"It's Meg, is it? We heard about it. It's a horrible, awful mistake."

Quill nodded, suddenly tearful. Raleigh turned off the stove. "Okay. I'll get Clare and I'll take over the class for her."

Quill led the way through the kitchen and into the large foyer. The classrooms were the first thing visitors saw when then walked through the huge oak double doors at the entrance. The walls facing the foyer were glass; behind them, Quill saw Clare at the Viking stove in the center of the room. She was surrounded by a group of late-middle-aged men and women.

Quill realized she was holding Raleigh's hand. "Could you tell Clare to meet me in her office?"

"Sure."

Clare had taken over Bernard LeVasque's sumptuous office when Madame had named her director. The floors were wide-planked cherry. Floor-to-ceiling windows overlooked Peterson Park. An elaborate cherry credenza in one corner was fitted with a bronze bar sink and a small refrigerator. The conference table was cherry, too, inlaid with fine bronze filament. The chairs around the table were executive style, in soft leather.

Quill sat down at the table, closed her eyes, and thought of the waterfall at the gorge and the cool green space that surrounded it.

"Quill?" Clare came into the room.

She opened her eyes. "Hey."

"Hey yourself." Clare sat down next to her. "I left a call

for you. We've heard all kinds of wild rumors. Is it true about Meg?"

"That she's been arrested for Mickey Greer's murder? Yes. Did she do it? No."

"Of course she didn't do it. I've talked to Madame, and you're probably going to need a bunch of cash to post bail. We can swing maybe fifty thousand if you need it."

For a moment, Quill was overwhelmed. "Thank you," she managed. "But I think we have it covered."

"Good," Clare said. "Because Madame wanted everything short of your firstborn son to guarantee it."

Quill laughed. Suddenly she felt much better.

"You look . . ." Clare hesitated.

"Fraught, probably. I didn't get much sleep, and Davy Kiddermeister is driving me crazy and I kind of lost it for a minute." She made herself smile. "But I've got it back, I think."

"Good. What can I do to help?"

"Tell me everything you know about Sophie Kilcannon."

She was clearly taken aback. "Sophie? Sophie has something to do with all this?"

"I'll know better after I talk with her. Why did you recruit her? Meg says she is a decent chef, but not a stellar one. Sophie herself can't quite believe she's here. You've got a national reputation. You could have any young genius chef you wanted."

"You're darn right we could," Clare said crossly. "I told Madame it was a mistake, but I got overruled. Put it down to Madame's well-known propensity to pinch pennies. That woman. Honest to God, Quill, I could tell you stories . . . anyhow. Now's not the time. The short answer to your question is we got bribed."

"Bribed?"

"Sophie's father approached us at the Miami Food Fair in November."

"Sophie's father?"

"Nice guy. A little eccentric. I got the impression that he'd inherited his millions . . . didn't seem to have too much on the ball but he sure had cash to splash around. Anyway, he didn't like Sophie's career choices, haring all over the oceans with a bunch of creeps, is how he put it. He offered a permanent scholarship fund to us if we took Sophie on for a year. I was totally against it. I mean, no offense to Sophie, she's a nice girl. A beautiful girl, and everyone loves her, but the girl just doesn't cut it in the kitchen. She's a decent chef. Maybe even a good chef. But not a brilliant one. Madame took one look at the slug of money Mr. Kilcannon waved in her face and it was all over."

Quill, perhaps because she'd been watching too many TV shows about elaborate international terrorist plots, said, "What did he look like?"

"Who?"

"Sophie's father. "

"Ummm." Clare spread her hands in a bewildered gesture. "Gosh, Quill. I don't really remember. Oh! Wait! He had a ponytail. I remember that. What did I say? You look weird."

Quill took out her sketch pad and her charcoal pencil. Her hand moved swiftly over the sheet. She held the pad up. "Was it this guy?"

Clare took the pad and stared earnestly at it. "No. He didn't have a bandana around his head. And he was much better dressed. And no earring."

Quill took the pad back, erased the earring, the bandana, and substituted a shirt and tie for the T-shirt. She made the ponytail neater.

"Yeah. That's the guy. Do you know him?"

Quill had stopped wondering years ago at the inability of most people to focus on the basics of visuals rather than the externals. It was one of the biggest reasons why prosecutors never depended on eyewitness accounts if they could help it. "You know him, too. It's George McIntyre."

"George . . . you mean that driver for Linda Connelly? Oh, my God. So it is!"

"I need to talk to Sophie. Now."

"Okay." Clare looked totally bewildered.

"And you have to get hold of Davy Kiddermeister. Immediately. Find him. Give him this sketch. And swear out whatever sort of statement he needs that you know this man as Whatever Kilcannon."

"Winston," Clare said faintly. "Winston Kilcannon."

"Madame will testify to his identity, too, won't she? Davy," Quill added, with a trace of bitterness, "has verification issues."

"Sure."

"It's important, Clare. I've got to get Meg out of that jail cell."

"I'm on my way."

"As for Sophie?"

"Umm . . ." Clare bit her lip. "Let's see. It's what—nine thirty? And this is Saturday? Sorry. This has really thrown me for a loop. Wait! I remember. She and Jim Chen went to the farmer's market in Trumansburg to buy produce. They took the van. She ought to be back right about now. You realize, Quill, if she finds out about her father's donation, we'll lose it. He was adamant about that."

But Quill was already out the door.

~

Jim Chen pulled into the employee parking lot just as Quill came out of the kitchen. Like everything else associated with Bonne Goute, the van was top of the line. The academy's logo was picked out in gold on both sides. Sophie waved hello from the passenger's side and bounced out onto the pavement to greet her. Her silver blond hair was caught up in a ponytail. She wore shorts and a T-shirt that read: *Fast Freight*.

"Quill! I was just devastated to hear about Meg. I left a call for you this morning. If there's anything I can do, just let me know."

"You bet there's something you can do," Quill said tightly. "You can tell Lieutenant Harker what you told me about Linda Connelly."

"Linda Connelly?" Sophie's blue eyes looked innocently into hers. "That's the event organizer that was murdered a couple of days ago?"

"You know very well who she is."

Sophie shrugged helplessly. "Um. Sorry, I don't know anything more about her than anyone else."

Quill rarely lost her temper, primarily because she was of an equitable disposition. She was close to losing it now.

"That is *not* going to work. Marge was there. She heard you. I heard you. You told both of use that Linda Connelly is really a Russian agent. Her name is Natalia Petroskova. Or was. I've already started an . . . an . . . inquiry into her background."

Sophie's shoulders relaxed a little. "Along with everyone else here, I'd be darned shocked if a Russian agent turned up in Hemlock Falls. But if there's anything to it, surely your inquiry will get results. Don't you think?"

Quill was good at body language. Better than most. She was suddenly certain that Sophie knew all about Myles and his work for the government. "I can see that you don't want to get involved, Sophie. But too bad. My sister's in jail for murder. I'm not going to let her sit there a minute longer, do you hear me?"

"I'm positive she didn't murder anybody," Sophie said earnestly. "And I'm really, really sorry, but I've got to help Jim unload these veggies." She turned, and Quill grabbed her shoulder. There was a lot of muscle under the T-shirt. Sophie gently removed Quill's hand. "Look," she said. "Everything's going to be just fine. Please don't worry."

"Don't you tell me not to worry. How do I know you're not part of this whole conspiracy, too? It's a little too coincidental that your father buys you a job here at the academy . . ."

"My father *what*?!" Sophie's eyes blazed. She clenched her fists.

Quill took two steps back. "Your father set up a scholarship fund with Madame in exchange for your job as a chef here. Of course you know all about it. Clare just identified him, and she's headed on over to the sheriff's office to tell them. He's right here in Hemlock Falls." She was aware, on some level, that a small circle of people had gathered around the van. Jim Chen, Raleigh Brewster, and Pietro Giancava had the look of spectators at a train wreck.

"My father . . ." Sophie stood as if struck by an awful blow. "My father. How do you know about my father? You mean he bribed Madame to let me have this job?" Two tears rolled down her cheeks. "Well, dammit all. Dammit all. I knew it was too good to be true."

"I didn't know until Clare told me." Quill took a deep breath. She felt awful. She shot a daggerlike glance at the rubberneckers and pulled Sophie across the lot, out of earshot. "If you're involved in whatever criminal conspiracy is going on here, you'd better tell me now. Davy's well aware of what's been going on, and Clare and Madame's statements are all he's going to need to arrest your father. It's pretty clear he didn't kill Mickey Greer, but Linda Connelly's another matter."

"Daddy? Daddy didn't kill Linda Connelly. But I just might kill *him*. Oh, I am so humiliated!" Sophie drew the backs of her hands across her wet cheeks. Quill dug into her skirt pocket and handed her a tissue. Sophie blew her nose.

Quill bit back the nasty comment she wanted to make— this is not all about you!—and said instead, "You're humiliated. I'm sorry. My sister's in jail. I want her out. Let's get your things together and go see the sheriff."

"Hang on." Sophie dug into the pocket of her shorts for her cell phone, her face flushed. She speed dialed a number.

"It's me, Daddy," she said. "I found out what you did. About getting me the job here. I am so royally pissed I can't believe it." She held the phone away from her ear. George McIntyre, or Winston Kilcannon or whatever his name was, sounded distressed, but not overly so.

She held the phone close to her ear and listened for several long seconds. Then she said, "You realize Meg Quilliam's in jail because of all of this." Then, after several minutes, she exploded, with a violent, negative shake of her head, "I'm not doin' it. I told you that in Miami, and I'm telling you now!"

She flipped the phone shut, stamped around three times in a circle, then opened the phone up again. "Okay," she said. "I'll do it. But I swear to God and the Twelve Apostles that this is the last freakin' time. Where did you say it was? All right. All right. Got it. I'll get my gear. I don't drive, you know, so you'll have to . . . what? Quill? She's right here. She might, but that's a big maybe. She is madder at you than I am. She wants her sister out of jail and so do I." Sophie held the phone away from her ear and looked beseechingly at Quill. "Can you drive me and the van somewhere right now?"

Quill had never been a fan of the Gothic heroines who persisted in going into the basement all by their virginal selves. "If the sheriff comes, too."

"Did you hear that Daddy? Okay. Fine. Oh, and by the way? Thanks for screwing up my life! Again!" She shut the phone off and shoved it back in her pocket. "Okay. I'm ready. I've got to go get my stuff. And you want a cop along with us? That's fine. You make whatever call you have to make, and meet me at my apartment."

"What stuff are you getting? Where are we going?"

"My scuba gear. We're going to Seneca Lake to retrieve the gun that shot Mickey Greer and Linda Connelly. Daddy's got a pretty good idea of where it went. I just hope I can find it."

It took longer to get to Seneca Lake than it should have, in Quill's opinion, but that was mostly her own fault. She wasn't about to get in a van alone with Sophie Kilcannon, who might be part of some terrorist conspiracy that had resulted in the death of two people. First, she couldn't reach Davy, who was in hot pursuit of George/Winston whomever.

When she did reach Davy, he informed her with some degree of asperity that George McIntyre/Winston Kilcannon was really an FBI agent Franklin Ruiz, who had the credentials to prove it, and to wait right there until he could accompany Sophie and Quill to Seneca Lake, himself. He hung up before Quill could tell him that McIntyre/Kilcannon/Ruiz was CIA, not FBI.

Whatever.

Confident that Sophie was at least, nominally, on the side of the good guys, she walked over to Sophie's apartment and knocked on the door.

Sophie opened it almost immediately. Quill could see that she'd been crying.

"The sheriff says your father's credentials check out."

Sophie rolled her eyes. "As an agent maybe. His, like, paternal credentials suck big-time."

"The sheriff asked us to wait for him."

"Just as well. Better to have an official witness if I can find the darn gun." She stepped back. "Come on in."

The living room was much the same as before, except for the pile of scuba gear heaped in the middle of the floor.

"You want anything to drink? Some wine, maybe?" She looked sympathetically at Quill. "You look like you could use it."

"I'd rather get some information."

"It'd be better if it came from Daddy."

"Just in a general way," Quill said. "I guess secrecy's important in some types of government work but unless lives are at stake, I think secrecy is a bad idea."

"You and me, both." Sophie flung herself on the sofa, stretched out her long legs, and put her hands behind her head. "And lives aren't at stake in this thing, or shouldn't have been. And anyhow, Daddy thinks Major McHale is a pretty decent guy. And my personal opinion is that we owe you one, because of poor Meg. It's fair to warn you that I won't volunteer any information, but I'll answer questions I can. So ask away."

"What does Myles have to do with this?"

"Not a thing. Except in the intelligence community, people tend to be pretty tight."

"Who killed Mickey Greer?"

"Brady Beale, most likely. We'll know for sure if I can find the gun."

"Did Brady kill Linda Connelly, too?"

"Probably. We'll know for sure . . ."

". . . If you can find the gun. Why? Why did *anybody* get killed?"

"Because Brady Beale is a stupid idiot. His grandfather worked at the underwater weapons depot during World War Two and talked a lot about the weapons that got dumped there. It's a deep lake, you know. Close to nine hundred feet at the deepest part. You could plunk the Eiffel Tower in there and just a little bit of the top would poke out."

"Sophie, please."

"Sure, no problem. Anyhow, Beale got convinced there was an atomic warhead down there. He's a diver, and he spent a lot of time looking around for stuff and finally found an old submarine."

"An atomic warhead? In Seneca Lake?"

"It's not totally bogus. The Manhattan Project had been underway since 1940, and they were working on all kinds of methods of delivery. So it's possible, as opposed to probable. Anyhow, as we all know, atomic weapons mean plutonium and plutonium is worth a lot of money.

"As near as Daddy can figure out, Brady met up with the Russians at this international car show in Miami and boasted about how he could sell them a pile of plutonium. It's illegal to sell it here, of course, and naturally, it belongs to the navy anyway."

"Naturally," Quill said, fascinated.

"So Natalia shows up with Mickey the Muscle. It looks like Brady and Natalia couldn't come to an agreement— she's got quite a reputation as a double-crosser, or did. So 'boom' (Sophie mimed a gun blast with both hands) Natalia gets killed, and then 'boom' Brady meets Mickey at the lake and they quarrel and Brady shoots Mickey and throws the gun in the lake. Like I said, stupid."

"But. Natalia shows up with Mickey? Just like that? And why did Brady have those pictures of you on his laptop? How do you know all this?"

"Daddy taped it on his cell phone. Brady's fight with Greer, that is, and his pitching the gun. That's how come he thinks I'll be able to find that darn gun in the middle of the deepest lake in the entire northeast. Otherwise, I'd be diving for weeks."

There was a fusillade of knocks on the door

"That'll be the sheriff?" Sophie asked. "I'd appreciate it if you'd do me a favor. There's no reason you should, except that I'm going to judge that pie contest for you even though it's a suicide mission that rates right up there with an assignment in Afghanistan."

"Quill? Are you in there?" Davy rattled the doorknob. His voice was ratcheted up a couple of notches with tension.

"Yes, Davy." Quill opened the door.

Davy shouldered past her into the room, his hand on his gun. "You all right?"

"I'm fine. Just fine. I'd like you to meet Sophie Kilcannon. She's going to save Meg."

He looked up at her, and nodded curtly. "Agent Kilcannon."

"I'm not an agent," Sophie said desperately. "I'm a chef. I never was an agent. I've just had to step into a few things because of my father. But I'm not, not, *not* an agent with the CIA."

Davy's cheeks flamed red. "I thought your father was with the FBI."

Sophie threw her hands up. "Whatever. Look. Did you get the transmission of the murder?"

"Yeah, I got that."

Quill knew better than to grab him by the arm, but she

stepped in front of Sophie and looked Davy directly in the eye. "And did you send it on to Harker?"

"I did better than that. Or rather, George whatever-the-hell-his-real-name-is did better than that. He called in a few favors. Meg will be released from police custody sometime this afternoon. If Agent Kilcannon finds the gun, all of the charges will be dropped."

"Chef," Sophie muttered. "I'm a chef."

Quill handed the air tanks to Sophie and picked up the face mask and the wet suit. "Okay. Let's go."

Davy's cheeks flamed again. He was out of his depth, Quill saw, and not happy at all. "Just hang on a second, Quill. I don't like this. I don't really understand what the hell is going on."

"Why don't you follow us in the cruiser? As soon as we get that gun and Meg's free, Sophie can explain everything." She nudged both of them out the door. "Let's move."

~

"You *can* explain everything, can't you?" Quill pulled out onto the highway. Dresden was less than ten miles away on the cross highway between Seneca and Cayuga Lakes. They could be there in five minutes if the road was clear.

Sophie stared glumly out the window. "Sure. I got set up. That explains it all in a nutshell. My father's a careful guy. He needed an extra agent in place and he knew I didn't want to do this anymore and he also knew I wouldn't let him down if he really needed me so he, what, arranged to *bribe* Clare Sparrow to take me on here. I suppose if things hadn't gone flooey with the operation, I'd still be barreling along happy as Larry thinking I'd been hired because I'm a damn good cook."

Quill looked in the rear window. Davy followed along behind her. She wished she'd thought to ride with him. He could have put on the siren.

"You were about to ask me a favor?"

Sophie tugged at a strand of hair and chewed on it. "Just that you not let everybody in town know about the bribe."

"It wasn't a bribe." They'd arrived at the intersection of Route 14 and 54. Dresden lay straight ahead. Quill glanced both ways and gunned across the road. Here, the highway remained two lanes, but the area was abruptly residential. The houses were mostly two-story clapboards and neatly kept with trim lawns and modest gardens. "It was more of a scholarship. And from what Clare and Madame LeVasque told me, your father was very concerned that you have a chance to settle down in one place for a while. I mean, it's obvious from what's happening now that he had another motive, too. But really Sophie, I'm sure that he had your best interests at heart."

Sophie chuckled to herself. "Maybe. He always says I have a gypsy soul. Maybe I do. And maybe I would have ended up feeling like I was in jail here. But darn it . . ." She leaned forward. "Stop here."

They were at the top of a steep hill that dropped directly down to the lake. To their right was an anonymous huddle of white buildings with corrugated metal roofs. To their left was a stand of sycamore trees that obscured the view of the lake. At the bottom of the hill, on the lakeshore itself, was a cluster of small lake cottages.

A long, massively built pier jutted straight out into the water.

Sophie peered through the windshield. "Okay. I've got it. The camera was over in the thickest part of the sycamores. They provide a lot of cover." She flipped open her cell phone and tapped at the small screen. "Beale must have parked over there and taken cover on the low side of the berm." She snapped the cell phone shut. "Park in front of the navy yard, if you don't mind. It's time to suit up."

20

"The dive was pretty amazing," Quill said to Meg and Justin late the next afternoon. "It took her a while to find the gun, but she kept going until she found it. I'm just thankful that Beale didn't have enough time to get out on the lake and pitch it into the really deep water. We might never have found it at all."

It was another brilliant day. The three of them sat on the patio of the Tavern Lounge. The chrysanthemums at the edge of the flagstones seemed to have bloomed overnight, and the scarlet, yellow, and purple flowers made the day a festival.

"Although it seemed to take hours, it wasn't more than forty-five minutes before she brought it up. Davy brought George/Winston/Franklin—how do spies keep all their identities straight, anyway? Whatever. Anyhow, Sophie didn't say one word to him. Not one. She just stared at him for a minute, then got her wet suit on and jumped into the water. But the cell phone tape helped a lot." She took her sister's hand and held it for a moment. "Horrible, but helpful. We could see where the gun sank. We also saw

Brady Beale shoot Mickey Greer, which was the worst part. Davy e-mailed a copy on to Harker as soon as he saw it, which is why you got out of jail so fast, thank God." She smiled at Justin. "That, plus Sophie's dad, and you calling in every favor you had in the justice system seemed to have done the trick."

"Howie had a lot more to do with it than I did," Justin said lightly. His arm was around Meg, and he tightened it briefly. His face bore the marks of more than one sleepless night. "I just camped out at the county jail."

"He did, too," Meg said. She shook her head. "Slept on the bench in the reception area. I don't know why they didn't throw him out."

Meg was pale, and very clean. Justin brought her back to the Inn late Saturday night, and the first thing she did was shower. Then she showered again. She fell into bed and slept for ten hours straight and began the morning with a third shower. "Thank goodness for that tape, though, as gruesome as it is. Without that I might have been toast. Mickey had my blood and skin under his nails. Nobody knew where the murder weapon was. And that witness who saw us arguing was pretty believable. He owns one of those little cottages right next to the navy depot." She shuddered.

Quill poured them all a second glass of wine. "I never thought I'd say it, but here's to cell phones." She raised her glass.

"Here's to scuba divers," Meg said. "I really ought to thank Sophie, too."

"She'll be along in a minute," Quill said. "She lost her

job at the academy, you know, and she's going back to Miami. Clare's taking her to the train, and she's catching a flight from New York."

"Here's to Sophie," Justin said. "Hail and farewell." He drained his glass. Meg drained hers. Quill poured them a third round, and decided that she herself had had enough. She wanted to take Jack to the park this afternoon.

Meg waved her glass merrily in the air. "And to George/Winston/Franklin, wherever he may be."

"I'd like to toast him with the toe of my boot," Justin said. "If he'd just alerted Kiddermeister to this operation, Meg wouldn't have spent those days in jail."

"Eighteen hours and twenty-three minutes actual jail time," Meg said proudly. "I was going to keep count of the days on the cell wall, like the Count of Monte Cristo. Anyhow, thank goodness he was hiding in the bushes surveilling those guys. Otherwise . . . what's the matter, Quill?"

"He wasn't hiding in the bushes. He couldn't have been hiding in the bushes." Quill set the remainder of her Riesling on the table. "Things have been going so fast, I haven't had a chance to think. Sophie's father was at the Croh Bar the day of Greer's murder. All afternoon. And he didn't pay his bar tab."

"*Somebody* took the video," Meg said.

"Sophie said her father took the video—I mean, you saw it. Davy saw it. I personally don't ever want to see it, but it exists."

The French doors to the lounge swung open and Sophie Kilcannon walked onto the patio. She was dressed for travel, in khaki pants and a long-sleeved T-shirt that read *If You Go You Can't Come Back*. Her guitar was over one shoulder and her knapsack was over the other.

"Hey, guys," she said. She looked tired and a little sad, but her smile was as bright as ever. "Sure glad to see you, Meg." She gave her a friendly bump on the shoulder, and sank down in the empty chair at the table. "Any of that wine left for me?"

Justin got up. "I'll tell Nate."

"And maybe a couple of cheese plates," Meg added. "Hang on. I'd better go and do them myself. Do you realize that I haven't been in the kitchen since Thursday afternoon? God knows what's been happening there without me. We'll be right back."

Quill waited until Justin and Meg disappeared inside. "Sophie, where were you the day that Mickey Greer was killed?"

"Thursday?" She frowned a little. "Let's see. I helped Jim Chen with a seafood class from three to five, and then I did prep work in the kitchen with Raleigh Brewster. Why?" Her eyebrows went up and she was quiet for a minute. "Oh. The cell phone tape. You're wondering who took that video, aren't you? I have a hunch you're a little confused about who's who, here. See? This is why I'm a lousy spy. I blurt. I'm impulsive. I don't think!" She pounded her head with the heel of her hand. "Next time somebody tries to pull me into one of these things, I've got four words for them: I'm not doin' it."

"Now, Sophie, dear, you don't mean it." Althea Quince sat down on Quill's left. Nolan Quince sat at Quill's right. Sophie snarled at both of them. It was, Quill noted, an affectionate snarl.

I won't volunteer anything, but I'll answer your questions.

Quill wanted to smack herself on the head, but didn't. Suddenly, it all made a cockeyed kind of sense. "There are one too many federal agents in Hemlock Falls." She slugged back the rest of her wine. "George McIntyre is really Ruiz, an agent from the FBI."

Nolan nodded yes.

"He thought you could talk Sophie into doing a bit of undercover work if he got her a job at the Academy, so he posed as you, Nolan, and talked Clare into hiring her."

Nolan nodded again.

Quill pointed at him. "You took the video footage of the murder at the lake."

"Yes," Nolan said. "I'm Sophie's father. Retired CIA."

He patted Quill's shoulder. "Both Althea and I realized it wouldn't take Myles McHale's wife too long to start asking some uncomfortable questions."

"Daddy," Sophie said between gritted teeth. "Quill would make a terrific agent all on her own. She is not, not, *not* an adjunct of her husband."

"Very true. My apologies for any apparent sexism." Nolan turned his mild gaze on Quill. "I don't suppose you would consider . . ."

Quill choked on the last of the Riesling. "No and no." She looked at Sophie and burst into laughter. "I'm not doin' it!"

~

"So they're gone, all three of the Kilcannons," Quill said to the image of Myles on her laptop. "Did my emergency message drag you away from anything important?"

"You're important," Myles said. "The name you sent on to me was a red flag. I was ready to order a platoon of Marines to come to your rescue, but it appears it wasn't necessary."

"Natalia Petroskova?"

"Althea Quince."

"Oh." Quill choked back a laugh. "She's the brains behind the operation?"

"She's quite the strategist."

"I should say she is. You know, she was the one who figured out Brady's scam early on. He hacked the money from the fete account to get Adela out of the picture and Natalia and Greer into town as the event organizers. The warhead, if there ever was a warhead, had to be transported in a lead-lined truck. Brady figured if Natalia and Greer were a normal part of the fete, it'd be less obvious to find a pair of strangers hauling around a tractor trailer. She had less than twenty-four hours to get Franklin Ruiz hired on as a driver. She wasn't about to tell me how she managed that.

"Althea knew about the possibility of the warhead early on, of course. Brady's inquiries about possible buyers weren't as discreet as he thought they were. So they put Sophie in place as soon as they could. They wanted her to shadow Brady and find out if there really was anything under the lake. She said the navy's records from that time were incomplete—and a lot of the documentation about the weapons testing had been destroyed. Althea admitted that she and Nolan were a bit past their diving days themselves, and Sophie's an expert."

"But Sophie refused?"

"She really wants a life of her own, poor girl. She loves them, that's clear. But like a lot of parents, they want their offspring to follow in their footsteps. It's a heck of a good life, if you don't mind the bullets, according to Althea. And Sophie doesn't mind the bullets, she says. Where else, she says, could you see as much of the world as she and Nolan have seen on somebody else's expense account?" Quill tugged at her hair. "The woman's a lunatic."

For a moment, they were both silent.

"We won't do that to Jack," Quill said finally. "Try and nudge him down a path he doesn't want to go."

"It sounds as if they did more than nudge."

"They did. You should have seen Sophie's face when she realized that she hadn't gotten the job at Bonne Goute on her own merits. She was crushed. On the other hand . . ." Quill put her hands lightly on the screen, framing Myles's face. "You should have seen her diving into the lake. She was having the time of her life. And that song she sang to Marge and me. It's called "Fast Freight" and she told me, before the three of them got on the train to head to New York, that she loves the song because it's about living with choices. If she doesn't make a choice, she said, she's free."

"Until she falls in love," Myles said. "Until she falls in love."

Epilogue

Quill sat in the Home-Cooked Foods tent of the Finger Lakes Autumn Fete and wondered if she could find a doctor who would excuse her from judging the Homemade Pies, berry and fruit division for the very sound medical reason that she was going to go stark staring crazy. She pulled a charcoal pencil from her skirt pocket and sketched a tiny Quill with wide-open mouth galloping madly off in all directions. Then she drew an even tinier Quill snatching herself bald.

She slipped her pencil back into her skirt and sighed.

The weather outside the tent was glorious. A bronze and beneficent sun shone on the grounds of Peterson Park. The aspens were in full gold glory. The maple trees glowed like crimson fire. It was the first day of the fete, and the week before, a stream of craftsmen and artisans had come from all over the northeast to set up their booths. Potters displayed clay dishes, pots, urns, jugs, and coffee cups in an astonishing array of vivid glazes. Quilters sat amid hangings of unique and marvelous colors. Exquisite wood carvings, handmade furniture, woven wool, hand-blown glass, and a dizzying variety of pictures in pastels, acrylics, oils, and charcoal were displayed in booths spread all over the velvety acres of the park.

The fete was thronged with tourists moving happily from the cheese tent to the wine-tasting tent and all of the booths beyond. The Home-Cooked Foods tent was thronged, too, mostly with the contestants and their supporters in the Homemade Pies, berry and fruit division. The Furry Friends pet show tent was immediately adjacent and the sound of bored puppies, cranky kittens, and irritable birds mingled with the chatter and gossip of the crowd around the display of pies.

Quill recognized a welcome face in the crowd and waved. "Mr. Swenson! How nice to see you!"

Jeeter raised his cane in response, made his way across the floor, and sat in the empty chair beside her. "It's my hostess with the most-ess," he said happily. "How come you're sitting all by your lonesome? I thought you knew most of the people here."

Marge Schmidt glanced at them and hastily away again. Adela Henry and Dolly Jean Attenborough cruised up and down the long, cloth-covered table that held a delicious-looking array of fruit and berry pies. Carol Ann Spinoza walked behind them, examining each pie entry with a big magnifying glass. Adela and Dolly Jean stopped every few feet, whispered furiously together, then glared back at Carol Ann, who reacted with superb indifference.

"I'm the judge," Quill said glumly. "Nobody's allowed to talk to the judge until the competition's over and the results are turned in to the awards committee. You may think that I'm on the awards committee because I'm on every other committee for this darned fete, but I'm not."

"You mean you get to pick the best out of all those pies?"

"I do. And then I'm dying my hair blond and moving to Detroit."

Jeeter laughed so hard he started to fall over. Quill righted him and resettled his cane firmly in his grasp. "Getting the hell out of Dodge, eh? Can't say as I blame you. 'Course, I'm gettin' out of Dodge, too. I expect you heard about that."

"I did." Quill put her hand over his. "You're moving to that nice adult community near Rochester."

"Sunwood," Jeeter said. "Yep. I am. You heard that I got a damn good offer for my cottage on the lake."

"Did you? That's wonderful!"

"Yeah, well, I thought the better of it. Don't need the money as much as I need peace in the family. I turned it over to Portly in return for his guarantee in writing, of course, to pay my way at Sunwood until I croak." He snickered. "Figure if I make it to one hundred and seventeen, like I intend to, I got the best part of that deal. I'll tell you, that place ain't too bad. Might just make it, with them takin' care of me."

"People have made it to one hundred and seventeen before. I'll bet you do it, too."

"Damn straight."

"Mr. Swenson. There's something I've been wondering about, since the events two weeks ago."

"Those murders."

"Those murders. Did you remember anything about that note? The one that told you to go out to the gorge the night you fell?"

"Sure. Came back to me a couple of days after I got concussed. Doc Bishop said that happens sometimes after a bump on the noggin. It said: 'Meet me at the gorge at one o'clock if you want the truth about the Seneca Lake Monster. Tell no one.' Something like that."

"Do you remember who you met?"

"Didn't know her. It was the one that got killed, or so she said."

"Linda Connelly?"

"That's the one. Except she wasn't any Linda. She was a Russian agent, right?"

"Apparently."

"I figure that's going to get me some attention at Sunwood. That I almost got taken out by a Russian agent. Pretty damn slick, isn't it? I guess she thought I was going to go public about the monster. That'd poke a pretty big spoke in her wheel."

Quill tightened her grasp on his hand. "I'm very glad she didn't take you out, Mr. Swenson." Then, as what she'd actually heard sank in, she asked. "Who said? Someone told you Linda Connelly tried to kill you?"

"That whacking tall pretty girl. The one with the bright blue eyes."

"Sophie Kilcannon?"

Jeeter shrugged. "Might have told me her name. If she did, I forgot. Came to visit me at the hospital. Said she was sorry I'd been in harm's way, but not to worry about Linda Connelly again. Did you know her name wasn't Linda Connelly at all? She was a Russian agent."

"Yes," Quill said.

"Anyway. She went away and didn't come back after that. That Sophie. I'd sure like to see her again."

"So would I," Quill said crossly. "She was supposed to judge this darn pie contest, not me."

Elmer bustled into the tent. He greeted Adela with an affectionate peck on the cheek, waved at Quill, tapped his wristwatch with an officious air, and prepared to bustle out again.

Quill got to her feet with a sigh.

"You stop right there, Elmer Henry!" Carol Ann said in a sweet, piercing, poisonous voice. "The piecrust in this entry is store-bought."

"So what?"

"This is the *Homemade* Pies division, that's so what."

"That is my blueberry pie and I made that piecrust with my own two hands!" Dolly Jean shouted. "How dare you accuse me of a cheap trick like that?"

"Did you hear that, Quill?" Carol Ann said. "I thought so. Mayor, these are supposed to be blind entries, aren't they? So the judge can't give the blue ribbon to her friends? Well, the judge just heard that this pie was made by Dolly Jean, and you have to disqualify her."

Quill stepped out of the tent, and into the mainstream of foot traffic. Parts of the squabble inside drifted out; the gist of it appeared to be that Dolly Jean was going to swap entry numbers with another blueberry pie entry and Quill didn't want to hear any more than that.

Suddenly, a slim, blue-eyed blonde a head taller than anyone else in the crowd appeared at the edge of the Furry Friends tent.

"Hey!" Quill shouted. "Sophie Kilcannon! Is that you?"

The figure turned and waved. It was Sophie. She was eating a corn dog. Quill raced toward her and grabbed her by the arm. "Hey!"

"Hey, Quill. How's it going?" Sophie wore tan cargo pants and a blue work shirt with the sleeves rolled up. A small knapsack was slung over her back. She looked tanned, healthy, and totally carefree. She gently disengaged Quill's hand from her arm and took a bite of her corn dog.

"You're back. Thank God. And you're back just in time."

"Raleigh Brewster had to take a couple of days off to get one of her kids settled in college. Clare asked me to come back for a few days to help out."

"You mean you've been here all along and you didn't tell us?" Quill wanted to strangle her.

"Not all along. Just since Tuesday."

"Good," Quill said grimly. "I'm supposed to be judging that bloody pie contest right this minute. Except that *you're* supposed to judge this contest, so come on and start judging."

"Who's in there?"

"Marge," Quill said reluctantly. "Adela. Dolly Jean."

"Carol Ann?"

"Carol Ann."

Sophie shook her head. "I'm not doin' it."

"Please, Sophie. I'll . . ." Quill tried to think of a suitable bribe, and couldn't. Sophie didn't care about money, didn't seem to care about clothes, and in general, had a take-it-or-leave-it attitude toward practically everything except her career as a chef, and Quill wasn't about to offer her a job. "I'll be in your debt forever. I'd do anything rather than judge those pies."

Sophie glanced over Quill's left shoulder and broke into a brilliant smile. Quill turned to see whoever it was that could get that sunny look; maybe he could talk Sophie into judging.

There wasn't anyone there—just the stream of tourists.

Quill turned back, a question half formed.

Sophie was gone.

Quill went back into the tent. The contestants were massed into a far corner, with a bellicose Carol Ann right in front.

She picked up her clipboard with a sigh. There was a shout behind her. Then a sharp, piercing whistle. A half-eaten corn dog rolled past her feet and came to rest under the table bearing the pies.

A puppy dashed after the corn dog. A mass of puppies followed the first one and they were followed by Nadine's poodle, Harvey Bozzel's schnauzer, and the rest of the uncaged occupants of the Furry Friends pet show.

~

"There were pies *everywhere*," Quill said to Myles's image on the computer screen. "It was an unholy mess. By the time Dr. McKenzie had rounded up the dogs, half of them were sick to their stomachs from gulping all that pastry down and the other half decided to roll in the pies that hadn't been eaten. Jeeter Swenson was laughing so hard I thought I was going to have to take him back to the hospital."

"So you were spared the judging." Myles shook his head with the first real smile Quill had seen from him all week. "I'm glad for your sake, dear heart."

"A lot of hard work went into those poor puppies' stomachs. Those poor ladies. It was awful. I have to admit it, though I never thought I'd say this. I'm truly grateful to Sophie Kilcannon, even if she is the daughter of spies."

Myles looked at his watch. "I have to go, Quill."

"Stay well. Keep safe."

She told him she loved him. She didn't tell him she missed him.

They'd agreed that they wouldn't do that.

And the Winners Are . . .

Every year, the Finger Lakes Autumn Fete provides the cooks, bakers, and amateur chefs of Hemlock Falls a wonderful venue to showcase their recipes. Recipes that featured local foods and produce were highly regarded by the judges.

Readers will be glad to know that despite the murderous activity leading up to this year's fete, the event itself was a splendid success. Well, except for the pies, fruit division, which ended in a free-for-all when Carol Ann Spinoza accused Adela Henry of using store-bought piecrust. In the ensuing melee, the pie table was turned over and the Furry Friends (puppy division) ate the entries. No ribbons were awarded in that division.

Division, Breads, Quick

TIED FOR FIRST PLACE:

~Cambridge Gingerbread~

⅓ cup butter
⅔ cup boiling water
1 cup molasses
1 egg
3 cups flour
1½ teaspoons soda
½ teaspoon salt
1 teaspoon ginger
¼ teaspoon clove

Melt butter in water, add molasses, egg, well beaten, and dry ingredients, mixed and sifted. Bake in an eight-by-eight buttered shallow pan at 350 for forty-five to fifty-five minutes. Serve with whipped cream. Serves four.

~Rebecca's Fruit Crumble~

2½ cups in-season fruit (blackberries, strawberries, apples, peaches, whatever is freshly picked; stone fruits should be peeled and sliced)
1 teaspoon cinnamon

2 teaspoons raw sugar (for topping)
½ cup melted butter
1 cup sugar
1 cup flour
2 teaspoons baking powder
1 cup fat-free milk
1 cup heavy cream

Add cinnamon and raw sugar to fruit and set aside. Melt the butter. Mix butter and sugar together. Add flour and baking powder. Stir until smooth. Add milk and stir until well blended. Spoon into ungreased eight-by-eight baking pan. Spoon fruit mixture over top. Bake for forty-five to fifty-five minutes in a 375-degree oven. Serve with heavy cream. Serves four.

Division, Breads, Yeast

~Beer Rye Bread~

1 package (2¼ teaspoons) fast-rising yeast
½ cup dark beer at 72 degrees F
⅓ cup water at 80 degrees F
1½ tablespoons softened salt-free butter
2 tablespoons dark molasses
1½ teaspoons Kosher salt
¼ teaspoon ground cloves

¼ teaspoon ground ginger

2 cups unsifted bread flour

1¼ cups unsifted rye flour

Combine yeast, butter, beer, water, molasses, and salt. Set aside. Combine cloves, ginger, and both flours. Add to yeast mixture and knead for five minutes or until smooth. Cover bowl with clean cloth and set in proofing oven (72 to 80 degrees F) until loaf has doubled in size. Knead for ten minutes and set aside to let rise. Bake in 375-degree oven forty-five minutes to an hour. Makes a one-and-a-half-pound loaf.

Division, Preserves

TIED FOR FIRST PLACE:

~Mary's Peach Chutney~

2½ cups red wine vinegar

1½ cups molasses sugar

1 cinnamon stick

½ tablespoon chopped, preserved ginger

1 teaspoon allspice

½ dozen cloves garlic, crushed

1 cup raisins

2 small sweet onions, peeled and sliced into thin
     rings
Six large slightly under-ripe peaches, peeled and
     sliced

**Combine all ingredients except peaches and sim-
mer for thirty minutes on low heat. Add peaches
and simmer until peaches are fork-tender, about
fifteen to twenty minutes. Let cool. Serve as condi-
ment with pork.**

*Note: Molasses sugar can be homemade by adding 1
tablespoon molasses to one cup white sugar. Put into
blender and pulse until combined.*

~Whit's Blueberry Chutney~

½ cup apple cider vinegar (or use white wine vinegar)
½ cup molasses sugar (or use light brown sugar)
1 medium onion, chopped
¼ cup minced fresh ginger, or ½ teaspoon
     powdered ginger, or ½ cup crystallized ginger
     (chopped)
*optional spices: ¼ teaspoon cinnamon, cloves,
     or allspice
*optional (but delicious): 1 tablespoon tamarind
     concentrate
1 teaspoon cornstarch, dissolved in 1 tablespoon
     vinegar or water

3 cups fresh or frozen blueberries or
    blackberries

In a two-quart saucepan, bring the vinegar, sugar, onion, and ginger to a simmer, stirring to dissolve the sugar. Cook about twenty minutes until onion is soft. Stir in optional spices and/or tamarind. Stir in dissolved cornstarch, cook another five minutes. Stir in the berries, simmer another five to seven minutes, until just starting to break up. Pour into hot, sterile jars and put lids on right away.

Division, Candies, Chocolate, and Confections

~Butter Taffy~

2 cups light brown sugar
¼ cup dark molasses
2 tablespoons white vinegar
2 tablespoons water
1 teaspoon salt
¼ cup sweet butter, unsalted
2 teaspoons vanilla

Simmer all ingredients except vanilla until a small amount dropped into cold water solidifies into a hard ball. Remove pan from heat, and quickly stir in vanilla. Pour into a greased jelly-roll pan and let cool.

Division, Canning, Vegetables

~Sauerkraut~

1 pound Kosher salt
1 40-pound cabbage

Remove outside leaves of cabbage, core the cabbage, and slice into fine shreds. Add salt and mix well. Pack firmly into stone crock, leaving about two inches to the top. Cover with a clean dishcloth and a heavy plate. Store at sixty degrees for a month or more. As soon as fermentation begins, remove the scum daily and re-cover with a clean cloth. When formation stops, pour a layer of hot paraffin over the top to seal and store at sixty degrees F.

Division, Canning, Fruit

~Arlene Peterson's Spaghetti Surprise~

6 pounds heirloom tomatoes, washed, blanched, and peeled

½ pound bacon, diced

2 large green peppers, washed, cleaned, and
diced

2 large sweet onions, peeled and diced

1 handful chopped fresh parsley

I handful fresh oregano

4 cloves garlic, peeled and mashed

Simmer tomatoes until done, about ten minutes. Strain through sieve and set aside. Cook bacon until just starting to crisp. Add peppers, onions, parsley, oregano, and garlic, and continue cooking until vegetables are al dente. Combine simmered tomato and vegetables/bacon mixture. Follow standard canning procedures.

Division, Jams and Jellies

~Tompkins County Cherry Jam~

15 pounds of pitted dark, sweet cherries

Juice from 8 large lemons, with 2 peels reserved

⅔ cup water

10½ pounds cane sugar

Wrap the cherries and two lemon peels into a large piece of cheesecloth. Put the lemon juice and two-thirds cup water into a large pan. Cook under very low heat for about thirty minutes. Remove bag and put cherries into pan, with the sugar. Bring the pan to a rolling boil. Turn off the heat. Let stand. Skim foam from surface. Pour into hot, sterile Mason jars. Cover with a layer of hot paraffin.

Division, Pickles and Relishes

~Pickled Carrots~

    1 pound peeled carrots, cut into evenly sized
        strips
    ¾ cup white wine vinegar
    ¾ cup water
    ½ cup white sugar
    1 teaspoon pickling spices; mixed dill seed,
        peppercorns, and flaked garlic

Simmer carrot sticks for ten minutes in boiling water. Pack into clean, sterilized jars. Combine the rest of the ingredients in a saucepan and oil. Pour over carrots in jars. Proceed with canning process.

Division, Condiments, Sauces, and Marinades

TIED FOR FIRST PLACE:

~Marge Schmidt's Tomato Catsup~

8 quarts of tomatoes, chopped, but not peeled

8 medium sweet onions, peeled and sliced into
medium widths

2 long red peppers, cleaned and sliced into
chunks

¾ cup dark brown sugar

**Simmer the vegetables until soft. Push through a
coarse sieve or process through a food mill. Add
dark brown sugar and set aside.**

SPICE BAG
1 tablespoon each:
whole allspice
whole cloves
mace
celery seed
black peppercorns
stick cinnamon
dry mustard
minced garlic
chopped bay leaves
cayenne pepper

2 cups white wine vinegar
1 pinch Kosher salt

Wrap all these ingredients in cheesecloth bag. Simmer in the tomato mixture until the amount of tomato is reduced by half. Remove the spice bag. Add two cups of white wine vinegar and a large pinch of Kosher salt to mixture. Simmer for ten minutes. Proceed with canning process.

~Citrus Vinaigrette~

Juice of 1 lime or lemon
1 cup pure olive oil
1/3 cup red wine vinegar*
1 pinch finely ground black pepper
1 pinch Kosher salt

*To make red wine vinegar, add 1 cup of red wine to 4 cups of white vinegar. Combine all ingredients, shake well and store.

Division, Salting, Smoking, and Drying

~Harland Peterson's Pork Butt~

1 large pork butt, 6 to 8 pounds
Several handfuls of Peterson's Pork Salt*

Rub pork butt well with salt mixture. Smoke for six to eight hours in a smoker stocked with apple wood chips. Remove pork butt from smoker and shred well, discarding fat. Add two cups of Marge Schmidt's Tomato Catsup. Mix well and simmer in a large pot for ten minutes.

*PETERSON'S PORK SALT

   1 cup Kosher salt
   1 tablespoon smoked Hungarian paprika
   ¼ cup finely ground green peppercorns

Division, Pies, Fruit and Berry

No award given this year, due to unsportsmanlike behavior of participants.

Division, Pies, Other

~Miriam's Luscious Lemon Meringue Pie~

   1 cup superfine sugar
   2 cups water
   ¼ cup flour

3 tablespoons cornstarch
¼ teaspoon salt
3 yolks, whisked to a smooth consistency
1 tablespoon butter
¼ cup lemon juice, plus grated lemon peel
9-inch piecrust, baked in a 375-degree oven for
    eight minutes*

Heat water and sugar in a pan until the mixture is clear. Combine flour, cornstarch, and salt, then whisk into the water and sugar mixture. Turn heat to medium and whisk until the mixture thickens to a thick, opaque pudding. Remove from heat. Whisk in egg yolks and put pan back on low heat for one minute, whisking all the while. Whisk in butter and lemon juice and when mixture is smooth, remove from heat. Let cool while you prepare the meringue.

MERINGUE

7 egg whites at room temperature
*¼ cup superfine sugar

Beat egg white to glossy peaks, adding sugar in a thin stream as soon as the mixture thickens. Spoon lemon custard into pie crust. Smooth meringue over top of the pie with a rubber spatula. Make sure that the edges of the pie are sealed. Sprinkle grated lemon peel over top and bake at 315 degrees for ten to fifteen minutes, or until meringue is nicely browned.

*PIECRUST

(It is a truth universally acknowledged that it is better to buy piecrust than make it. But Miriam Doncaster plays fair—and she made this herself.)

⅔ cup shortening, such as Crisco
2 tablespoons chilled butter
2 cups flour
1 teaspoon salt
4 tablespoons water

Cut shortening and butter into flour with a pastry cutter. Sprinkle the dough with the water. Form into a ball. Roll out with a rolling pin. Makes two nine-inch piecrusts.

Division, Cookies and Bars

~Claudia's Ambrosia Cookies~

1 cup salted butter, slightly cool
¾ cup dark brown sugar
¾ cup white sugar
2 eggs
2¾ cups flour
¾ teaspoon baking powder
¾ teaspoon baking soda
1 14-ounce package semisweet chocolate chips

1 cup toasted coconut flakes
1 cup chopped pecans

Cream the butter and sugar together, which will be a pain, because the butter is cool. The resulting mixture should be light in color and fluffy. Add the eggs and beat them well in. Mix the flour, baking powder, and baking soda together. Combine butter/egg mixture and flour. Beat at low speed until well combined. Add the chocolate chips, coconut flakes, and chopped pecans. Chill dough for an hour.

Drop by tablespoonful on greased cookie sheet. Bake at 375 degrees F for twelve to seventeen minutes. Doneness will depend on your oven and on the size of the cookie.

Division, Fry Off, Sweet

~Cider Fry Cakes~

2 eggs
1 cup sugar
1 cup sweet apple cider
5 tablespoons melted shortening, such as Crisco
4 cups flour
4 teaspoons baking powder
½ teaspoon each cinnamon, nutmeg, allspice,
    grated lemon rind, cloves

Beat eggs and add sugar slowly while beating. Stir in milk, apple cider, and shortening. Mix all dry ingredients, and then add to the liquid mixture. Fry in deep fat at 375 degrees F until golden brown. Frost with cider glaze.*

*CIDER GLAZE

   1 cup confectioner's sugar
   1 tablespoon melted butter
   1 tablespoon heavy cream
   Enough apple cider to make a medium thick
      glaze

Division, Fry Off, Savory

~Double-Fried Potatoes~

   1 pound firm white potatoes (do not use baking
      potatoes or any mealy potato)
   ½ cup flour seasoned with a heavy pinch of
      Kosher salt

Cut potatoes in squared-off quarter-inch strips. Place in bowl of ice water for about thirty minutes. Drain potatoes and roll carefully in paper towels to dry. Fry in 350-degree shortening until pale brown.

Remove from fryer. Heat shortening to 375 degrees. Dredge the potatoes in peanut oil, then in the seasoned flour. Fry until golden brown, then dredge in Kosher salt.

Division, Cakes and Cupcakes

~Julie's Amazing All-Occasion Cake~

You will need five nine-inch-round pie pans for this cake.

7 cups cake flour

8 teaspoons baking powder

2 cups salted butter

4 cups sifted white sugar

2 cups full-fat milk

16 egg whites

2 teaspoons rum

Mix the flour and baking powder and set aside. Beat the butter and sugar together until creamy. Add the dry ingredients to the butter/sugar mixture. Pour in the milk, beating continually. Beat the egg whites to soft, glossy peaks. Carefully fold egg whites into batter. Add the rum. Pour into greased pie plates and bake at 375 degrees F for twenty-five minutes. Let cakes cool. Frost with 7-Minute Icing* and decorate.

And the Winners Are . . .

*7-MINUTE ICING

    4 unbeaten egg whites
    3 cups sugar
    10 tablespoons cold water
    ½ teaspoon cream of tartar

Blend all ingredients in a sauce pan. Put sauce pan over boiling water, and beat with electric beater for seven minutes.

Touring the Finger Lakes

Many readers have e-mailed me to inquire about the actual location of Hemlock Falls and Summersville, where Quill and Austin McKenzie have their adventures. They lie somewhere between the real-life villages of Trumansburg and Hector in the Finger Lakes region of upstate New York. If you check out the map, Hemlock Falls is on the lower northwest side of Cayuga Lake (or would be, if it existed). I've located Summersville on the lower southeast side of Seneca. Savvy readers will notice right away that I needed to relocate Dresden to the southeast side of Seneca; for that, I hope you will forgive me!

With its gorges, waterfalls, freshwater lakes, and rich farmland, the Finger Lakes region is extraordinarily beautiful. At the time I write this, the region's vineyards are producing some of the best Rieslings in the world. The area has bountiful peach, apple, and cherry orchards, cheese- and homemade-ice-cream-producing dairies, and wonderful organic farms that grow a cornucopia of vegetables. Our jellies, jams, and relishes are unique.

We don't have an annual Finger Lakes Autumn Fete; we do have summerlong festivals showcasing our area's rich food and wine bounty. We have wonderful places to stay overnight, even lovelier than the Inn I created for Meg and Quill. And there is a place much like my fictional Bonne Goute Culinary Academy; it's the New York Wine & Culinary Center, on the shores of Canandaigua Lake. Interested readers can search the Internet for the Finger Lakes Tourism Bureau.

Believe It or Not,
There Is an
Underwater Weapons
Naval Testing Facility

I've lived in upstate New York for more than thirty years—
and to my amazement, the United States government created an underwater weapons testing facility on the shores
of Seneca Lake. It's tucked away in the little town of
Dresden. The facility never tested nuclear weapons—
that's a function of my imagination—but the site exists
and is in operation as of this writing.

The first slice is magic . . .
The second slice is murder . . .

FROM
Ellery Adams

Pies and Prejudice
A Charmed Pie Shoppe Mystery

When the going gets tough, Ella Mae LeFaye bakes pie. So when she catches her husband cheating in New York, she heads back home to Havenwood, Georgia, where she can drown her sorrows in fresh fruit filling and flaky crust. But her pies aren't just delicious. They're having magical effects on the people who eat them—and the public is hungry for more.

Ella Mae decides to grant her own wish by opening The Charmed Pie Shoppe. But with her old nemesis Loralyn Gaynor making trouble, and her old crush Hugh Dylan making nice, she has more than pie on her plate. And when Loralyn's fiancé is found dead—killed with Ella Mae's rolling pin—it'll take all her sweet magic to clear her name.

Includes pie recipes!

PRAISE FOR THE CHARMED PIE SHOPPE MYSTERIES

"This Charmed Pie Shoppe Mystery
will leave readers longing for seconds."
—Jenn McKinlay, *New York Times* bestselling author

"Enchanting! As sweet and tangy as a warm Georgia peach pie."
—Krista Davis

facebook.com/ellery.adams
facebook.com/TheCrimeSceneBooks
penguin.com

M1198T1012

Someone wants to bake a killing.

FROM *NEW YORK TIMES* BESTSELLING AUTHOR

JENN MCKINLAY

RED VELVET REVENGE

A Cupcake Bakery Mystery

It may be summertime, but sales at Fairy Tale Cupcakes are below zero—and owners Melanie Cooper and Angie DeLaura are willing to try anything to heat things up. So when local legend Slim Hazard offers them the chance to sell cupcakes at the annual Juniper Pass Rodeo, they're determined to rope in a pretty payday!

But not everyone at Juniper Pass is as sweet for Fairy Tale Cupcakes as Slim—including star bull-rider Ty Stokes. Mel and Angie try to steer clear of the cowboy's short fuse, but when his dead body is found facedown in the hay, it's a whole different rodeo…

INCLUDES SCRUMPTIOUS RECIPES!

"I gobbled it up."
—Julie Hyzy, bestselling author of the
White House Chef Mysteries

facebook.com/TheCrimeSceneBooks
penguin.com